This story is a work of fiction. Nar
incidents are fictitious and any si
locations, or events is coincidentai.

ISBN: 978-1-989206-52-2

WITHDRAWN

"Cold on the outside, burning with love at the center, this debut from Mackenzie Kiera is as good a time as it's possible to have on the page, with dead people. With sexy dead people."

– Stephen Graham Jones,
author of THE ONLY GOOD INDIANS

"Mackenzie Kiera's electrifying debut novella is laugh-out-loud funny, over-the-top gory, totally insane, and just what the doctor ordered to chill you for the summer and leave you begging for more."

– Bob Pastorella, co-host of THIS IS HORROR.

"Sadie Snow is the twisted lovechild of Patrick Bateman and Victor Frankenstein but sexier. Mackenzie Kiera's *All You Need is Love and a Strong Electric Current* does not hold back. It's sexy, extreme, unflinching, in your face, and hilarious. This will in equal-parts turn people's stomachs and excite their Lady Elizabeths and King Henrys. So, go ahead. Read. Mackenzie Kiera will show you a good time and then she'll make you bleed."

– Michael David Wilson, author of THE GIRL IN THE
VIDEO and founder of THIS IS HORROR

ALL YOU NEED IS LOVE AND A STRONG ELECTRIC CURRENT

(a Frankenstein retelling, but sexier)

MACKENZIE KIERA

Let it go, let it go, and I'll rise like the break of dawn.
Let it go, let it go, that perfect girl is gone.
Here I stand, in the light of day, let the storm rage on.
The cold never bothered me anyway.

– Elsa

For Papa. If he wasn't dead, this would have killed him.

And, too, for my son, who turned me into something fearless.

1999. Michigan.

I'm naked, straddling Michael's corpse on a gurney, and he's wired to every single defibrillator unit I, as a paramedic, have access to. That's including the ones at the lifeguard station at the therapy pool, so I'm totaled out at thirty. That's thirty thousand watts of electricity.

Fuck lightning bolts, Dr. Frankenstein. Lightning never strikes the same place twice. I, however, can keep pushing my de-fib button over and over and over again.

Clear?

Michael? Oh. He hasn't held together so well. Sewing has never been my strongest suit. He's cold and just the thought of him being inside me, covering my insides with a freezing, numbing feeling is enough to make me grind against him.

Not yet, though. Here's the thing. I don't want him dead and cold. I want him alive and cold, bridging that gap between here and there. Like the rainbow bridge, but sexier.

I've always liked cold things. Cold water, ice, popsicles, you name it. Is there anything better than jumping into a cold pool and having your breath get taken away? Have you ever floated there and let the sun beat down on you, perfectly chilled water rising up, touching everywhere, threatening to pull you down and keep you?

Why would anyone want to sweat when they could freeze, be slippery when they could be jagged? Maybe I'm wrong. The few times I've flipped through a porno magazine, the stories featured throbbing hot members and passionate sex that leaves you sweating outside the bedsheets, panting for air.

Gross.

But I love sex. I love the bond, how two bodies work together like machines, straining and writhing with each other. The problem? I can't get off. After sex—when only the guy has had an orgasm—I reluctantly go to my freezer, pull out the vibrator I keep between two ice packs, let that work, and it always does. Most times, I don't even go back into the bedroom. I stay out in the kitchen with an ice-cold dildo deep inside me.

I've tried dolls, like, the fuck-me-Ken-dolls that are as large as a man and have a permanently erect schlong. But, they don't love me back. No voice muttering into my ear, no mouth and nose nuzzling against my neck.

And? No matter how cold I make their synthetically engineered cock, it's all in the arms. They don't hold me unless I move them (one arm hugging my waist, the other slung protectively over my shoulders).

Before you get any ideas, know this: I don't want to fuck dead things. Let me repeat that for emphasis. *I don't want to fuck dead things.* That's not where this is going. I like the cold. Not the corpse. Michael, I still love him, but each time I bring him back, he's less and less pleased with the way his body moves; how it doesn't hold muscle and drips strange fluids. His dick still comes back from the dead harder and colder than the iceberg that sank the Titanic, so I guess there's a compromise in every relationship. Tonight, I'm really excited because I gave him some upgrades.

Don't tell anyone, but I, Sadie Snow, procured some bodies.

Fit bodies. (Yes, yes, I know. Sadie *Snow.* It's way ultra cliché for someone who likes it cold, but riddle me this: is it cliché, or just meant to be?)

I can't wait to show Michael his new parts. Instead of weak, shriveled arms, he now has big, tan biceps. And his legs, when I'm riding him and reach back, I won't feel skeleton, but my fingernails will dig into overly testosteroned meat. Sewing limbs onto Michael's stringy body was tricky but shows I care.

Last time I brought him back from the dead, I needed enough electricity to revive an elephant, but we were able to fuck for hours. I came three times on his cold prick and his climax was so intense he bit me. Left a solid mark on my left boob—a perfect mold of his mouth with a beautiful purple bruise around it. This time, I'm bringing him back for real. For always.

Before we light up this Christmas Tree, I want you to know that I was normal. Sort of.

Every killer has an origin story, right? Well, lucky

for you, I happen to have a pen and a bright yellow legal pad. It's perfect, really. I feel like it's important to write this all down. For, you know, science and stuff.

Chapter One
1994. Michigan.

I'm out on the frozen pond behind my house and I'm, I don't know, maybe sixteen? I say maybe sixteen because the night hadn't quite turned to day yet and the next day was my seventeenth birthday. My boyfriend had convinced me to sneak out of my house so I could 'turn seventeen' with him. Don't laugh. It was a dumb romantic gesture I swallowed whole. It's hard to ignore that mushy, lovely stuff when you're raised to want it—to BE that Disney princess—even if you don't really.

That December night, there was this excellent frigidity to the air. I felt like I could slice through it with my hand, heat up the very atmosphere if I moved slow enough, let everything just gather around me in perfect frozen pieces, and I was their God. The one deciding factor if things stayed frozen or melted and died. Snowflakes gathered lightly in my hair, sunk to my scalp in tiny rivulets of cold. I closed my eyes and did the quintessential *stick out your tongue* to catch the unique bits of frozen. It's so human, isn't it? To want to taste. To try it. That's what infants do to learn about the world. When did we stop? When is it that we stop tasting everything because we feel like we've learned? Like we know? How could we possibly ever really know?

I wondered what it would feel like to put my hand through frozen sky.

"Sadie!" A heavy weight blocked the snow and ice and trapped my warmth against me. I felt sticky instantly, like I'd been dipped into bubble gum. Brandon. He had blankets, and the one draped across my shoulders ruined everything. "Aren't you cold?" Brandon asked.

I looked down and was greeted with the bare whiteness of my legs. My skin had barely bothered to bloom goosebumps. Running shorts are so short, aren't they? Yet, it's the cheerleaders who get all of the attention because of the skirts. Are skirts more feminine than shorts? That's probably the reason. Everyone can say it's because you can sometimes see their underwear, but that's normally built into the skirts because, you know, religion.

The blanket Brandon slung around me was wool, pink, and scratchy. Not sure if you can tell from just hearing my voice, but I don't do pink.

The smell was worse than the color. It had that musty mothball stay-in-your-nose smell. It reminded me of a hot attic with boxes full of tea sets and blazers sporting shoulder pads. And his mother.

Brandon pressed his body against me, kissing me with lips that were sort of spongy and warm.

"Happy almost birthday, babe. Let's get our skates

on."

We did. His were snap-ons. Mine were lace-ups because I'm a real skater, but I'd never say that to him. I didn't want to hurt his feelings, which means maybe I liked him better than I'm remembering? I know he held my hand as we skated around the pond, which was sweet, but I was annoyed about only skating forward.

I don't mean to put him in a bad light. He tried to do cute things. He tried to twirl me around, blow snow out of my hair, and a million other nice things any other sixteen-year-old girl would have enjoyed. And I was a sixteen-year-old girl, so I should have liked all of that, right?

See, I'm not saying I'd have rather been in the back of some beat-up truck, doing blow with the bad boy from detention. Except I totally am. Bad boy from detention had a ponytail.

I have a type. Okay? Sue me.

So, what was it that drew me to Brandon if he wasn't *my type?* Well, Brandon was six feet of solid muscle. And even though he was sort of always sweaty, he was a good kisser. Ultimately, though, his time was limited. I mean, he liked No Doubt for Christ's sake. I wish they'd listen to their own advice and you know, don't speak.

So, it wasn't entirely unwelcome when the ice beneath Brandon cracked.

In the movies, the ice swallows you whole. The person just disappears. There, then gone.

In real life, the ice started to crack around us, just

splintered. It shouted the same warning a tree makes when it's about to fall. Brandon and I locked eyes, and then he slipped in. Like going back into an icy womb.

Screams. The kind that boil up and out, pour from you like lava. No choice but to release.

Those were the first in-pain screams I'd ever heard. In-pain screams are different than scared screams. Scared screams have this sort of adrenaline about them—they make you faster. They make you think and send blue fire racing through your veins. In-pain screams, though. You just want to make those stop because they're in your head ringing and ringing and ringing, pressing on all sides and it's all you can think about.

I didn't run. I didn't start yelling for help. I surprised myself by dropping down with him. Not into the water, but on the ice. My knees hit so hard there'd be bruises on my knee caps for the next week. Brandon screamed and clawed at the sides of the hole, but I had a tight grip on his sweater-vest.

"Just hold on! I've got you." The ice beneath me gave a high-pitched crack of protest, but held.

"Kick!" I ordered Brandon. He did. Water sloshed over the hole, pouring out, soaking me.

The cold was pain and pleasure. It was fire without the burn. It was air without having to do the arduous work of breathing.

Life.

Just having my lower body—more specifically, my Lady Elizabeth Von Trapp—pushed up against the hard, crisp ice woke something up. And I wanted more.

Can you understand it now?

You will.

"Kick!" I screamed, and I knew, I knew it wasn't love keeping me there helping him. It was something else, something bigger at work. And that something bigger was underneath the ice, was probably all the way sucked back into his body because isn't that what dicks do? Asking for a friend.

Steam rose from our bodies and even though I'm small, even though I'm light, I remember gritting my teeth and pulling as he kicked and suddenly we were both on the ice. I helped him scramble over to the side of the pond. We lay there, panting. Well, I was panting. He was crying. Which is fine. Men can totally cry. Just, the way he cried was freaking gross. There was clear, stringy snot running from his nose. His clothes were soaked—starting to harden. He was freezing.

I pulled his sweater-vest over his head and ran my hands along his arms fast-like, to warm him up, to make the blood hot again. But my hands, they had a mind of their own and they were going to his pants, unbuttoning, and Brandon, well, he was a seventeen-year-old boy. He was shivering so hard he'd bitten his tongue and even though the world was blue and white with frost, at the corner of his mouth, there was a touch of ruby red.

"Did you think you lost me?" he asked. A smile trembled at the corner of his lips.

"Uh-huh." I pulled his pants down to his ankles.

Red fruit of the loom boxers were next. "Yep. That's what I thought."

"Out here?" he said, teeth still chattering. Brandon was coughing too because he'd fallen in up to his chest and his lungs were probably constricting.

"It might be the only way to warm your blood up," I lied. I wanted him. Hell, I *needed* to drag him back onto the pond and ravage him on the ice underneath the stars like something primal. Would the pond crack again beneath our combined weight? Would the cold swallow us up?

I stood up long enough to pull my shorts down, pull my tank top over my head. My skin had taken on a fine blue hue and I'd lie if I said I didn't feel beautiful. Only a blizzard—another frozen, formidable force—could understand how I felt.

Brandon and I had sexed it up a couple of times before, but I was wet in a whole new way. I'd always thought that one song in Aladdin was stupid, but I can truly say as I lowered down onto Brandon's cock, I understood completely. This was indeed a whole new world.

Everyone else can keep their sweat and their fire. Give me snow, give me frost. Give me frigid and stiff.

We did it out there, even though Brandon's skin was turning purple. Even though my body was telling me I was crazy, that I needed to get inside. My legs had cramped and my fingers felt like they were taped together and would never bend again.

All for nothing.

Brandon came in a long groan. His hands were so polite. Even though he was trembling and probably in a great deal of pain, he was still light and delicate. He was still trying to be so loving. To caress.

And I remember, at that exact moment, I'd wondered how the bad boy from detention came.

I bet he'd gasp into my neck if we banged. I bet he'd hold me in place as he spasmed. I bet he'd bite my lip until it bled crimson heat. I bet he'd let me tug a little on his ponytail.

But, he probably had a cock that was an impossibly stubborn 98.7 degrees. Just like Brandon. Clearly, that wasn't going to work for me. I could feel the hot sticky semen inside of me and all I could do was think about peeing, wiping the goop off and out of me.

Ew.

I did everything I was morally obligated to do after that. I helped Brandon into the house. I put him in a warm (not hot yet, got to go slow so you don't shock the body) shower. I left some of my brother's spare clothes on the lip of the sink. Tyler wouldn't miss them. He was two years older than me and away at boot camp.

I went upstairs and woke up my parents. I told them (almost) everything that had happened. I sat quietly at the kitchen table and even cried a little when they yelled at me. I'd been foolish and stupid and did I know what the temperature was? How could I? And in my running shorts for crying out loud, Sadie!

But then my dad made me hot tea to drink and my

mother pulled me in for one of those big hugs parents give you when you've scared them, like, really scared them.

They told me I was brave for staying and pulling Brandon out of the icy water, that they'd raised a good, kind girl, but to never do that again, okay? We'd talk about boys and curfew later.

After they left, I pulled some ice cubes from the freezer and went to my room. I imagined the bad boy from detention. I imagined that he had an erect, cold tallywacker and it was just for me and I came hard and fast and it was glorious and needed.

But then...then.

What did that mean? Was I a freak? Was I weird? The ice cubes I'd just rubbed up and down and almost inside of my Lady Elizabeth were already melting in my hands. I felt a sob hitch in my throat.

Who would understand this...this...*perversion*?

Boys at school called girls who were putting out sluts. Maybe that's why I was with Brandon. Safe, kind, Brandon. He'd never turn against me, say we sometimes did it behind the baseball dugout or the back of my car.

Would I ever have the chance to love and to be loved for who I was? Who I am? Would there ever be a guy who would be willing to, I don't know, I mean, how do you turn a prick cold and keep it cold? How could I get that and still have the companionship I so desired? The companionship I felt I needed? The breath against my neck, the long, perfect kisses?

What would people call me? Frigid bitch?

Later, I promise.

But, something else came that night. No pun intended.

See, it was when I grabbed Brandon. When I was fighting along the slick, cracking ice to keep him. The reaction. The adrenaline. How I saved him despite the dropping temperature and splintering shards. Despite the danger.

It was the electricity. It was the pins and needles decorated in blue and purple light stabbing me in all the right places. It was a strong electric current of excitement, of need and want and desire to do a good thing, to do the right thing.

Some people take years to know what they want to be when they grow up. Some people take thousands and thousands of dollars from their parents or the government for school before they figure out how they will contribute to society. Me? I knew right then, that moment on the ice, what I wanted to be when I grew up.

Chapter Two

Poof! Back to 1999. Still Michigan

The day before Michael died, Hank and I were doing it. Like, really doing it. The word *jackhammer* should be enough to paint the picture.

I want to say we were both making the good

noises, but to be totally honest, the only noise bouncing off the chipped, sad, blue walls was the hard slap of his pelvis against my ass. Sometimes I'd give a groan or whatever, just so he knew it was wanted. And it totally was, but mostly because I wanted to keep fucking him in the walk-in freezer at his work and every now and then he'd get all: No, I don't want to do it at my work's walk-in anymore. That's what they call it. A walk-in. So dumb.

But, like I've said: every relationship has compromise. See, the next day his boss was going out of town, which meant no one would be checking the freezer, doing inventory on all of the boxes, making sure all of the Hungry-Mans made it there safe, letting all of that magically perfect cold air slip out of the doors. I was looking forward to some almost pleasurable sex with Hank, where the air around me could sink down into my bones. Ice, ice baby.

Until then, I had to endure Hank's hot, sweaty embrace. This sort of sex is just so blah. I mean, I know it can't ALL be perfect. It can't all be that moment we assume happens at the end of Princess Bride, after Wesley and Buttercup ride off into the sunset. I bet they totally Humperdink each other.

More slapping and I want to say something like "lovemaking is so dead," "finesse is so dead," "chivalry is so dead," but I'm a feminist, and I don't need those things.

I don't.

It's the other way that confuses me. I get the love.

The pure, unadulterated romance. How do I say this? Okay, so, for sex, on one end we have the supposed sex between Wesley and Buttercup, right? On the other, would it be like, full-scale BDSM gear complete with a ball-gag like the one that dude was wearing in Pulp Fiction? I mean, how does that even start? Is it a husband and wife couple, or same-sex partners? (I'm an equality for all sort of person, duh) But, how do you start that sort of thing? Do they just wake up one morning and say: Hey, honey. I want you so bad. Your skin looks so fair in the new morning sun. Get the ball-gag and cape. I'm about to blow my creamy, creamy load all over your starched black pleather.

Also? Hank used to snuggle his entire body around me at night, and I swear I had more room to move when I was in-utero. He slept naked and sticky; all pressed up against me. He didn't snore. I wish he did. His breaths were too light and dainty. I'm not saying a man can't be light and dainty. I'm saying I, Sadie Snow, wanted to sleep next to someone who sawed some serious logs. I lived next to train tracks my whole life so noise at night comforts me. That steady, airy song makes me feel like I'm not the only one lying there in the dark.

Yeah, I'm using past tense regarding Hank. Stay with me.

Hank's fraternity smelled funny and the bathroom was something out of a goddamn nightmare, but the overripe scent of man, his chiseled, perfect abs kept me coming back. He didn't have a ponytail, but not everyone is perfect.

I mentioned I have a type.

Maybe I was using him a little. Maybe he was using me a little? I don't know. These things are so hard to figure out.

A grunt behind me followed by a spasm that can only be described as startling and he crashed next to me the same way you used to fall down after London Bridge was over as a kid. A whole-body thing. His landing shook the bed, and his dick leaked cum onto the quilt someone made for him. A grandma, I think. I wasn't really listening.

"Did you?" Hank panted.

"Sure did." I lied because I didn't want to hurt his feelings.

Hank reached his sweaty hand across my belly, pulled me in and kissed me gently on the lips. See, that's the good stuff. That's the part I love. It's just the *heat* of it that I detest.

All at once, his tongue that was roaming around my mouth kindly, exploring, sort of forced itself all the way in and felt too big—I couldn't help but gag. I was basically being choked. And his body against mine had that kind of unexplained stickiness of child hands. You know it? When those little kiddo hands touch you and your mind thinks: oh, lord, what *is* that? Only, with kids, it's cute and entirely excusable. A grown man? I mean, does he bathe? *Did* he bathe? Sorry. The tense is messing me up. I pulled away, far as I could without being rude, and thank god, a horn sounded outside.

Just a light tap, but it was my absolute saving grace. Time for work.

"That's Michael."

"How does he always know where to find you?"

"I called him last night to let him know. You were already asleep."

And I knew I would only be able to handle a few more hours of Hank before I wanted to leap out of my skin.

"Do you have to go?" Hank pouted out his thick, pink bottom lip. "Stay in bed with me?" Only, when he said with it was that baby talk: wifth. See what I mean?

I threw up a little in my mouth. A shiver sent my skin into a ripple effect.

"Sorry, Hank," I said after I swallowed. "The world awaits, and even if I called out, sick people don't. Michael would be on the rig by himself."

"I don't know what you see in him. He's so skinny."

Rude.

"He's my friend. We work together. That's it."

That wasn't entirely true. Just the other day, Michael and I had an all-out war in regards to *The Phantom Menace*. Michael said that while it sucked, it was necessary. I'd told him that I was going to pretend that the movie and his comment about the movie had never happened. I'm not super into space movies, but I'd heard Ewan McGregor was in it, and if I'm totally honest, I wanted to see his lightsaber.

Michael had thrown an old, empty coffee cup at me. I threw it back. We stopped when we almost hit a lamppost. All in all, it was a good time, and just remembering it made me smile. Sure, okay, I had a crush on Michael. But he wasn't my *type*. He didn't look at all like the bad boy from detention or a hulked-out jock. Not yet. He was destined to be the Julia Roberts to my Richard Gere. In other words, he Pretty Womaned me and I'm totally *not* ashamed. I'm all for switching stereotypical gender-roles. But that's later.

Hank rolled over. His limp meat-whistle flopped against his leg. Gross. Show it to me hard or put it away. No one wants to see the Urinator when we're after the Terminator.

"What if I called in an emergency," he asked, "then you would have to come save me?"

"You should never do that."

"Why not?"

"That's, like, the worst thing you could do. You never cry wolf. Ever. Plus, I think it's a huge felony, so there's that."

"Will I see you soon?"

"When are you going to be at work?" Cold-sex!

"Work? Aw, babe. Really? I'm done doing it in the walk-in. It's cold in there."

Sigh.

Guys? I never played Barbie and Ken get married. I played Barbie and Ken buy a house. Barbie and Ken decide to have a baby. Barbie and Ken fight about money (because Barbie isn't getting paid as much as Ken even though she has a higher education, shocking) and maybe they don't always get along and maybe sometimes Ken forgets to load the fucking dishwasher, but at the base of it all, they love each other. See, I played Barbie and Ken were *already* married.

Although, technically, it was Barbie and Aladdin because Aladdin had dark black hair, a really cute smile, and a bare, muscular chest. His hand was even facing up, like when he asked Jasmine to 'trust me' on his magic carpet. Yum.

Ken. Poor Ken. He wore pastel sweaters around his shoulders and sported a pink visor. Come on, Barbie. You can do better. The only way he could have been a bigger douche is if his other outfit came complete with a moto-cross shirt and neon green dirt bike.

The problem was Aladdin's head kept falling off, so I had to use some toothpicks and tape to keep him together. But it didn't matter. He and Barbie didn't fight about it because that's who he was and they were happy and *so* in love.

A relationship. A bond. We're all after the same thing, I guess. But I had The Lady Elizabeth Von Trapp to please, and the bitch likes it cold. Would I ever find someone who I could love who also didn't just endure the cold, but embraced it?

—

Michael was waiting for me in the ambulance that bore our company's name: *Lightning Response!* It was still a little dark outside because it was the dead middle of winter. Being up before everyone else is delicious, isn't it? I mean, I know you're not *really* up before everyone else, but that quiet feeling? The calm? It's the best.

Makes me snuggle with the memory of being at home in my room I'd covered with posters of Metallica while they were still cool. You know, before Enter fucking Sandman ruined it all. You can't put out something as incredible and awe-inspiring as Fade to Black and then think that Enter fucking Sandman is okay.

I don't want to talk about it.

"Wow. Big house." Michael rolled down the window. He was wearing one of those hats with the floppy, fuzzy ear protectors and his glasses were all fogged up from the hot coffee he'd been drinking. I hoped he'd brought some for me. He normally did, which was sweet. "Different location," he said, speaking out of the window. "Normally, I'm picking you up outside of the Safeway."

That was where the walk-in freezers were. Don't judge me.

"This is the fraternity where Hank lives," I explained.

I hopped into the ambulance and took the steaming cup of coffee Michael handed me. Hot drinks are okay. Unlike men, my stomach and libido aren't tied together. Although, I did feed Lady Elizabeth ice cream once. I dated one dude who thought fucking with food might be fun. Obviously, I chose popsicles and ice cream. Well, that adventure ended with both of us just feeling sticky, smelling weird, and needing a shower. Everything melts, especially if you put it in warm, dark places.

"Must be serious?" Michael asked, pulling out onto

the frost encrusted road. I closed my eyes, let the sway of the ambulance reach into my bones. The crunch of the tires against the fresh snow was so nice. *Home.* I imagine in some different life I'd have been a pirate. But like, a sexy pirate. You know? With the leggings and the guns stashed away in odd places? I don't so much say this for the outfit, but more for the motion. I love the sway of the rig. I imagine the rock-a-bye motion of a large ship with the ocean underneath me would have a similar feel. I'd sleep in a hammock, arms and legs hanging over the ends. Maybe a hat on my face even though I wouldn't need it down there below the decks because it would be so cool and shady.

"Dude. I don't know what I'm doing with him." I was talking about Hank.

The ambulance went a little faster.

"Oh, is it...um..." Michael's face got a little red, and he tried to swallow the coffee to maybe give himself more time to think, but the liquid must have been too hot. He sputtered coffee all over the inside of the ambulance. Droplets of brown liquid splattered the windshield. I reached into our glove compartment and grabbed some left-over brown napkins from yesterday's Burger King lunch (I just had fries because I, Sadie Snow, am a vegetarian) and started mopping up his drink. Some of his spit was probably in there too. I didn't mind. We'd shared bottles of water and energy drinks on several occasions, so his saliva had that bit of friend familiarity to it. No, I didn't want to bathe in the stuff, but it wasn't repulsive either. Come on. You know what I mean.

"No," I told Michael, "Hank is like, SO sexy, but the actual doing it part is just like…"

"Bad?"

"So bad." I cringed. He cringed. Together, we passed words back and forth using only our eyes and sidelong glances. That was something I loved about Michael from the start. We had a similar train of thought. Our conversations were never strange or awkward, and when we worked together, it was like we had one single brain.

"How bad, er, I mean, what makes it bad?"

"Think about a jackhammer."

"Oh. Oh!" And he started laughing. It was a deep, guttural noise. From his belly, kind of. But it was real and something in my heart leaped a little. Real felt so good after all the pretending I'd been doing with Hank. If I'm being honest, I think that's when I felt those first butterflies in my belly. You know, the kind where if they had a color they would be bright, electric blue? Maybe I'd always liked him, but that was when grey turned to turquoise. When he wasn't just Michael, my ambulance partner and friend. When he was *Michael*. Someone I liked.

"Vehicle eighty-oh-eight, this is dispatch, come in vehicle eighty-oh-eight."

Michael muttered: "Type that on a calculator and it will spell boob."

Now it was my turn to laugh. I picked up the walkie.

"This is vehicle eighty-oh-eight, what's up dispatch?"

"Guys?" A little blonde named Victoria, or Vicky with an i was working dispatch today, and she was never that informal. Something was up.

Michael and I looked at each other. I clicked the radio to speak.

"Victoria?" I said her full name because I'm sorry, even hearing her name with an i is just wrong. I bet she does that stupid heart i too. I once tried it out on my name. It didn't stick. "What's wrong?"

"It's the plant."

Michael gave a choked sound. He was going to spew a mouthful of coffee again. I myself felt like hurling. My stomach had that awful battery acid anxiety that burns the insides and tugs on your throat.

The plant. Otherwise known as the slaughterhouse. Let me explain. One hundred words or less. Promise.

So, the plant is this big awful cattle farm where they slaughter all of the old cows from the nearby dairy farms. Yeah, so sad. It's why I'm a vegetarian. Anyway. That plant sees a decent amount of critters trek across its bloody lines. Lots of critters mean lots of poop. Lots of poop means lots of fertilizer. The catch? That fertilizer has to be rendered down. Now, I'm just a paramedic, not a chemist. I don't know much about chemicals and I sure as hell don't get paid enough to find out (we make, like, barely above minimum wage) BUT this rendering requires nitrates; the kind that can explode. The kind where if they explode, there's a fire for days. And, it's a chemical fire. Which means we can't help anyone until the victims of the accident are decontaminated.

No one takes any fucking chances after that Chernobyl shit went down. I swallowed bile. Michael's mittened hands on the steering wheel clenched and unclenched. I looked over to him. He gave me the smallest *yep* nod.

"We're on our way."

Chapter Three

It was just smoke and field. Could have been a tornado, the way the sky was all full of dark grey. Michael and I pulled up. The fire trucks and hoses reminded me of whales spouting water. A helicopter flew overhead and dumped some of that white shit (retardant, right?) all over the plant.

A cop ran up to us, a man with a short, grizzled brown beard. His name tag said he was something super boring and normal, so let's jazz it up and call him Officer Randy. Get it? *Randy.*

Officer Randy said to us: "They're set up in there."

The 'they' were the people who had been decontaminated. Michael and I followed him. The cop jogged, but we didn't run. You get trained at the beginning of your EMT courses to never, ever run. It does a whole bunch of shit to your body (boosts your adrenaline, sends you into your fight or flight response—basically it fogs your brain and burns a ton of calories) and it's also unprofessional. I'm not saying you should stop and sniff the flowers. Get there, get there fast, but do it professionally. A quick, well-intentioned walk should be used.

There was a smell on the air. I mean, yeah, it was totally bull shit (haha!), but there was more. I knew that smell. I *know* that smell.

"Death," I said to Michael. He nodded. The decontaminated people had been set up inside the slaughterhouse.

At least fifteen men waited for us. To their credit, no one was screaming. There was cussing, sure. Burns suck. But it wasn't as bad as I thought. I had been expecting full-on bubonic plague status. Bodies of the untreatable just lined up next to each other. I wonder if they held hands? I hope the nurses in the days of yore placed the beds close enough together so the affected people could hold hands.

I would have. I'd have held their hands. And then promptly died right after them because they knew, like, nothing about sterilizing and anti-bacterial stuff and they only took, like, one bath a year (or less if you were way poor), so maybe not. It wasn't until Florence Nightingale came along and checked out where doctors were tending to wounded soldiers and was all: Um, guys? Maybe, we, like, crack a window?

Nurses get their jollies off to Florence Nightingale. I have nothing against her, but really all she did was suggest that we treat the wounded in a cleaner environment. Wow. So smart. I'm all for women making headway in the workplace—it's so hard for us. But Florence Nightingale wasn't a fucking pioneer in medicine. She was just a neat freak.

Michael nudged my side with an elbow and leaned down to whisper into my ear.

"We need one of those masks."

"What do you mean?" There are just so many options.

"Like, a plague doctor's mask."

"With the bird beak?"

"Yeah, those. Did you know doctors back then had a cane? It was so they could keep a safe distance from their patients."

I haven't mentioned this, but I love people who have *fun facts!* Being with them is like constantly learning. I'm a *fun fact!* person. I'm not saying you'll be learning from me all the time, but I can occasionally drop some really juicy fruit from my knowledge tree.

"We haven't triaged," Officer Randy said.

Cool. I ran my hand through my hair. I hated triaging. It's particularly difficult in an accident of that magnitude too because you'll have people in shock but minus an appendage wandering around, claiming they're totally good to go home if we could just package up their arm, please? Lots of head trauma goes unnoticed too. Lots of internal bleeding. Most important thing is if you tourniquet someone, scrawl a T across their forehead in anything. (I keep a bright red lipstick in my pocket for such emergencies. You ask why I don't keep a sharpie? Because everyone everyone everyone steals sharpies. Am I wrong? No one steals clearly used lipstick.) This big T across the forehead lets the hospital know there's a tourniquet somewhere. They'll look. ER doctors are great that way. They translate the garbled mess I send them because my job is to get these people to the doctors alive however I can. Sometimes that means Macgyvering some shit. Think the weirdest thing I've sent someone into ER with was a wooden baseball bat splint with dog collars keeping it in place. Shit went down at the park. Let's just say he'd been the last call after a long day and I was so, so out of supplies. I had to come up with something.

"I'll go right?" Michael said. I nodded. Yep. That meant I was going left. Got it.

The first person I approached had angry, red and white welts going from his shoulder to just above his wrist. Looked like he got sprayed with something the way the skin puckered around the patches of white. I sat down next to him for further inspection. Bits of black shirt poked out of the weeping wounds. Fuck. That was going to hurt when someone took that shit out of him. Looked awful. Truly, I was surprised he wasn't screaming. Either he was a tough bastard, or he was already going into shock.

"Hi, sir. I'm Sadie Snow. I'm a paramedic, and I'm here to help."

"Richie," he managed through chattering teeth.

Nothing will make you colder than a solid burn.

Noted!

"So, how's your day going?" I asked, smiling. You're not supposed to joke on the job, but I've found it's better to make people laugh than cry.

I went through the motions. Took his blood pressure, which was a little high, got his heart rate— also a little high. All of that is indicative of shock. I pulled out my lightweight bandages that are great for burns. Their fine, butterfly wing-like fabric keeps the bacteria out but still allows some airflow. Last thing you want to do with a burn is cover it and leave it to its own devices. Buns are nasty, clever little devils.

I gave him a quick patch-up and helped him lie on the ground with his feet up. I covered him with a shiny shock blanket and patted his shoulder.

"I'll be back to check on you."

I left him with a yellow sticker. I probably shouldn't have treated him. Not yet. That's not the way triage works, but the shock made me want to stick with him just to make sure he would be with us a while longer.

See? That's who I am. I'll break the rules if I feel it's right. What I won't tell you about? How I had to put black stickers on toes that day. I won't tell you how Michael and I both had to work, really work to keep a red sticker red and not black. Those are things no one else can really understand. Those are things we keep between us at the company and between other medical professionals because somehow, after a call like that, we have to suck it up buttercup and go to the next call. We have to go to the little old lady who THOUGHT she was having a heart attack and you can't yell at her and ask why in god's name would she pull you away from other people for a thing like that.

But see? I'm telling you this because I want you to know that being crazy is part of the job. Insanity is a job requirement because one of our duties is to walk from person to person putting damning stickers on them as they watch.

I'm telling you this because I was there to help. My work was my life, and I hope, hope I was decent at it. Have your opinions about me, sure. But you know what they say about assholes and opinions, right?

Chapter Four

After the plant, Michael and I were granted a twelve-hour reprieve. I'm not super big on eating late dinners, but Michael and I had been ferrying wounded men to the hospital all day and hadn't stopped for food or water or caffeine or bathroom breaks or, well, you get the idea. We were pretty fucking fried. Toasted enough for me to agree to a late dinner. Late dinners mean all those carbs and calories stay in your gut. Granted, ever since my hours went way crazy weird (curse of the job) I've become a little more lenient. But let's be honest with ourselves here. There just isn't a wrong time for donuts. The best kind have sprinkles.

Michael got one of those weird apple fritter things and a kid-sized carton of milk. It looked even smaller inside his big gloved hand. I got apple juice and a strawberry sprinkle donut. Generally, I chug three things to keep me going—coffee, water, and if I'm off work, margaritas. Like, the big ones. It's not a real drink unless it can sport several umbrellas between the ice—but I needed sugar to the brain pronto.

For the next few hours, we weren't on call. After you get something gnarly, you get emotional reprieve time. Tends to be after something traumatic. Everyone says: "Oh, sure. Like after a kid dies." And while yes, that's true, I also needed an emotional reprieve day after I responded to this one dude who'd taken some bad acid and ate his friend's face off. Barbara Bush is right, kids. Don't do drugs. You might eat your friend's face. I'd be lying if I said I didn't spend a day in my apartment away from everybody because what if I somehow got some of that bad acid on me and I was just a few hours away from eating a chin, cheekbones, the works.

I know you have to, like, ingest it, but the job has made me a little paranoid about Hepatitis B (Not HIV, you ask? HIV dies once it hits the oxygen. Hep B can stay on stuff for days and still infect you. So, Hep B, and eating faces. Just a big solid No Thanks.)

Generally, on a break, I'd have called Hank, but I was in a lone-wolf mood. After you go through something like the plant, the only person you really want to talk to is the someone who went through it with you.

It's a misery loves company thing.

If I sound subdued, it's because I was. I am. Thinking about that hole-in-the-wall shop. It's one of those memories I go back to. Not this one necessarily, but the place. Michael and I were in there so often I can kind of just imagine sitting in there and have any conversation I want to have with Michael and be at peace.

Peace.

Wow.

Excuse me while I put my sage and healing crystals away. I went a little hippie there for a moment. I mean, I know I sound like a glitz and glam sort of girl, and in another life, I totally could have been. I could have rocked the elegant hairstyles, the tight pink dresses, the pearl necklaces, but really, I pride myself on being down to earth.

No, not the *semen* pearl necklaces. Gross. Do people actually like that? Not to harp on the people who do, because I, Sadie Snow, believe that you should do whatever you want as long as no one gets hurt, BUT, if your dream is to have someone say: oh baby, I want your salty, gacky splooge on my neckline, you should probably just jerk one out and rub it across your own face because no one *wants* that shit. Like, ew.

Where was I? Oh, yeah. Tight pink dress, REAL pearls, and some fancy hairdo. Ruby red lipstick. A diamond necklace would just be too flashy, but diamond earrings because why match and be all boring? I'm in my own field of dreams and it doesn't involve baseball.

A ring, though? I want a ring. With a rock so big I have to take it off before I clock in. Can't have people at work thinking our credit is that good, that we make too much money.

I'm getting ahead of myself.

Michael wiped his napkin across his lips. They were a little greasy from the fritter thing, but they were nice. Men shouldn't have big, pouting lips. Is there anything grosser than a dude with Angelina Jolie lips? Barf. No. Ew. Men should have thin lips that extend into broad smiles. Like Michael's.

He must have caught me staring because he grinned and I felt my heart plummet and splash into my stomach. Damnit. Why was I feeling like that? It's not like simple, dorky Michael would ever know what to do with the Lady Elizabeth. No one would ever know what to do with her. I felt like giving up. I'd never have both worlds: someone who simultaneously loved me and liked it (and could keep it) cold.

I was doomed to a world of frost-covered, frozen dildos. Some of us are just not meant to be the Disney Princess society told us we should be. The Barbie we wanted to be.

"Weren't you supposed to call Henry?"

It took me a moment.

"Oh, Hank?" I felt my brows furrow in confusion and remembered not to because, you know, wrinkles.

"Yeah, that's what I said."

A blush crept up to my cheeks. He was making fun of my boyfriend. Was that flirting? It was funny.

Michael inserted his sugary fingers into his mouth one at a time to clean them. The act made small popping, sucking sounds. Somehow, it wasn't gross. Was more just a human thing. A habitual thing. "Go phone Herbert," he said. "Might not get another chance if we get a call."

Ha! Herbert.

"I don't really want to."

"Oh. Um. Is it because of what you were talking about before. The uh...the...you know."

I didn't.

"Sex?" I asked. Was he afraid to say it?

"Jackhammer is how you described it." A long draw from his milk carton. I watched his Adam's apple rise and fall. His skin was smooth—that's the part of the neck men always have a weird razor burn on, but not Michael. Either good genes or good hygiene. Or both. Oh my.

"Yeah, yeah, that's pretty much right. Super accurate." Sometimes I surprise myself.

"Okay, well, I'm not a relationship expert, but have you tried talking to him about it?"

I shrugged. "Thing is, we have. He knows what I like, and he'll do it...but, he doesn't, like, want to."

"Doesn't want to?" A final swig of his milk. He wiped off the remaining white liquid from his thin lips with a napkin.

"Well," I started, shifting uncomfortably. Yeah, I'm

pretty open-minded and all. I mean, I have to be if I want any chance of getting my jollies off. But I'd only ever told boyfriends. Never a friend. No, let me rephrase. Never someone who I wanted to think well of me. And I did. I wanted him to think I was, well, *good*. Not like a fairy princess kind of good, but more from a moral standpoint. A quintessential good person. Could good people have weird sex fetishes?

Let's not go there. Not yet.

To tell or not to tell? I supposed I wasn't risking much if he thought I was weird, right? Weird sex stuff only sends lovers running for the hills. Not friends. Thing is, what if I wanted him as more of a friend? That was a giant, cold sea of emotions I didn't want to deal with. Honesty is always best though, right? I took a breath and dove into that frozen bitch of a sea.

"What I like isn't exactly normal," I said.

"Well, if you really think about it, none of it is 'normal.'"

"What does that mean?" Did he have *thoughts*? No one had ever had thoughts before.

Michael pushed back a little bit from the table. "We are spoonfed this fall in love, get married, have babies algorithm. It's awful. It's deviant. We spend our lives searching for this one person."

Ouch.

"You don't believe in the one person?" I asked, a little hurt. "You don't believe in love?"

"Well, yeah, I do, but there's got to be thousands of people who would make a great match for each other."

"Not for me. My odds are much, much slimmer." I took the last bite of my donut, rolled it around in my mouth. Somehow, it felt like we were negotiating and I wanted something sweet inside me for this part.

"Look, what I'm saying is you are way, way too cool to be with someone who doesn't at least try. Other fish in the sea and all that stuff."

"He sort of tries," I said.

"Yeah, but you can't stand him."

"He totally grosses me out and he doesn't even have a ponytail." It felt so good to get that off my chest.

"Okay, so tell me. What is it that makes you stay? Are you into bondage?"

"What? No! Gag me. I mean, no. No."

He stood up, leaned over the table, his hands flat against the surface. He squinted his eyes, like trying to solve a math problem. One of those really hard ones where letters get involved.

"Okay, um, are you into feet?"

Was this crouching tiger hiding a dragon? I stood up too, copied his stance.

"Nope." I stuck my tongue out. Feet? Ew.

"Tell me."

"You want to know?"

His face was inches away from mine. I could smell his milk and donut breath, and even the stubble and enlarged pores around his face were taunting me.

"So bad," he said.

"Okay. I like it cold."

"Cold?" he barely blinked. His eyebrows arched a little. Just a little, though. Almost undetectable. Although, if he developed wrinkles, he wouldn't be ugly. It would just give him an air of sophistication. Totally marriageable.

"Yep. Cold." I reached over, took the final bite of his apple fritter. But oh, god, the thing spurted its stupid jelly into my mouth, so I spat it back out on the table. How do people eat the jelly-filled ones?

Michael didn't move. I wiped my mouth, told him: "When I was sixteen I saved my boyfriend from a freezing ice pit and ever since I felt that frozen ice along the inside folds of my Lady Elizabeth's dress, it's all I've wanted. I dream about it but there isn't a Mr. Goodwrench out there that can get cold and stay cold because everything, everything eventually gets warm if it has a stupid fucking heartbeat. I would kill just to cum on something cold that stayed cold. Something that loved me back or even just liked me a little because that love that you say might not exist is the only thing I really want in life. It's easy. I want to help people, fall in love, and finally, finally fuck something that will stay fucking ice cold!"

"What have you tried?"

"Tried? Oh, let's see, walk-in fridges, frozen dolls, frozen dildos, walk-in freezers, frozen strap-ons, popsicles, frozen giant Ken dolls, one regular-sized Aladdin—don't ask—and a variety of produce. I've even tried zel gel. Ever heard of it? It's for fire stunts. It leaves you cold, yeah, but it more removes your heat, so it's not like being in something frozen, it's like being cold and not having a jacket. And, oh-my-god the texture? It's basically the last thing I'd ever give to the Lady, thanks.

"The frozen dolls thaw surprisingly fast, I don't like wasting food, and while the frozen dildos do work, they don't cum. I want to wrap my legs around someone as they blow an ice-filled load of slushie cum into my waiting Lady Elizabeth. I then want to have an orgasm with this someone that could shatter a whole world the way the Death Star destroys Leia's home planet Alderaan. I want to do this with someone I love and who loves me in return. Why can't I have both: love and pleasure? Is it because I'm a woman? It's always the woman who is expected to compromise, isn't it? So, the reason why I'm with Hank, why I deal with him, is because until I find that someone, I may as well get off even if it's not cold. I may as well have the companionship, regardless of how annoying he is."

"So, are you saying you're like Snow White? Thinking that someday your prince will come?"

He smiled a little like the double entendre was super intentional, and I won't lie, I loved it.

"Let me tell you," I said to him. "If I ever find *that* someone, if one day my prince does *arrive*, I will grab his ponytail and ride him better than the ice witch from Narnia rides Mr. Tomnus in the land of everlasting winter. Don't look so surprised. We all know she does. He plays that flute way too seductively."

"Okay." Michael made a noise that was somewhere between a choke and a nervous laugh. "First off, that sounds a little rapey. Like Mr. Tomnus was asking for it. Secondly," Michael continued, "her name is Jadis. And she's the *White* Witch, not the *Ice* Witch."

We were both standing, slightly bent over the table like dogs about to fight. Our sweaty palms were flat against the sugary table. "Can you stand me?" Michael asked.

"You're my partner. We're friends."

"Can you stand me as more?"

"You're not my type," I responded, inches, no, millimeters away from him. I wanted to bite him. I wanted to grab his utility belt and see what sort of tools he was carrying. But I wasn't going to get into another situation like the one I was in with Herbert. Hank! I mean Hank.

Damnit.

Michael nodded. Like admitting defeat. The hopeful part of my emotions that had been swimming around inside my throat went right back down to my belly again. I wanted to throw up. I'd be lying if I said I wasn't a little surprised. Like that one song proclaims, I'd apparently wanted him to want me.

And I mean the version from *10 Things I Hate About You* because Heath Ledger. Duh.

And then.

Then.

Michael took off his glasses.

Behind them were the same, clear blue eyes I'd

come to know so well, only without the glasses framing his eyes I could see something else. Most blue eyes are just expressionless and dead. Only psychopaths have blue eyes. Not Michael's. Behind those glasses, there was a serious spark to them. Something electrifying. A small dot of brown in the iris. A hand reaching up and out through frigid, crystally December water.

He folded his glasses and placed them on the table. Next, he reached up for his hat. I'd never seen him without his weird Russian wooly mammoth hat; it was just part of Michael. Like the glasses. Like the uniform. Like the boots.

"You mentioned you like ponytails?"

In one fell swoop, Michael tore his stupid furry Russian snow hat off and wooft. Guys, let me just say? It was better than a shampoo commercial.

Perfect, deep brown locks cascaded around Michael. They piled at his shoulders, framed his face, and brought out his eyes. The Beast just became the Prince and I was Belle, unable to do anything but swoon and breathe heavily. I was incredibly aware of how tight my uniform was. How even the back of my neck was sweaty.

Michael pulled his hair back in a quick, practiced movement. From his wrist, he snaked up a hair tie I'd never seen there before. It was black and worn with bits of the white rubber band poking through. He moved his perfect mane into a smooth, long ponytail and said, "Let's play *Titanic*."

Chapter Five

I suppose you can guess what happens next? Right? I mean, I don't know if you can tell, but I'm not one to gossip. A lady doesn't discuss what happens with her love behind closed doors, so you'll just have to imagine.

Ha! As if.

We wanted to take each other there in the donut shop. Michael did the swoop to clear the table of everything, but there was only a napkin holder, my spit-out chunk of fritter, and his milk carton. They clattered to the floor, and it was such a sad, pathetic sound I laughed a little.

Okay, a lot, but Michael grabbed my hand and pulled me from the booth.

We made it out to the rig and he flipped on the lights and sirens. With blood pumping down to the Lady Elizabeth, I want to say it was unpleasant or something because of the heat. But really it wasn't. It more tickled. Felt like pins and needles and I just *wanted* him.

That's never happened before. Before the Lady had just been like, yeah, sure, I suppose I can receive some guests. Now? Now she was out of her throne and practically begging. And? Play Titanic? Would I be Rose or Jack? Obviously I'd rather be Rose because of the whole female thing (we have that in common, me and her) but I imagine I could be Jack too. I'd need to make a stop by my place, but I've mentioned I can MacGyver things? You'd be shocked how many things are shaped like a giant meat stick. It's like the human race suffers from little dick syndrome and needs to make as many things as huge and pointy as possible.

Fun fact! Ambulances are only in a crazy rush if the lights AND the sirens are on. If they just have lights, that means they're heading somewhere, or, they have a passenger but the person in the back isn't dying. Those lights are just there to warn the public, make sure everyone is being careful.

It's way, way illegal and we could have lost our jobs but like Stephen Wolfe, I just felt so born to be wild.

I clung to the oh shit handle in the ambulance even though I wanted to hang my body outside the window. I wanted to feel the winter air on my skin but people would surely report an ambulance with a paramedic hanging out of the side, right? I used to do that, on frozen nights. My brother, Tyler, would let me sit on the lip of the window to his white mustang and take turns too tight, go down hills crazy fast, so I could feel the wind in my hair and against my neck and tears would prickle at the corner of my eyes.

He joined the military because he's stupid and I miss him. Oh, sorry. I'm getting sentimental and I don't mean to. It's a bad look and makes my eyebrows do that weird crinkle in the middle thing. I fight the urge to look in the vanity and try to peek at the side mirror instead and hope that like Jurassic Park, objects in the mirror are closer than they appear. I'm too young to get wrinkles. I'll just die when my totally naturally blonde hair goes grey. Not that anyone will know. Come on, let's get real.

"Where are we going?" I asked.

"Back to the plant," Michael answered, eyes on the road.

"Back there? Why?"

"Everyone has been evacuated."

"Duh! Isn't there, like, radiation?"

Look, it's so very rare that I'm the voice of reason, but I don't fucking want cancer from the radiation or the chemicals or the cow fats on my pristine body. (I'm not full of myself. There's a gym at our home base. On slow days you can either sleep, work out, or jerk off, and I'm not going to sleep all day, so that leaves two things and they both burn calories, so I'm just calling it like it is.)

"I got a chance to see their walk-in freezer. It's been totally cleaned out of meat."

Oh, I hope *some* meat will survive in sub-zero temperatures, if you know what I mean. What was he planning? I may like it cold, but I'm not heartless. I'm a paramedic for Christ's sake. What I'm saying is, I give a shit. Several, in fact. I may like the cold, but come on. I'm aware of the effects. It's painful. If it wasn't, I would have just stuffed Brandon through the ice hole again and again and kept him as my personal frozen-dick Loch Ness monster, but you know what they say about hindsight.

"Listen," I placed a hand on Michael's arm. It was

firm. His arm. I mean, I'm sure my grip was too because only awful people grasp with a dead fish hand, but let's get back to his arms. Firm with a capital F. I wanted to see them outside of his faux fur-lined paramedic parka. "I like it cold," I told him, "but I don't want you to get hurt." I made sure to give his meat stick a pointed glance.

And you know what? I waited to feel like I was lying. I waited for that sinking feeling in the back of my throat I'd always get with the other men when I'd say that yeah, yeah, they were really good at pounding my Lady Elizabeth. But the feeling never came. I honestly didn't want him hurt.

I sat back, mouth open in wonder. I cared? I cared.

"Don't worry, Sadie. I'm fond of my King Henry. I wouldn't hurt him. But I do want to try something."

We pulled up to the plant and I can honestly say I had no idea what he had in mind.

—

We walked into the freezer, and thank god all of the animals were cleared out. Probably to be boxed up and sent to the highest bidder. You have to hand it to America; nary a carcass goes unsold.

Watch your burgers. I don't know. What I'm saying is I'd give the market a minute to clear out. Maybe a year just to be safe. Just saying, Michael and I ended up wearing oxygen masks at the end of shift because we were having a hard time breathing, and the meat that was present for all of that, well, you're slathering it with a healthy amount of ketchup and feeding it to

Junior.

"What are you thinking about?" Michael said.

"Fast food and children."

Michael nodded knowingly. "Yeah, me too. We have to make healthy food more accessible."

He was so sweet!

Michael kissed me lightly (our first kiss!) and suddenly, the only frozen meat I was thinking of was his. He lay me down on the cold, hard floor. Both of us fumbled in our clothes because the shitty thing about being a paramedic is we have these ridiculous lace-up boots, and we also have to tuck everything in. I mean, the hours are shitty too, but that's not what I'm talking about right now. What was I talking about?

Clothes! Off! Not on. Yes!

He was out of his parka, hat, and over-shirt first. Underneath his attire, he sported a fantastically tight white T-shirt.

Can I just say? I love a man who can wear the fuck out of those T-shirts. Not the wife beaters, but the other ones. They come in a three-pack at Target.

Michael's biceps and forearms seemed that much bigger, that much darker and broad against his clean white shirt. Also, in our line of work, if he's maintained the whiteness in his shirts, he fucking knows how to do laundry.

I bet he even hangs it up. No one hangs their laundry up. My GOD. Would he hang my laundry up too? It was mostly uniforms, despite what you might think. I know I sound like I have a plethora of crotchless panties and a washable sex swing, but that's you thinking that just because I want to get off, I'm a total sex/freak/addict. You should really see a therapist. Society has done a number on you.

So, I'm watching him there, seeing him whip off his glasses, unleash his mane of amazing, thick hair again, and I let my crazy out.

"I can't wait until we move in together."

He lay down on top of me, one hand sliding through my hair to find purchase and the other one keeping him up so all of his weight wasn't on my perfect, petite body because he had MUSCLES and he kissed me with purpose. His tongue wasn't forceful and our teeth only accidentally knocked together once.

"If you think about it," he said, a little breathlessly, tugging at my pants, "we already live together half of the week."

"Oh, keep saying things like that."

The Lady Elizabeth was feeling a deep, deep need to be touched, to be prodded, and then fucking ravaged. And he hadn't even made his dick cold yet. What sort of sorcery was this? What magic did he possess over me?

Michael kissed me again and I could feel a smile curl the corners of his perfectly thin lips. "Sometimes I watch you sleep."

He lifted up my shirt and began to lightly kiss my belly, then traveled up to nipples that were tight and hard from the cold air but also from him being so, so fucking sexy.

"More!" I said, somewhere between a moan and a squeal. I know those things are opposite, but I'm telling the story, not you. You want to hear the sexy stuff or what?

My hands went to his pants and then we were both undoing belts. I kicked my pants off, let him see all of me because I don't wear underwear. The Lady Elizabeth likes to be free. Michael didn't even blink, but ran a hand between my thighs, her lips.

"I've heard you fart in your sleep and it was so bad I left the room."

I laughed, leaned up and bit his neck, just to mark him. Just to let him know he was mine. I felt a couple of fingers enter me, feeling around experimentally. They were long and thick, which was a good sign.

"More," I said, with a little gasp afterwards.

Michael leaned in. I didn't mind his breath against my ear. See, his heat, while it did kill it a little bit for me, his breath landed on my freezing ears so it felt different. Didn't feel like he was ruining anything, but more, sending pulses of lightning through me. Like the heat and cold were meeting and formed this new perfect baby named desire.

His words came out in a rush, all hot and breathy: "Tell me your credit score, Blondie. I want to make sure we can buy a big house one day."

Oh. My. God.

"And what would we do with such a big house and fabulous credit scores?"

"Fill it with babies."

"Get your fucking clothes off."

He kicked at his own pants. There was a massive *thunk* from his trouser snake hitting the ground.

Hallelujah!

Guys? As a lady, I have to tell you. There is a moment before sex, before we succumb to our desire, before we decide that hell, whatever you have in your pants will do? We dare to hope you are about to unveil Thor, the Rod of Thunder. I'm sorry, but we don't want your sad penis. Notice how I used the clinical term? Picture me saying this through a megaphone. *We don't want your sad penis! We want the Third Leg Lancelot to sate our Queen Guinevere!*

Moving on.

Michael stood up, pulled me up with him. "Come with me."

I did. We went into the back room I hadn't been in before. Naked, holding my hand, Michael nodded. He put his glasses back on, leaned in, and kissed me.

"If this doesn't work, I'm not out of ideas. Okay? Stay with me. I'll figure it out."

Michael's one-eyed monster heaved just above my Lady Elizabeth in time with Michael's breaths.

And then he left me there, in the dark. I mean, it wasn't totally dark. It was still light outside, but it made me very aware of my skin. How alone I was. How I didn't really know what to do with my arms.

A noise through the walls and above me. I jumped a little in surprise. Water rained down from unseen spigots overhead. Cold, cold water rushed down me. It felt like the icy water from the pond was splashing over me again. The pipes must have been near freezing— considering it was winter outside. The water, my god, it was like I was in the middle of a crystalized blizzard and the cold was wrapping around me, touching everywhere. It sunk into my bones, spread its icy hold along them, gripped at my teeth and the back of my head where spine meets skull.

Yes.

Michael was heading towards me, his walk could only be described as Terminator and I was super, super ready to come with him. To, you know, live.

Buckets of water rained down on him. His hair was already plastered against the back of his neck and the sides of his face. In the dim light, the water made him sparkle.

I was going to have to promote the Lady. After this, she just might be a Queen.

He pulled me to him, and that's how we did it. In the freezer with the water on. It was like we were on top of the ice. It's like we were every splendid thing. He lifted me up. I grabbed one of the hooks that probably had a dead animal on it not six hours ago. I wrapped my legs around Michael's waist, and when he entered me, his King Henry was cold and it's sort of like what Jack said in Titanic. I was on top of the world.

Chapter Six? I think?

It totally didn't work. It wasn't frozen enough. But, that can take a knee, because the lovemaking itself was off the goddamn charts. Michael was all around me. His arms and back could hold me. His lips almost never left mine and never once did I think of a jackhammer. No. We were two bodies moving as one. We were intertwined. We existed together.

Together.

He knew my weirdness and hadn't left. He knew what I wanted and had tried. Really tried. Seriously. King Henry even turned a little blue at one point, but he'd kept going. He'd even snaked his icy fingers down to play around with the Lady, but those, too, became too warm.

Sigh.

Didn't stop us from doing it everywhere in the slaughterhouse. And at the end, we lay down on the cold floor. Michael kissed me one final time, and then pulled his clothes on and snuggled up next to me in full uniform plus his parka and his weird Russian hat.

"Cold?" I asked him, laughing a little. I didn't want to get dressed yet. I was sprawled out, butterfly open.

"Freezing," he said. "I'm sorry it didn't work."

I leaned on my elbow to see him, to really look into his clear blue non-psychopathic eyes.

"It's okay. I mean, I'm sad, because I'd have been way stoked if it worked. But this was still...there's something else happening."

"With the Lady?" He smiled and the edges of his lips crinkled. That alone made my cold heart melt a little. Not that melting is good; it was sweet is all.

"No, like, with us." I bit my lip, wondering if my

Barbie could finally get her Prince Ali.

Michael looked away. Oh god. I wanted to bury my head in my hands. For shame! I'd gone too far. Of course he'd just been playing when he talked about wanting to share credit.

"It's like..." he started, and I held my breath, "it's like an invisible shield, or cloak almost." He rolled back over to me, wrapped his clothed arm around my waist, and pulled me in. "I feel it everywhere. Even in my fingertips."

I nodded against his parka. Yes, yes. That's what it was. How it felt.

And we rested there, breathing each other in, letting that first touch of love descend upon us like the best blanket. The kind that keeps the wind off you, but still wraps around all nice and makes you feel like you're getting a gentle hug.

I can like blankets. What, just because I like it cold I can't enjoy a nice blankie? I'm not a monster. Gosh. And it's how it felt, okay? Fuck. I'm not good at describing stuff, okay? Not like I'm a writer. Plus, everyone describes love differently. It's called perspective. I learned about it in my photography class in college. Did you know it only takes a year to become an EMT-Paramedic? It takes way longer to get an English degree, and who uses that?

So, to describe love? Hm. Okay, how about this. Music is the universal language, right? Let's put it this way. In that moment, I believed the Beatles. It was true. All you need is love. All *we* needed was love.

Chapter um...Seven? Crap.

"Guys? Unit eight-oh-oh-eight, do you copy?" Vicki-with-an-i spoke up from the radio out of the dark.

"Guess we're back on," Michael huffed.

"I still feel traumatized. I think we should get longer than twelve hours to deal with our feelings," I said, sniggering a little. Michael kissed me.

"Ambulance eight-zero-zero-eight, do you copy?"

"Let's deal with our feelings some more tomorrow? After shift?" I asked.

"Guys! Seriously. What the hell?"

"Deal. Also, say it's ambulance 'Boob,'" Michael dared.

"I'm not saying that."

"Come on!" His smile was too big and reminded me too much of Health Ledger. I'd have done anything for that smile.

"Michael! Sadie! I swear I will so tell on you, pick up the goddamn radio."

"Yeah, this is ambulance Boob. What can I do for you?"

"Lord, give me strength..."

"See? She loved it."

I swatted at Michael who probably didn't feel much through his layers and layers of clothing. Such a pussy. Adorable, though.

"Thank sweet Jesus that God judges all because he's

saving me some trouble right now."

"Tell her I turned her crosses upside down when she wasn't looking." Michael snickered.

"That just means you corrected them. I turned them upside down six months ago." When I learned she dots her *is* with a heart. What I'm saying is, she had it coming.

"There's been an incident at the UM fraternity."

Actually? That fraternity is important. Let's name it for emphasis. I know! Frat house douche-canoe. Perfect.

Anyway.

My eyes went wide. Hank! He said he would call in an accident. No. He didn't. I'll kill him.

Michael took the radio from my hands, clicked it on to talk to Vicky-with-an-i (no, I'm not doing it. It's not natural).

"Can't you send the other rig? Jorge and Kyle? We're still distraught."

"You guys are closest."

"All right, we're on our way." I stood up to pull my uniform on.

"Listen," Michael said. "This will at least give you a chance to break up with him."

"Oh, oh yeah." I'd forgotten that I needed to end things with him. Now that I'd found Michael, every other relationship I'd ever had paled in comparison. Had Hector (no! Hank) and I even been in a relationship? Did I even know what love felt like until Michael?

No. No, I didn't. Not really. And you know? The truth of that should have made me feel naïve, but it didn't. Instead, I felt this sense of chilled relief swirl around inside. Like it was all going to be okay. Like the loneliness and longing I'd felt before, I'd never feel again.

Ugh. But, the right thing to do was to break it off with Hank. He was 50% of the relationship, after all, regardless of how I felt.

Morals.

Also. What if someone was, like, actually hurt? Do no harm, right?

Chapter Eight? Yes! Chapter Eight.

We arrived at the Fraternity Douche-Canoe (don't you love how that just rolls off your tongue?) Generally, when you pull up in an ambulance, there's someone waiting outside. To, you know, flag it down. That wasn't the case with this because we knew where we were going.

We were lights and sirens until we got to the house.

It was quiet. Too quiet.

"Think we'll need the backboard?" Michael was looking through the windshield, his glasses a little fogged up from the heat inside the rig.

"No. I think I know what's going down. Bring your pad and pen though, okay? We're writing down a statement and this motherfucker is going to refuse treatment."

"Glad you don't go into every call like that."

Michael and I left the rig and climbed up to the frat house. Hard to believe it had already been over twenty-four hours. It seemed like Michael had just picked me up from out front. The door was cracked, so I nudged it to open a bit so we could see inside.

"Hello?" I called into the house. No one answered. I opened the door completely. The large common room that was normally way over its maximum capacity was barren and dark. "What the Hell?"

And then, from the floor above, a big white bedsheet unfurled at the bottom corners. Displayed like a banner across the rails for all to see were the words *I love you* scrawled in pink, cursive letters.

And it wasn't just pink.

It was baby pink.

It was the color of cheap bubble gum that loses its flavor. The color of a little girl's bedroom. It looked like how those tiny heart-shaped candies taste.

And then the song *Hey Baby* by No Doubt blared. You guys know how I feel about No fucking Doubt. Hank stood at the top of the stairs with a giant black boom box on his shoulders.

Barf. Throw up. Gag me. What in all that is good and holy was this?

"Surprise!" he called. Everyone called. Frat jocks appeared from the hallways, popped out of closets, opened their room doors.

And what the fuck was Hank dressed in? I narrowed my eyes (my faraway vision isn't so great anymore from staring at tiny stitches. I'd say tiny dicks to be funny, but I can't even say it. Be real. I don't fuck dudes with little dicks) so it took me a moment to realize he was in a goddamn man thong. Lingerie?

Because nothing says MAN in all caps like cupping a limp dick in fancy silk. Lord, give me a half-dressed Viking with blood from a battle smeared across his face before you give me this fluffy version of God's supposed image. I'd rather fuck against a rough tree with snow falling than be softly fluffed in a bed of feathers and pillows and fucking goose down or whatever people have. It's sanded down and unsalted. It's smooth and easy. It's society trying to sell us shit for something that should be natural. This is, dare I say it?

Warm.

Warm as tepid bathwater. (Showers are for winners. No one older than five should take a bath.)

I'd been on a cold floor with Michael. I'd been nestled and happy. My Lady Elizabeth had been full of Michael's King Henry, and my belly had been full of sprinkled donuts. What. The. Fuck.

Deep inside my gut there was something bubbling and it went all the way to my head and I'm sure it turned my face and ears red. Rage. Michael and I were just already so connected that he must have sensed my discontent.

"Sadie? Sadie, don't explode. We're on a call."

"What the fuck *is* this?"

"Money in the swear jar for you. If the boss hears you've been cussing on a call again..."

I couldn't unclench my fists. To be fair, the anger wasn't only at Hank, but it was against the world. For doing this to sex. For watering down and taming something that should be wild. Did my supposed boyfriend know me so little? What a big, terrible gesture to do for someone you think you know. Michael cleared his throat.

"You must be Hector?" he asked.

"Hank."

"Cool. Listen, Harry, we got a call?"

"It was for my lady love. I have an ache only she can fix." He pressed his hips to the railing so his man thong showed through the bars.

I needed to break it off with him. I needed to be calm and act rationally. I was, as Michael kindly pointed out, working.

"Take your satin covered dick back to your frat boys for your nightly circle-jerk, you watered-down version of a man! Do the world a favor and hang yourself with your greasy jockstrap!"

Okay, let me explain.

If Hank had been into dudes and enjoyed circle-jerks, I would have supported him completely because I, Sadie Snow, think all love is beautiful. I was—and I'm not proud of it—getting cheap shots in by poking at his outdated sense of masculinity. I'm not saying this is how men should be. I'm just saying Hank was that kind of jock.

Yeah, was. Past tense. Don't worry.

So, I was somewhere between throwing up and screaming. There was an ax next to the fire extinguisher and I was thinking I could pull both out? I could pressure blast this cock-sucking shit-eating cum bucket of human waste and then just start hacking away and the blood—

"Sadie?" Michael's voice cut through my important thoughts. I turned to him. His eyes gave me a thousand questions and nothing, nothing I could say could make this any better, and maybe he understood because he didn't wait, he just nodded.

"Listen, Harold. I'm not going to report you, but if no one's hurt, we are leaving."

My future husband took my shoulders, turned me around, and we headed back outside. Hank's voice followed.

"But, I thought we were in love!"

Michael stopped tugging on me and tossed me over his shoulder in a fireman carry. From my new position—slung across Michael's shoulder—I shouted the final, most hurtful thing I could think of to Hank.

"You suck at football!"

His face turned upside down. His brow furrowed, his smile curved down into a frown, and even his nostrils sagged a little. Fucking pathetic.

"Whatever, freak!" he called, loud enough for anyone who hadn't already heard use could hear him now. "Only freaks like what you like. You're a frigid bitch!"

It was my exact fear. It was everything I was worried people would say about me. It was my secret. And he told.

I heard them.

"Wait, she likes it cold?"

"Yeah, man. She likes cold stuff shoved up her pussy. Have fun with your ice queen, fucking queer!"

"Fri-gid bitch! Fri-gid bitch!"

Their chants followed me and I wanted to simultaneously hide my face and shove my fist down Hank's fat throat. But then we were outside by the rig and Michael had set me down. His grip on my shoulders was strong, his hands held me steady.

"Don't listen. Whatever they say, it doesn't matter. You've got me now."

I nodded against his jacket. I didn't even realize I was crying, like really sobbing. I didn't realize they could hurt me like that.

"I'm fine!" I sputtered.

"Funny how we will always care about what people think of us, huh?" God, he really was perfect. He just got everything. I pushed away from him a little, just so I could look up into his eyes that I actually really liked even if they were blue.

"And you don't care? About me?"

Michael smiled a wonderful smile that crinkled at the corners and there was snow on his glasses and his funny hat and the ice collected on his jacket and melted against my skin and in the moment of cold and weather and taunts, I felt home.

I think that's what love is. I think love is feeling at home wherever you are, as long as you're with that person.

We released each other. I went over to my side of the rig. Michael always drove. Even though the frat house was still yelling, was still jeering, I felt okay. No, better than okay. I felt at peace. It was okay. I'd found love and we were together now. My Lady Elizabeth had her Dudley. The Prince Ali to my Barbie. We opened our doors and looked at each other. I smiled.

"What?" he asked.

"Be the Jack to my Rose?" I said.

"Oh, babe." His eyes glittered. As the snow piled onto his funny hat he said those perfect, wonderful words I'd been waiting to hear since I saw *Titanic*. "I'll never let—"

And then a snowplow ran him the fuck over.

———

I don't know how we didn't hear it. I don't know how the plow didn't see us. I don't know why the fuck it was going so fast. Just don't ask hard questions, okay?

I do remember white. The world went dark and then light and then it was just fast and bright. I remember screaming. I know I did that.

The plow had gobbled Michael's legs, had taken him down like a goddamn lion on the Serengeti. His legs were eaten, and from the force of going down, he'd hit his head. There was blood under the back of his skull, but he was awake.

I want to put quotes here. I do. I wish I could tell you we had a moment of loving perfect words.

Instead, it was more like N'Sync and it was all just tearing up my heart.

Our words were quick. They were business. They were work. They were desperate.

I grabbed my medic pack from the back of the rig and slid to my knees in front of Michael. I threaded ace bandages around his legs and pulled. I held one side tight with my teeth, cinching it so my hands could get a good grip and tie double knots.

"The joint, my knee. Save it?" he was saying.

"I don't know if I can. I'll try. I think I have to go higher..."

"Something, something's wrong. Something's crushed..."

"I know, I know, just stay still. I've got you." I scrawled a big T across his forehead with my lipstick. For the ER doctors. For when they went in and repaired everything that was busted.

Fun fact! Soldiers have built-in tourniquets in their uniform arms and legs. Honestly, I think we should all have that. I mean, if you're worried about the cost of a little more cloth, stop giving us girls the stupid fake pockets. It's just confusing.

Tears sprouted from Michael's eyes. His hands grabbed at air. "Sadie? Help me. Get me out. Sadie?" His eyes were starting to go far away. It was too quick. I'd heard of people living with crush injuries for days. Something else was bleeding. Something I couldn't see.

Think think think.

The plow driver was talking, but Michael had all my attention. At some point, someone must have called another ambulance because I heard sirens.

"Something's wrong. Take my leg. Cut me free. Get me away." Tears down his cheeks and his eyes were going glassy and the snow around us was turning a dark crimson.

"This isn't the fucking eighteen-hundreds," I hissed at him. "I'm not sawing off your leg. You're going to be okay, just stay with me, all right?"

"Something's wrong. Something's wrong."

"What? What?" When someone is telling you something is wrong, believe them. It's their body, after all.

I looked at his legs again. Fuck, we had a bone saw, but a fucking amputation without narcotics? And awake? That was some medieval shit. In the movies, the person getting their foot sawed off bites down on something so they don't bite their tongue off because yay old fashioned medicine. See? Fucking Florence Nightingale could have done, like, a thousand other things that would have been more helpful than opening a fucking window.

Something to bite down on.

I'd have to go above the knees which would suck and his snowboarding days were so over. But wait, one of his legs looked bigger somehow. He had thinner legs, so why was just one leg straining at the cloth?

I pulled my pocket knife out. I did a quick cut and

then tore through the rest of his pant leg. His left leg was bulbous and pulsating.

"No."

"Sadie..."

I moved the tourniquet up and tightened it but if his femoral artery was dumping blood into his leg it was probably because a busted bone had ripped it, which meant there was nothing, nothing I could do without a way to get in and stop the bleeding and I'm so, so not a surgeon. That's, like, a ten-year degree. I sat in class for two semesters and took one hard test. What I'm saying is, I have room to improve.

You have maybe four minutes before you bleed out. Maybe seven if you have crazy low blood pressure, but that's pushing it and he'd already lost so much.

Cold! Cold can slow the blood.

I stood up and started packing snow around him. I'm O negative and hypothetically, I could have done a field transfusion which is literally sticking me with a needle, sticking him with a needle and his heart sucks up my blood. But, the blood would have just poured out alongside his, and at that point, I realized I was totally, unforgivably grasping at straws because I was thinking about a fucking field transfusion in 19 goddamn 99.

"Sadie...Blondie..." His breath was hitching and I say hitching and not hitched because it kept happening. Like his lungs were hiccupping. Like he was my very own mermaid gasping for air.

"I'm here, keep talking." I worked. I checked his

pulse and tightened his tourniquets and checked the superficial wound on the back of his head. I checked his eyes for concussion, his ears for brain discharge (not the technical term, but basically what it is) and then...and then there was nothing left to do but sit back on my heels, run my hands through my hair. Something else. Something else. Something else.

"Michael, tell me where it's worse? I can, I can maybe..."

A breath. A blink.

"Michael?"

And then the hand I didn't realize I was holding became heavy the way the other side of the bed goes heavy when your partner falls asleep.

"Michael!"

He loved me. We loved each other. And it was only beginning. He'd accepted me and we were going to play Barbie and Aladdin get married and have a mortgage and I would have taken care of him because he was taking care of me and we'd have been together for all the fights and the not fights and I don't know if we'd have opted for kids but of COURSE we'd have had dogs and he was leaving me. Leaving me before we could even start.

And something cracked. The ice pond that was my brain fractured down the middle. Some part of me that I didn't even know existed packed up her bags and left.

"Michael!" I left his side and I got the d-fib unit. "Come back!"

I knew it wouldn't fix anything. I could restart his

heart all I wanted. He was still out of blood.

I placed the pads in their allotted spots (below the heart and another on the right chest plate) and I didn't do CPR because I could have just been forcing more blood out of his body because when you do CPR you're circulating the blood so if someone is way, way bleeding out then it's just not right. But I could shock him. I could maybe keep him. I could tell him what he meant to me. I could bring him back.

I armed the de-fib unit and the familiar lady's voice checked for heart rhythms.

"Shock advised," she proclaimed. "Stand clear." I could bring him back with the press of a button. I could do it. I could bring him back. I stood clear, button in hand.

And then I got tackled.

Chapter, um Nine? Whatever.

The official report states that I wouldn't stop CPR. Just that one sentence. So easy, so contrite. You could spell almost every word wrong and people would still understand what it meant.

The reason why that's what the official report says? It's to protect me. The other ambulance on call (I'd mentioned Kyle and Jorge) wrote out a statement. They were nice guys. Kyle was long as a string bean. He was a little douchey—probably because his parents named him Kyle. The other one was a squat dude named Jorge. He's the one who grabbed me and pulled me off Michael. Kyle saw to Michael, helped the plow back off of my one true love and load him up into the back of a rig; all closed up in a black body bag. I fought against Jorge the whole time. I struggled and bit and screamed.

Someone has a recording of this on their video camera, I know it.

Kyle and Jorge brought me to the hospital. I rode in between them because they wouldn't let me in the back. I tried. I grabbed the wheel. I bit Kyle. And then I remember going still. Going very, very still. Just staring ahead. Kyle and Jorge had passed a few glances over my head, I'm sure, but I don't remember if it looked like concern or fear.

At the hospital, I sat with my feet on the floor, my hands gripping the armrests. My hair was loose and hung straight down. This stands out to me because I'm more of an all-business severe ponytail person.

Shock does strange things to a person. Before, I'd never been cruel and asked someone to 'snap out of it' or 'pull through,' but now, going through it myself, I'm sure I'd done or said something highly inappropriate to someone at some point. For that, I'm sorry.

"Hon?" Nurse Nancy was in front of me. I liked her kind brown eyes. I like brown eyes better than blue. I've mentioned that, right? I don't mean to make the blue-eyed community angry or anything. Just, blue eyes look like you're dead inside. No offense. Don't get me started on green eyes.

Since you asked.

Everyone with green eyes always flaunts them like it's their only good quality and moment of truth? Most of the time, they are one-hundred percent right.

"My green eyes are so beautiful! So *rare*," green-eyed people say.

"Good, because the rest of you is regular," is what I want to say back.

Do I sound judgy? It's because I am. I was. I sat across from the body of the only person who had loved me, who I felt all the right things with, and he was so, so still underneath that sheet, so excuse me if I was a little disenchanted with society and everyone in it. Especially green-eyed people.

"Hon? Sadie?" Nurse Nancy patted my hand. I blinked and some tears rolled away from my eyes. I wasn't sobbing, more just perpetually leaking. Nurse Nancy went behind me and pulled my hair away from my face. She knew me so well. A couple of years back, when I was brand new, she was the only nurse who was kind to me. Nurses tend to be bitches because they are overworked and underpaid and super high on their own shit, but not Nurse Nancy. She'd whispered instructions to me on how to transfer patients from gurney to hospital bed, told me which doctors to avoid because they'd had to clean up my MacGyvers. (Why get mad if it kept the patient alive?)

Nurse Nancy used one of her own rubber bands to secure the end of a braid she'd comfortingly weaved my hair into. I felt a little less crazed.

"I have to go, love. But is there someone you can call? I'm so sorry. You were such a pair."

Someone to talk to. Yes. Yes, that's what you are supposed to do in a crisis. When your world falls apart.

The only person I wanted to talk to was my brother, Tyler, who was an active duty Marine. Fortunately, he lived off base. I could call him. I could see if he in a place where he could maybe talk.

I felt like if I called Tyler that would take the last, little popsicle stick bit of strength I still had.

But the fear of being alone? That's just this empty blackness that stretches on eternally. And maybe that's why I was using all the Hanks of the world (well, not THAT many, but it's also not like I'm going to go and count all the marks on my bedpost or anything. Go ahead. Call me a slut. If I were a man, you'd call me a player, so fuck you and your thoughts. Eat my Lady Elizabeth) because I'd been too afraid to look down that long, dark empty hallway of isolation.

Michael could have been a light. Or we could have just held hands in the dark.

Being all by yourself, it's not good for the soul. I know that much and in hindsight, maybe that's what got me into this mess.

I stepped outside to the payphones. My Nokia cellphone was back at my apartment. No reason to take it everywhere with me, right? Some people are attached to the damn things, but it's like, if no one's calling you, there's only so much Tetris and Snake you can play. Plus, texting is SO annoying. And don't get me started on computers these days.

I popped a couple of quarters into the payphone, dialed by heart.

"Sadie? Hang on."

My favorite thing about my brother? His voice. It's so deep some people have a hard time understanding him when he's mumbling or tired. I've never had that problem. His voice is more like a heartbeat. A low lullaby I know all the words to. It took twenty minutes of a dark, quiet hold until my brother's voice came back.

"Sadie?"

"Hey, Ty."

"Everything okay? You never call me in the middle of the day."

"My partner on my ambulance...he was just killed."

"Oh. Oh! The guy we met last Christmas?"

Michael had indeed stopped by. He'd been wearing a Santa hat instead of his wooly mammoth hat and an ugly Christmas sweater. God, I'd crushed on him even then. I remember finding his Christmas sweater adorable. Had anyone else been wearing something as ridiculous as that, I'd have judged them hard. Not Michael. He was cute in his Santa Hat and weird sweater. How had we really just been friends? How much time did we lose? I wish I'd ripped his stupid reindeer sweater off then and there. Made his Rudolph nose glow.

"I'm sorry, Sadie. I didn't know, I mean, were you more than friends? What can I do?"

I was stupid. So dumb. I shouldn't have called him. How could he understand?

"I tried everything, Ty."

"I'm sure you did."

A commotion behind me. Were they already coming for the body?

"Ty, sorry. I have to go."

"Wait, Sadie. You called me."

"I know, I'm sorry. I just needed to hear your voice." Yeah, it's cliché and whatever but seriously? My family has been the only normal part of my life. I mean, Tyler and I were two years apart. We spent every Christmas opening up presents side by side. We helped each other sneak out of the house at night. He started driving first and got saddled with having to take me to school and track meets. He stopped complaining after he saw the varsity girls. They trained in spandex and sports bras.

So yeah, I needed to hear my big brothers' voice. I won't apologize. Fuck you.

"Do you need me to come out? I'm a flight away. I have some time saved."

I bit my lip. Tyler leaving was a big deal. I wasn't sure I wanted him to go through the headache of getting leave approved.

"Can I let you know later?"

"Of course. I'm here whenever, okay? Turn your cell on. I'll call in the next couple of days to check on you. All right?"

I bit back tears, rubbed my face real hard to get the

emotion good and gone. Hearing his voice was sometimes too much and everything would just come forward. Before long, I'd be telling him. I'd be telling him I was afraid I was going to die alone and how close I got to finding my person. My lobster. Watch *Friends* if you don't get the reference. Not that there is much hope for you or your soul if you haven't seen *Friends*.

A sob erupted from the bottom of my throat. I thought I clasped my hand over my mouth quickly enough, but damn him, he heard. Or he just knew.

"I'll fly out tomorrow."

"No, no. Tyler, it's okay."

"It's not like we're at war or anything. I'm sitting on my thumbs in San Diego." I nodded but still wasn't sure if I wanted someone else to feel this grief with me.

"I'll watch for your call," I told him. He sighed over the phone.

"How about this. I have leave for New Year's. That's in three days. Can I come check on you? We'll hang out. You can drink that awful tequila shit you enjoy."

"But the plane ticket, it's going to be expensive."

"I'll be fine. You're worth it."

"Thanks. I'll see you then. I mean, unless the computers crash and we all die."

"Would make everything easier, living in a post-apocalyptic world. May Y-two-K bring the end of the world as we know it."

"Totally." Tyler was such a nihilist. It always made me happy to hear how much he hated people.

"Love you, stupid," he said. "I'll see you for New Years'?"

"Sure. Love you too."

We hung up.

Understand that I did love him. Okay? Maybe he didn't know about me, but he was my brother, and I loved him.

I dragged my feet into Michael's room—into the room of the only man who would ever accept me. The person I was supposed to be with.

We never should have left that slaughterhouse.

And I almost giggled because all those other movie actor people have those lines of 'we still have Paris' or whatever. God. That's what we had. A slaughterhouse because we needed somewhere cold to fuck so he could try to please me.

I wanted to see him. No, I needed to see him, even if he was just a body underneath the sheet.

I held my breath and pulled the sheet away from my one true love.

His legs had stopped bleeding. Where there should have been something meatier, it was just sort of flat. Like it was Michael, and then a bunch of hamburger from the knees down.

I took another step closer to Michael. No. Michael's body. *He* was long gone. I had to remember that. He was nothing more than worm food.

His face was all contorted, frozen in an O shape that was all death and no sex. His eyes were open and glassed over—they belonged to something that should be on a wall, all stuffed and hung up.

Just that morning he'd brought me coffee. Just that day I'd felt those arms around me. He'd been everything I wanted.

No. It wasn't him. Not anymore.

I was supposed to be saying goodbye. They would come for his body soon, no matter what.

So, it was time to do the worst, hardest thing, right? I took a deep, brave breath.

"Bye, Michael. Thank you for being the Jack to my Rose, however brief." I sat down on his bed, held his hand, and stared into those dead, depthless eyes. I leaned down. I kissed him goodbye and thank you and a million other things I'd have thought or said throughout our lifetime together.

And then the words I'd told Tyler crept into the back of my head.

I tried everything.

But I hadn't. Right? Not really. No, they'd stopped me. Jorge and Kyle had arrived and wrote that I'd been doing CPR when really I'd been screaming at them to stand clear of him because he was wired up to the de-fib unit and he was my friend, my partner, mine to revive.

Mine.

I had to try. Understand?

Lucky me, there were two full crash kits just to the left of his bed.

I ripped the sheet off his body, opened his shirt, and placed the de-fib pads in the places you're not supposed to: directly over his heart and another behind his neck—the spot where spine meets brain.

Never try this when saving someone. It *will* kill them. But, to bring them back to life? All bets are off. I pressed the button.

"Shock advised. Stand clear."

Yes, ma'am!

I pressed the button and sent a shock that slithered through him. Was kind of like that flop a fish does when you take it out of its bowl.

Really? You've never done that? Just me?

There was the smell of burning hair and then nothing. He was still just as dead. And not even sexy dead like Jack when he was in the water. (They both totally could have fit on that door, by the way.)

No. He was loose and floppy. He was sagging. He was temperate.

Of course, because what did I expect? Stupid. Clearly, he needed more electricity.

I unwrapped the other unit. I had no idea what plugging two of the units into the same wall would do, so I plugged that next one into the far wall away from Michael's bed. It would reach. Just barely, but I made it work because I cared. I should have been worried about blowing a fuse and plunging the hospital into darkness, but considering the state I was in? Everyone else on the ward could have burned and I wouldn't have batted an eye if it's what would have brought Michael back.

Yeah, not something you want your paramedic to say, but it's not like those people were *my* patients. Not like anyone else was *my* Michael.

I hooked up the other kit, pads to wires, wires to unit, and upped the watts.

Clear?

Crystal, bitches.

The machines worked together to send electric pulses up and down Michael's body. I killed the juice when he started twitching, when one side of his face drooped. Nothing.

Damnit.

I went to leave—to find Nurse Nancy and ugly cry on her shoulder, but when I pushed by Michael's bed, his hand shot out, grabbed mine, and pulled me in. His lips pressed against mine, his hands ran through my hair, tugging on the ends. His lips were ice cold like your first gulp of water after a long run. Like a pond in the middle of winter. Like a snowstorm and I was the motherfucking Ice Queen.

Alive. He was alive.

"I'm so cold for you," is what he said, into my ear. I knew he was smiling.

Michael was back. The Ross to my Rachel. The Batman to my Robin.

I pulled his pants off. What greeted me was his splendid, wonderfully sized God of Love. I wrapped my fingers around it, knowing if I licked that pole, my tongue would get stuck.

Shaking, I pulled my uniform pants down. I knew what he would feel like; he'd been inside of me before but not dead, or, dead-alive. Cold alive. Oh god, what was I doing? What was happening?

No, no. Don't leave. Stay with me. It's getting good.

I straddled him. Michael pulled me in. He bit at my lip and unbuttoned my shirt. He pinched at my nipples with fingertips colder than ice because these, these fingers weren't from the cold. They were from somewhere else entirely.

I slid onto his cock, couldn't help but moan into his neck. He held me and just having him inside me froze me from my toes to the place behind my eyes.

"Michael," I said into him. Being with him? It was breathing for the first time.

We rocked back and forth. The hospital bed started to slide a little around the room because they're on wheels, but then Michael and I were so pressed, so perfectly pieced together. Then, somewhere deep inside the Lady Elizabeth, there was a crash, a rush of winter and tingles that left that middle part of just above my legs shaking and pinging. I screamed into Michael. It was everything I'd ever wanted. Not only did his Jolly Rodger stay cold, but his arms were strong and held me.

A breath. A minute. Or was it eternity passing me by?

"I'd wanted to make you cum so bad," he said, a little breathless. "I'm leaving, Blondie. I can feel it. But bring me back again? Let's do this forever."

I know it's all in my head, but in that last, final kiss, I felt sparks and energy stronger than lightning dance around the room in blues and whites.

"Bring me back again?" he said, slipping away. His eyes blinked from that clear blue to a hazy, cloudy day grey. I kissed him while letting my lips linger so we could be joined as long as possible.

"I'll never let go," I said, hoping he could feel my smile.

He could. I know it.

And then Michael died in my arms for the second time that day.

Chapter, um, crap.

Okay, so. First lesson today, class! How to steal a body. Like my relationship, it's complicated, but so, so worth it, even if it's just for the adrenaline rush. I wouldn't say I recommend it, but maybe if you need to lose a few pounds super quick?

First, he was heavy. Like, crazy dead sack of potatoes heavy. I swear, if his Prince Ali wasn't so good, if he hadn't been so perfect, I'd have left him there in the hospital for the coroner to handle.

I dismounted Michael's dead body and redid my uniform. It was sticky and starting to go a little stiff from Michael's blood. You know what they say about girls. We just want to have fun.

Hell, I didn't have a way to get him out but however I was going to do it, it would be by the grace of my uniform and my hospital key-card. I'd covered his face, sure, but even though I was a paramedic, they weren't just going to let me heft a body bag all Santa Claus-like out of the hospital because dead or not, it was clearly a body. (Side note, ever wonder if Mr. and Mrs. Claus still do it? I mean, if there was a couple who might like it cold like me, they might be my best bet. Do they even have heat? Probably not. Which leads me to believe that Mr. Claus has totally used his Christmas Tree in sub-zero. Fiction or supernatural, those bitches are CHOOSING to live in the North Pole. And they're, like, *old*. Maybe they have some pointers for me!)

Sorry. That was a hell of a side-note. So! Leaving the hospital, right.

It's not like I'd ever left the hospital with someone. That's not my job.

Unless.

What if I was transporting? EMT's transfer all the time. It was something I got saddled with once or twice in training. The reason why EMT's get stuck with that is because the next hospital is, like, forty-five minutes away and no one wants to do that in the winter. You could get stuck and die and who wants that?

Jorge had mentioned he was going to go back and get my rig. We couldn't leave it there. I wonder if he'd already brought it back? Where would he have put it? Probably somewhere in the sea of ER visitor parking.

"I know what to do!" I kissed Michael through the sheet, through the veil of here and now, of dead and alive. I tucked the starchy fabric around his arms. Thankfully, all of the hospital beds roll just in case there's an emergency. It wasn't the kind of bed I was used to, not the kind that would fit in the back of my ambulance comfortably, but we were all about to do things that we weren't supposed to do. Don't see why I'd pussyfoot around the rig. Plus. I just needed him out. Then, I could heave-ho his body into the back of the rig.

Okay. But then I still just had a body. Not my thriving, writhing Prince of Love. If I was Dr. Frankenstein, I needed my lightning. I grabbed the crash kits and stowed them underneath the dumb, ditchable hospital bed.

Know that one scene in that really old movie, *Nightmare on Elm Street,* where the body bag holding Tina gets dragged away down the hall feet first?

Okay, now take away the blonde and replace it with my frozen, super dead but still super sexy lover. Take the blood away too because the ER surgeons had tried to save him (maybe for me? Maybe because he was a paramedic? Or hell, maybe they were just bored and needed something to cut? Surgeons are weird).

Would two be enough?

It was enough electricity this time, but later? I should grab a few more. But the hospital only had so many portable ones...crap. My home base at the ambulance company was only a few blocks away, but take that chance after stealing a body? No. The ones I was taking would have to be enough.

I pushed Michael out of the door, past the nurses' station (no Nurse Nancy, phew!) and all the way down the hall. It shook his body a bit when I used the end of the gurney to open the heavy, metal doors, but no lasting damage. He'd be fine.

We walked that way all the way to the rig, which, thankfully, stuck out like a sore thumb in the ER parking lot. My white and red island in a lake of tan and white Volvos and hippie vans.

But if that was my sea, where was my port? Where would the power still be on with enough voltage to bring my dead-dicked lover back from the grave?

Other heroines get a floating door, or a horse, or a carpet.

What do I get?

A slaughterhouse. No better place to take my hunk of man-meat than to a place that used to store meat, right?

Like, duh.

Chapter Ten. See? Back on track.

So, safe space? Dead bodies are really, really heavy. I hefted Michael off the hospital bed and onto the rig, which was really, really hard. Because I am not the biggest gal in the room, I devised a way to carry people bigger than me a long time ago. Think of a horse harness? I loop a stretch of rope around the person's (man's, in this case) chest, snake it under his arms and cross it at the back, and then I loop it around myself, crossed at my back and hold it tight with my arms in that ready for business L-shape bodybuilders have when they lift up the big weights.

I have to back up all squatty, but it works, and I have, like, the best-looking thighs because of it. Let's just say I've Sarah Connored myself without the awful diet they had the poor actress on. I'm not as muscly as her, but I imagine I could do some seriously attractive pullups if I were ever thrown into the big house.

Yeah, I'm a paramedic and I should have known how heavy dead bodies were, but I've always had a big strapping, manly specimen of a dude to help me heave ho.

Once inside, I strapped him down and tried not to look at his legs. Thankfully, they were still pretty much covered by the body bag. Michael and I had already made sweet love and I was stealing his body so we could ravage each other again, but that doesn't mean his hamburger meat legs were suddenly beautiful like some Cinderella magic.

After that, I got behind the wheel. I'd be lying if I said I didn't have to do a few deep breaths before clicking my seatbelt in place because safety first.

I drove from the hospital all stealthy like to the slaughterhouse.

I realize that's a rocky transition, but I just don't feel like you need to know all about me driving? Maybe I took a wrong turn and got a little lost, but I got there and that's what's important. Don't fight it. It's better this way and not as boring.

So, poof! Got to the slaughterhouse. Wasn't pulled

over and I even figured out where the headlights button was!

Look, I'm not here to fight *all* the blonde stereotypes, okay?

The slaughterhouse was totally abandoned. I vaguely wondered about things like electricity and when the water would get shut off, or would anyone come looking to lock up or if a worker forgot their lucky gloves here or whatever. But what else could I do? I may have mentioned before that paramedics don't make a ton of money, and cramming my future husband into one of those open freezers just didn't seem right. No, this would be the place. This would be our home. Couples bought weird, retro fixer-uppers all the time. This would be ours. Sure, it needed a fresh coat of paint and you know, to not smell like carcass, but this was just all part of my relationship now and I'd need to be flexible. If anyone was getting the short end of the stick, it was Michael. He was the one not breathing after all.

I'll spare you the details because it's pretty straightforward. The doors were unlocked. Michael was on a gurney. I mean, do you really need me to describe taking him through all the doors? Do you really want to know how he was beginning to seep a sort of weird human snail-trail into what had been our frozen seduction nest?

I guess what I'm saying is: it wasn't Michael's sexiest hour and I'd like to protect his privacy. Plus, why remember him like that when he would soon be a grunting, pulsing excellent exhibit of a man.

My man.

If he was super gross and disgusting, well, that's between us. I'd say between us and God, but I brought Michael back from the dead. Is that supposed to happen? Was someone sleeping on the job? I guess what I'm saying is, to my knowledge, there's no God in this story. And if there is, he's a total perv because I brought Michael back, like, so many times to fuck. If there was a deity in the room—sent to condemn us for breaking the laws of nature!—said deity was sitting in the corner watching us and double-fist beating his God Stick like it owed him money.

I didn't waste any time. I'd placed the de-fib units in the gurney, so I hauled them out and placed the pads in the same places as before, only this time I added the second de-fib pads next to the first set.

Six thousand watts of electricity. That's enough to light this entire place up for about fifty seconds. I could run, like, a huge shop vac on what I was about to send into Michael's heart and brain.

I pressed both buttons, (which was going to get tricky as soon as I needed more. I'd have to get a surge protector or something and an extension cord. Eventually, I'd find the right amount of electricity to bring him back for a full day. Maybe days! And things could go back to normal.

I pressed both buttons at the same time.

Clear?

Uh huh. Yep.

Shocks went through Michael's body. His arms flapped and his hips bucked. I killed the electricity when his eyes kind of rolled back and got really, really big. Sort of how a bubble looks when you're blowing it out of the bubble wand. All stretchy and shiny like.

"Wake up!"

I remember yelling at him once or twice.

"Life! Come back to life!"

Not in anger because you should never yell at your spouse in anger, but more just swearing because the room—our room—seemed to spin. I couldn't remember the last time I'd eaten or had anything to drink. Had Nurse Nancy brought me something? If I was running off adrenaline and adrenaline alone, I'd have to eat something soon. What I'm saying is, I was hangry and taking it out on my love. I'm not proud, but we've all done it.

Again.

Again.

Again.

And then he groaned, moved a little after I'd killed the juice.

"Michael!"

I ran to his side and kissed him hard. His ice-cold lips made my Lady Elizabeth stand at soldier-like attention.

"Sadie?" He kind of croaked. His eyes wouldn't hold still. "More..." he breathed. I know a person can't breathe and speak, but you know what I'm talking about. It's when words sort of hitch a ride on breath alone. When the person speaking could just be super horse from nursing a really horrible sore throat.

"More?"

He nodded, and then closed his eyes. His right hand reached up, let his knuckles glide across my cheek. I kissed the palm of his hand before it got heavy and fell.

"But where am I going to get more?" I'm glad he was already dead at that point, because a sob sort of went past my lips and I never want Michael to hear me like that. Yes, yes, you should be vulnerable in front of your significant other, but there is also a time when you need to be the strong one in your relationship, and that means *handling it*, whatever the *it* is. And preferably without crying.

He needed more. Much more. But from where? I couldn't go back to the hospital. I mean, could I? I was going to have to truly embrace my Dr. Frankenstein side and steal electricity, but from where? The fucking sky?

Chapter 11. Feeling pretty confident about it. The chapter numbering, I mean.

I made a list of all the units I knew about.

1) *Lightning Response!* We had one on each rig. But we only had four rigs. Considering that the two I had weren't enough to keep him going, four probably wouldn't last very long. So, I'd have to make this an

endeavor. A voyage of sorts. But how? I'd been planning on keeping Michael here in our slaughterhouse, attending to the Lady Elizabeth's needs for a while until I figured out how to keep him going. How to fix him. Let's remember, regardless of this miracle, I had just stolen a body. In order for all of this to work out, for Michael and I to get our picket fence one day, he needed to come back to life and stay living. At least for a while. So you know, the public could see and I could be excused from jail time and we could get married.

2) Next place with de-fib units: the gym I went to. They had one at the front desk and another at the pool; I know because I placed them there after they introduced a plus-size water aerobics class. I'd told them the de-fib units were 'on the house.' Really it was to save me a lights and sirens trip. It would be easy to sneak that one out of there. Their lifeguard was a short brown-haired girl who stared at the pool like she was in Hell and watching the water was her eternal punishment.

Fun fact: Most of the time, your lifeguards are praying for an accident to break up the monotony of their day. Know what they say about a watched pot? Well, no matter how long you stare, a pool never boils. Think about it.

Final one: the hospital. I knew I could rely on at least six new units. ER had a ton of portable ones. Really it was just a matter of how many I could carry.

That would be tricky. Nurse Nancy, my fabulous

fairy godmother ER nurse, could spot me. Was probably worried about me too, so she would be hypersensitive to my whereabouts.

But then, could all of these de-fib units run from the same outlet? No. okay, so I'd need to go and get a power strip too. Can't have my boyfriend shorting out, right? No way. We'd be in the middle of doing it and then, what? Would he just fade away? That would be more confusing than trying to figure out why Nicole Kidman married Tom Cruz.

Okay. Mom always said if you do the worst first, the rest isn't that bad. So, I'd be going to the hospital first.

Lights and sirens because it's a total emergency.

An emergency of love. No, no that's not good. Sorry. I must be getting tired. Are there any songs about driving an ambulance through the snow to steal electricity? Dr. Frankenstein had it so easy. What did he do, fly a kite? And yeah, I know that's the movie, not the book. Right? It's been so long since I faked reading it.

No one would ever arrest you for flying a kite in a thunderstorm. Me? I could totally get arrested for this. Not only was I way, way truant for check-in at the ambulance company (hopefully they'd just assume I was somewhere crying my girlish eyeballs out in unrelenting grief for my dead partner) and while some things were going to be unrelenting (his joystick-love muscle!) I wasn't grieving. Quite the opposite. I was taking action! I was doing something about it! This, looked at in some different, grey lighting, was actually healthy.

Hospital. Yes.

I don't really like driving and I don't like talking about it either.

I'm not saying I'm so bad I mix up the brake and the gas pedal—haven't done that since, like, a couple of Thanksgivings ago. Long story, but it involved gravy and that's how I remember. Don't ask. My hands still do get super sweaty. And left-hand turns are hard. Present tense. Left-hand turns will always be hard. But that's okay. We have to be brave, especially when it's all for love.

Before I got to the hospital, I could see the lights. It's pretty when the city is all lit up in Christmas lights, but the circular, continuous movement of police lights gave the scene a different ambiance. Not only was ER straining at the drive-up Emergencies Only parking section from the number of cop cars, but the doors around back were guarded too. Of course they were. I'd stolen a body, after all.

If they saw the ambulance, they didn't notice.

"Goddammit."

Michael was back in the slaughterhouse on ice. If they took me away from him, no one would ever know, and he'd be left there in the cold forever, halfway between living and dead. Like a strange hibernation. If someone took me away from him, what kind of horror would that do to him? I should tell you, while God and I don't get along (I mean, is he even real?) I know there's a soul. Something leaves when people die. I've seen it. And that one dude did an experiment where he was able to weigh the soul. We don't know what leaves or how it works, but whatever it is, it weighs ¾ of an ounce.

So, with the hospital out of the question (for now) that left the gym and *Lightning Response*.

—

Just, picture me driving, for this transition, okay? I obeyed stoplights. I kept my head down. I'd say I was nervous and drove all incognito, but truthfully? Only thing I was nervous about was the actual driving part. Getting de-fib units from work would be a cinch. I had my keys and with a little bit of luck, Kyle and Jorge would be out on a run. No one else would be there. Dispatch (Vicky-with-an-i) was at the Sheriff's station and the company was in this way super old farmhouse built in, like, the thirties. The company snagged it because I guess it's better if an ambulance company doesn't have neighbors. Not because we're loud partiers, but it does seem like accidents always, always happen at night. Especially when there's a full moon. I turned my radio up when the Proclaimers swore they'd walk a thousand miles because I, Sadie Snow, know the feeling.

—

Lightning Response! had zero lights on. My ultra-cool digital watch said it was close to four AM on a Thursday. Michael and I had Thursday off—this company embraces the four on, three off policy, and then once a month it flips so you get four off, three on. It works well, except that if you're only on calls for those three-four days, then you just spend the other days sleeping. I'll have to work for a hospital with 12-hour shifts before Michael and I settle down and get married. Because babies. Could I be away from babies for 12 hours? That sounds like such a long time. Maybe I'll take an extended leave. I imagine money would be tight because America hates maternity leave and women, but we'd manage.

Sidenote? There was a husband and wife team who got pregnant on our crew not too long ago. Everyone was whispering about if SHE was going to go back to work after having a baby. I remember shutting the door to my rig extra loudly on that conversation because, like, do women have much of a choice? Maternity leave is considered a 'disability' in a society that jerks itself off to Christmas, elves, and Jesus. Like, how is it a disability? If you, church, don't support birth control, then it should be called 'life happens' leave. Not *disability* leave. How does that make sense? If anything, you are twice as able because you're growing a human. Jesus fucking Christ. And then! The choices are to pay out the ass for childcare and go back to work six-twelve weeks later and miss your baby and drip breast milk, or, succumb to the stereotype and stay at home with your new baby and have no money.

And our society shames you by whispering *think she's coming back?* Fuck you. I'm not a mom yet, but I've seen this shit, and I have a brain.

Why the Hell were we ever called the fairer sex? We deal with more. Should make us the stronger, ballsier ones.

Basically, eat shit, society.

Where was I? Michael and I living together. Right. We would have to make some sacrifices, though, because I can't imagine what our electric bill would look like. Perhaps I could make some sort of low voltage charger for Michael. I realize that might mean no middle of the night sex, but I bet our morning sex would be *shockingly* great.

I parked the ambulance down the road a little. We're pretty rural, so the road was full of potholes and whatnot. I didn't want to alert anyone to my super sexy presence. Kyle and Jorge were on shift. Their rig was parked out front, close to the door. The snow had turned the ground into just mud and the going was way, way slow.

My boots stuck and I really needed to wrench and jerk at my feet. We'd have to get this paved before next winter. The high-ups are always promising that we will, but then they take care of the fireman first.

Can't say I blame them. Maybe that's who Michael and I will go work for when we want babies. I hear they pay better too because, you know, fireMAN.

My boots were making an awful sucking noise as I approached the other rig. I tried the back door, but it was totally locked. Damn Kyle for always being so rule-booky. I'd have to sneak into the house and pray they were asleep.

I pulled my keys from my pocket and tried not to make the door squeak or anything. We had one of those awful rinky-dink screens because during the summer there wasn't any AC. I slid in.

Kyle and Jorge were asleep on their bunks, snoring loudly. I almost smiled. And then a rush of uncomfortable, hot, awful sticky air hit me, pressed itself against my face and bare arms. Yuck! How come I'd never felt it before? And then it clicked, how Michael was always dressed so warmly. How I'd never seen really much of his body before. Hell, how I'd never seen his hair. It's because we never turned the heater on or lit the stove. Nothing. He never did because I never did. He must have seen me walk around in my uniform pants and tank top. Figured I was warm enough and that he was the problem! That's why he was always dressed like a wooly mammoth.

Is there anything better than a man letting the woman control the environment. Those Amazonian women had the right idea.

Back to business. The boys' jackets were hanging up. I rummaged through for keys. In his bunk, Jorge shifted, mumbled a little in his sleep.

They couldn't see me here. What would they do? Turn me in because when I disappeared, so did Michael's body? Not to mention I'd left in the middle of what was technically my shift. If they woke up and caught me, Michael and I would never be together. They'd either put me away for body snatching (is that a thing?) or worse, make me go back to work!

Sharp and metal greeted my fingertips. Got the keys! I never thought I could be so excited to grab something small and metal. I breathed a sigh of relief. And then in the corner of the room, there was a muffled:

"Oh, lord in Heaven."

No. I knew that perfect southern bell voice! Sounded like she couldn't wait to bring me iced tea and place a pie in the window to cool.

I turned around and was greeted by a tiny little blonde creature. I knew that bob cut. The swell of her hips and her huge, incompatible-with-her-tiny-waist tits. This was, dare I say it? Vicky-with-an-i. Former cheerleader. And can I just say? No one's legs should be that skinny. No one. How do they not snap when a strong gust of wind puffs along?

"Sadie Snow, what are you doing?" Her voice roused Kyle. Jorge's legs were already over the edge of the bed. He must have been just barely awake. I registered that both Jorge and Vicky were only in the bare-essentials—underwear and an undershirt. Wow. Totally hadn't seen that one coming. Interprofessional relationships are normally so rare. Poor Kyle, top bunks can really suck, but his name is Kyle, after all. He's basically asking for awful weird crap to happen to him.

"Did you do it? Did you really steal his body? Where is it?" Vicky asked.

"His body is gone?" I did my best to look confused. "So weird. I had no idea. I'm taking some time to, uh, mourn. I just need to get something out of the rig and then I'll go back to crying. Bye." I slipped out the door.

Damn ex-cheerleader followed me.

"We haven't seen your rig," she squeaked in that awful gaudy drawl. "And that's the only one you could have left something in."

"Not true!" I gave her the finger as I walked over to Kyle and Jorge's ride. "They gave me and Michael a lift the other day."

I opened the back door and score! Three de-fib units. They must have grabbed two from the hospital for service. My lucky day.

I closed the doors and despite the cold, despite her name being spelled so fucking wrong, Vicky with an i was waiting for me. I jumped a little. Can you blame me? No one ever wants to see a tiny blonde with a bob haircut.

That primal, animal gut instinct we all have whispered to me hard that it wasn't just Vicky; the boys were behind me, too. And not in a sexy way. I turned around. They were blocking the way back to *my* rig.

"Sadie, come back inside."

"Let me pass, guys."

"No way."

I swung a de-fib unit straight at Vicky's head. I heard the wet spat and crunch of the hard plastic against her nose. Blood spurted from what was surely broken. I jumped over her, grabbed the unit and ran. Running with three AED units is just not super easy. It would be akin to running with three medium-sized cat carriers.

Don't ask how I know this.

Jorge and Kyle caught up to me easily. Kyle wrapped long, skinny arms around me and Jorge slugged me right in the jaw.

"Fuck!" Although it sounded more like *uck!* because moving it wasn't an option yet. Fortunately, I have always been ready to be kidnapped. It's just part of being a woman. I stomped on Kyle's foot with the heel of my boot (he was barefoot) and I threw my head back into his nose. I was getting good at breaking noses!

"Ow! Goddammit!" Kyle reached his right hand up to staunch the blood flow, which means I was released! I dropped the de-fib units and with a wild, carnal cry I attacked Jorge with keys I held like my very own womanly brass knuckles in-between my fingers. I was Wolverine. I was Terminator. I was motherfucking Ripley!

But when the keys came in contact with Jorge's face, they slipped a little and raked at the tender meat of my palms.

"Ahh!" I held my injured hand to my middle. Fuck fuck fuck. I was going to have to stitch myself up, and I hate hate hate giving myself stitches. Maybe Michael would do it for me! We could have that scene from Terminator where Sarah Connor bandages Reese up and they bang and make John Connor.

Oh, sorry. Spoiler.

Jorge's meaty hands grabbed my collar and I felt

my sagging body get pulled. But I wasn't done yet. I used my toned abs to rear up like the lioness I was, break his hold on me, and then I kicked him in the dick and *ran*.

In my haste, I could only grab two of the de-fib units. My cut hand tricked little rivulets of blood down onto the red plastic of the AED machines.

The third machine was by Vicky. She stared at it like she was trying to figure something out. Like why I was after them. Why I was willing to risk being caught for them.

Chapter UG. Look, I'm not good with numbers, and this part of the story is really, really hard for me to talk about, okay?

It's hard for me to talk about it because I have sympathy pains for myself. See, my jaw was on fire. Moving it was awful, and I sort of wanted to be like a corpse in a funeral home with their cold/dead jaws wired shut. Just holding it up felt terrible. Like most things on me (and in me) it just needed some ice. Get the swelling down.

Bringing Michael back was first, though, even if I was in pain. I wanted to see him, to talk with him and tell him this whole thing was getting really, really hard.

I dragged the de-fib units into the freezer with Michael and stripped off my bloody uniform coat. My cut hand had stopped dripping blood, but it stung and looked like I'd tried to wrench apart a barbed wire fence by gripping it and pulling. Who thought we, the fairer sex, should use fucking keys to stop our attackers? Honest question for the attackers out there? Come on. You put this idea out there so you could laugh as we brandished our keys and ended up slicing the meaty, sensitive flesh of our fingers.

Ladies? Word of the wise? Don't use your keys for anything but the ignition. Kick him in the dick, run to your car, and then hit the bastard again and again and again and put it in reverse and make sure the fucker's head is squished again and again and again and when the cops say: "Did you have to kill him? Boys will be boys (insert douche bag laugh from probably overweight, unattractive white man cop). You say: "I didn't see him, officer!"

Trust me.

I hooked up the de-fib units, but only two reached. The third one (one I super needed, I was sure) wouldn't reach. Damn. I didn't have extension cords and it wasn't exactly the right time to run to the Do-It center.

The Do-It center. So I could Do-It. Ha!

Later.

I was exhausted. My stomach hurt from Jorge's excellent punch to my gut and my eyes hurt from seeing Kyle and my ears hurt from hearing Vicky-with-an-i. My hand was ribbons and my jaw, well, I've already complained about that. I guess the physical work was really getting to me, you know? Maintaining a relationship is so hard!

I placed the de-fib pads on Michael and pressed the On button.

"Shock advised. Stand clear."

I pressed for the shock.

Michael's body jostled a little from the electricity. Nothing. I'd expected that. It took a moment in the hospital too. I hit it again, and this time Michael came roaring to life.

"Whoa!" He looked around, like trying to get his bearing. "Shit! Where…"

"I'm here." I walked in front of him to he could see me, fucked up as I was.

"Sadie! You did it, you brought me back, oh." His hand went up to my jaw and touched it gingerly. "Blondie. Babe. What happened?"

I took his hand and held it against my face. I wouldn't cry. I wouldn't. But I was so tired and everything just hurt.

"I'm fine. Nothing compared to you." He was dead most of the time, after all.

Michael shook his head, took my injured hand in his.

"It's not a competition. What happened? Here, wait. Can you put me on the floor? We can sit together? Is the ambulance here? I can at least bandage your hand if we have a kit."

I threw my arms around him and cried. He held me, even let his fingers graze over my arms and neck in a soothing, loving way. He was back. I had my friend, my partner, back. Our thoughts were on the same train they'd always been on. Not everyone gets as lucky as us, but I really, really hope some people do.

We used the meat hooks to get him all the way to the ground. I could lower the gurney, but moving him all sore and beat up as I was hurt like hell, so Michael suggested to use the hooks. So selfless of him. He's so conscience of my feelings and well-being. He gripped the ends so we could sort of swing him down.

I told him about dragging his body and about stealing the units as he patched up my hand. I held some icicles broken off from the inside of the meat freezer to my jaw and it was already feeling better. Not broken, that was good.

"I can't believe you did all of that for me," Michael said.

"Well, of course I did."

"But also for the Lady?"

He knew me so well.

"I mean..."

"I should thank you. If I may, there's something I've been wanting to try."

Michael pushed away from me and crawled down, tugging at my shirt, kissing my belly, and undoing my pants.

Oh, oh shit.

I lifted my butt off the concrete so he could pull my pants all the way down. I leaned back, closed my eyes, and holy shit.

Winter licked my Lady Elizabeth. Ice that would

never unfreeze surrounded me. I was sinking into that frigid pond I'd saved Brandon from all those years ago. Michael was slow at first, like tasting, and then when I couldn't help myself anymore, I reached for his ponytail.

Because we were totally MFEO like Tom Hanks and Meg Ryan, he understood.

His lapping became faster and rhythmic and when I came, I wished I had a belt to bite down on because the ecstasy scream that tore out of me surely echoed around through the slaughterhouse and bounced off the hillsides even though Michigan is, like, totally flat.

Michael crawled up and kissed me deeply. His thrumming icicle was so close to the Lady Elizabeth Von Trapp's trap and yes if this was a drug, I guess you could say I was like Britney Spears, saying: hit me baby, one more time.

Again.

And again.

A couple of times I felt his legs. I won't lie. It was sort of like touching a run-over, bloated worm after heavy rainfall. How it was slimy but also sort of tough? I don't think Michael noticed me make a face or anything. What I'm saying is, I feel confident that I handled myself with grace.

We lay there in the dark after I don't know how many times. Michael's teeth were really white against his greying skin in the dark. Made me think of the Cheshire Cat.

We're all so, so mad here. Madly *in love*.

"Sadie?"

"Hm?"

"It's happening again."

"Wow! Really?" I hadn't expected this much sex! "Excellent."

"No, no." He shook his head. "Not that. I think I'm dying again."

"Oh." If my heart had been a balloon, it would have deflated. I was about to be alone again. But, I shouldn't make it about me, right? No. It was about Michael. "Okay. Sure. What can I do?"

"Hold me?"

I nodded. I sat up and cradled Michael's head in my lap. I smoothed his hair and kissed his nose.

"I love you," I told him.

"Love you," he replied. I smiled and pressed my forehead to his, felt like I could just sink into him. "Sadie?"

"Hm?"

"Something's wrong."

"How do you mean?"

"I can't recall...I mean. I don't remember? I feel like parts are going away. Like pieces of me are leaving."

"What? No. No, you're all here." That wasn't super true. His legs were more crushed than Spanish grapes at one of those grape-wine-stomping-events. And his skin was starting to get a little, well, smelly.

Oh! We could share a shower. That was always super fun!

"What's missing? How can I help?"

But he was leaving. He was dying in my arms for, what, the third time?

"Do you need legs?" I asked him, trying to be quick. Trying to get the answers before we he was gone again.

"Legs?" he repeated.

"Is that it? You need more parts?"

"Parts..."

His head rolled to the side, his eyes closed this time, and his tongue lolled a little. Ugh. Let me tell you. It is, like so emotionally draining watching the Prince Eric to your Arielle die over and over again.

I sat alone for a minute with dead Michael at my side. Yeah, we'd been able to bang, but what if I wanted him around for a whole day? He'd need more electricity, that much was clear. But he said he needed *parts*.

Well, I'd just have to go and get those parts. He would have done it for me, had our roles been reversed. And I'm totally a role reversal kind of gal. Like, if he one day wants to stay at home with the kids while I work, that's so totally okay with me. Maybe he can start a woodworking hobby. Or install solar panels because I am seriously beginning to worry about our electric bill.

My first thought was to dig up the dead because it's not like anything would be missed, but how would more dead bits help Michael? No, he needed his new pieces to be alive. He needed fresh, all-organic meat.

But who deserved to be chopped up and used as spare parts?

Chapter 12 AKA: The best chapter where I get some bodies for the sexy, sexy Han Solo to my gold bikini-wearing Princess Leia.

Side note: Ask me before I met Michael if there was anyone in the world hotter than Harrison Ford and I would have answered yes, only one person. Han Solo with a ponytail. I think I really would have lost my shit if that spaceship captain had a mane to pull back from his face. I'd have become a total, total stalker. So glad I never got to that level of crazy.

So. We're at the frat house and I'm about to get Michael some of those parts we talked about.

I, Sadie Snow, don't know much about football, but I have always wondered how the really, really big dudes with big guts get on the team. Is it just solid weight? I'd think they were a liability. I mean, they are at, like, total risk for a heart attack on the field. I know the NFL doesn't allow the big fat dudes, but high school and college sure as hell do. Whatever. I'd just avoid them. They'll die young anyway. Trust me. This one time I had to help cut a fat bastard out of his trailer. He'd been dead for days, just liquifying in his own bountiful fluids. We cut the trailer down the middle, and it took six firefighters (and they were the strong, yummy kind) to lift this hippo. Originally, Michael had lifted me up and stuffed me in through the bathroom window so I could open the door. (We could smell it from outside and just sort of figured). Upon going in there and seeing Jabba the Hutt, I'd called out to Michael through the paper-thin walls of the double wide, "we're going to need some help with this!"

It was things like that that made me want to bring Michael back for just more than sex. More than marriage or a mortgage, shared credit, or even babies.

He was my friend.

Is that the secret? To be with the person you not only have fallen in love with, but laugh with, talk to, and just understand?

I opened the back of the rig to grab my favorite tool. But that made me pause and think. A lot of my plan relied on me not getting caught and going to jail, at least until I could get Michael up and running again. I've seen enough crime shows to know they always catch the killer from bits of hair, pieces of clothing, fingerprints. So, it was only rational to strip down to my fabulous birthday suit. Besides, name me one thing that men find scarier than a naked, empowered woman.

Outside in the cold, I stripped. Everything could stay naked, except for my shoes. Michael's boots were in the back. It's important to always have an extra pair of boots in our line of work. Let's just say human liquids have a way of getting on you and seeping down into your boots, and if you don't have a change of shoes, you'll squelch around in that human nasty until shift change, which could be 72 hours.

And I hate, *hate* getting my feet wet. Have I mentioned that? After slipping my super dainty feet into Michael's boots (so much room because, well, big feet and all) I pulled my hair back into my usual severe ponytail because why fix what's not broken? I held a protective mask over my mouth because old habits die hard. But did I really need it? I'd say I was going for the *killer with a mask* look but really I just didn't want hepatitis. Or syphilis. What were the chances of one of those motherfuckers having syphilis? Syphilis makes you crazy and I really, really wanted to keep my sanity.

I know what you're thinking right now. If anyone had a disease, it was probably me, the girl who was fucking something that was dead most of the time.

But look, we were in love, okay? Love does weird things to a person. Exhibit A: OJ. Exhibit B: MJ. Hm. Seeing a trend. Don't go by your initials. I mean, I never would because my initials are SS and I want to stay away from that one because you know, the Nazis.

I stood in front of the door. This felt wrong. If I was going to make them pay, it should be with the very thing that initially, partially, killed my love...but who would loan a snowplow to a naked woman? Plus, I wasn't here to ruin more body parts.

But I did have an ax.

Well, society. It was time to do what women do best.

Go shopping.

—

Michael and I hadn't been properly introduced. He was

filling in on my rig after my last partner accidentally ran over his own foot and somehow managed to hit his head, too.

Most men weren't thrilled to see a woman as their partner. And I get it. We can't lift as much and we smell like posies. Michael, however, walked towards me, waving. He blew into his hands before extending his right out to me.

"I'm Michael. Sorry, my hands are still a little wet. I just washed them."

"Sadie."

"Cool. Nice. I don't hear *Sadie* a lot."

"Yeah, yeah, my parents liked it too."

"Same. I mean, my parents, and with Michael, obviously."

We rocked on our boot heels for a moment.

"Do you mind?" he asked, pointing. I remember feeling a huge letdown. He was going to say some manly dick thing. "Do you mind if I chew sunflower seeds and spit them out in the rig? It helps me heal people." Or worse: "Look, sweetheart, I don't know how this company runs, but I ain't stopping every couple of hours so you can pee, okay? You'll pee outside whenever we have a free second like the rest of us."

Shockingly, he didn't have a disgusting habit to divulge, nor did he try to control me. Instead, he sort of pointed with his chin towards the driver's side door.

"I know it's your company and your rig, but can I drive?"

"Really?"

"Yeah, I uh, I get really seasick in the passenger side."

"Oh!"

"I don't have to. I just..."

"No, no. That's perfect. I hate driving, actually." I do. I hate it so much.

"Yeah?"

"Yeah."

"Thank god." He pulled his glasses off, rubbed at his temple, across his shut eyes. "If you said no, I wasn't sure what I was going to do. I can't throw up outside a window again. Or on a partner."

"Ha! You've done that?" I knew then he was going to be fun. He made his way to the driver side door. Michael bounced a little when he walked, that first day. Maybe he was nervous?

"I'll tell you all about it over breakfast," he said.

"What fabulous breakfast conversation material." I got into the passenger side, set the seat up so I could rest my feet comfortably against the dash and hang one arm out the window. "Where should we go?"

"Breakfast sandwiches? Hole in the wall spot. Best sausage you'll ever taste."

"Oh, I'm actually a vegetarian." This is when my partners and I would usually argue and I would get stuck with lettuce between two slices of bread because I'm the one being difficult. Me and my love of nature and animals, always getting in the way of things. Michael surprised me.

"Oh, okay," he said, nodding. "Totally. Um. You like

donuts? I know this great corner bakery."

—

When the door opened, I guess you can say I was ready.

"Whoa…" the new frat recruit said, his eyes lighting up at my nakedness (I think) and yeah, it's super flattering, I mean, I do sit-ups and some light running and whatnot, but really I think it's my awesome rack. Men. I should have known how easy this would be. And can I just say? You should have seen what he was wearing! He was practically asking for it— khaki cargo shorts, a white pooka shell necklace, and a bright green long-sleeved polo. And his hair? He had that stupid haircut. You know it. The spiked hair with bleached blonde tips?

Barf.

I got the ax almost all the way through his head before his eyes even went up to my face. First try. Yay me! I mean, I don't want to brag, but I did try out for softball once.

Can I just say? The insides of cactus head were crazy super interesting because I'd never actually seen a brain. Yeah, okay, I'm a paramedic, but we get the crap cadavers that have been there longer than the frogs (poor frogs!). It's the doctors who get the pristine and recently deceased. I doubt nurses do because nurses are predominantly female and we know how things turn out for women in the workplace.

A bit of hot blood spattered against my super flat amazing belly. It would have made a great tattoo. Couldn't help but think about *Alien*. Love me some

Ripley. Now there's a bad bitch. A good role model for girls.

I pulled the ax out of the new recruit. It made a sort of sucking sound. And hey, because I'm telling you this in hindsight, in past tense, let's cue the thunder and lightning. I bet I was framed in the doorway. Can't you see it? Michael's boots, an ax, and a mask? Turn me to the side and *boom!* Strike a pose. That would be a killer silhouette. Ha! Get it? *Killer* silhouette?

But, like, a sexy killer.

I didn't bother to look at the recruit's extremities. I could tell from the build, Michael wouldn't like any of those parts. Also? I wasn't here to re-create my boyfriend. I was here to *improve* him. Which meant I needed to figure out where my tight ends were. I, Sadie Snow, don't know much about football, but I know who the runners are. Also. I like the name *tight ends*.

I walked up the stairs and of *course* the lightning illuminated me on the stairs. I'd say I dragged my ax, just to be super creepy (sexy creepy) but with all the adrenaline I had and the motivation to make my love whole again, I could have juggled six firemen axes at once using one hand. And no, for the first time, that's not a euphemism.

Can you imagine? Six firemen? That doesn't even sound fun. Sounds like work.

Also, I feel like I say *sexy* too much. I need a synonym. How about *Britney Spears*.

"Hank!" I kicked his door open. The Lady Elizabeth got a solid draft of cold air from the kick and it was magnificent. Every woman should try it.

"Sadie?" It was super dark and quiet. Hank slept without white noise, which means he was probably secretly a serial killer. He shifted on his bed and I could tell where his curled-up form was.

"Hey, Hank."

"Sadie? Are you in a...what are you...?"

"Call me frigid bitch?"

He didn't even have time to scream. Ax to the head.

It was hard.

Oh, I mean getting in through the doorway. Killing Hank was fine. This was harder because the damn doorway sort of limited my movements, really made my swing less efficient. My ax only made it through part of his skull. His eyes sort of rolled together and even in death, he made this really pathetic but loud squeak.

Christ. Man can't even die attractively. What did I ever see in him? Was it really just for the access to the walk-in freezer? I set my boot against his shoulder so I could wrench the ax from his skull. It separated in a spray of blood and grey drippings that reminded me of snot. How it was all bumpy but sort of glistened?

I've got a pretty strong stomach, but something about snot has always really grossed me out. The slimy, stickiness of it. Like everything disgusting is leaving a human in the form of goop.

A scream from downstairs. It was a little high pitched to come from a man whose balls have dropped.

Considering where the scream had originated (like, downstairs, not like, where the scream came from on the person. His throat, obviously. Sorry, told you I'm not a writer). And then the heavy slams of doors opening, the frantic scramble of men finding pants because dudes always sleep naked. I don't know why, but they do.

I gripped my ax with both hands, maybe slid them up and down and up and down the big, hard shaft.

Oh, it was on like Donkey Kong.

Ladies and Gentlemen, this Y2K, I, Sadie Snow, will be crashing your computers. Only, not, like, real computers—I can't work those much less crash them—but the ones inside your skulls! Cue my amazingly attractive but still victoriously evil laugh.

"Muahahaha-ha!"

I backed into the hallway, my ass pressed against the banister and maybe, maybe if they could get to me, they could throw me over the edge, but they'd have to catch me first. I stood my ground outside of my dead ex's room (how many people can say that? Oh! It's a great feeling and it almost, almost made my Lady Elizabeth pay attention).

The first one I swung at, my ax cut right through the bottom of his chin. He had the BEST arms, so once he fell, I hit him again in the back of his head because I'd like to take those fabulously solid bits of concrete back to my beloved. Those arms would hold me, could pick me up and keep me suspended in the air as we fucked like frozen little snow bats.

119

Wait, no, I was thinking about snow bunnies. And they don't hang in the air. Whatever. Bats or bunnies, just think of us as two animals doing it—as the Bloodhound Gang says—doing things that only Prince would sing about.

The next one had the perfect shoulders and neck. They were square, but weren't so huge they suggested steroids. I'd hang off of those as Michael and I made out with tongue. Wrap my legs around them when Michael licked the folds of the Lady Elizabeth's dress.

Know who the shoulders reminded me of? Jeff Goldblum in *Jurassic Park*. Don't play coy with me. You know the scene. When Jeff's on the floor, bare-chested and heaving from the pain and morphine. Hubba hubba. Yes, I must have those shoulders. I could dress them up or dress them down. Would literally go with anything. They were perfect.

I swung my weapon across his face so as not to ruin my new meaty acquisitions. The shiny, silver blade cut across his nose and into his nasal cavity. All kinds of awful clear gunk spewed out and thank god I was wearing a mask and boots. Don't want things to get too messy.

Let's get another thunder rumble and a deep, reverberating boom. Another jock down! And another. That one was only in shorts and his legs were exactly what I needed. They had perfect calves and his thighs weren't fleshy. They were carved.

A track runner. No. Those calves could only come from riding a bike and kicking in water. This was a triathlon *champion!* No way he came in anything but first place.

Come to Mama.

Because he was a runner, there was another part of him that Michael would like. That would be perfect and supple and grabbable. You know the saying. I hate to see you leave, but I love to watch you walk away?

Slice!

The top half of the runner's torso fell to the ground below and it must have hit the boom box on the lower level because over the loud stereo the song I hadn't realized my soul needed blared across the room. There's a lot of copyright laws about writing down song lyrics, so let's say that yes, yes, MJ.

I was, indeed feeling like I could just beat it.

I was finishing my cut job on Michael's new legs (maybe we could go for walks!) when a shadow loomed over me.

I was standing in a pile of dead jocks. I'm just a paramedic and a vegetarian, I wasn't super sure what the next steps would be, but I felt confident that I had almost everything I needed. Who could this be? What could I still need?

I turned around to see a large, Adonis of a man. The naked yin to my naked yang. A weight lifter. A gym rat. Could probably crack a walnut with one perfectly sculpted ass cheek. Don't ask me how.

Oh, if I hadn't already grabbed the butt from the runner, but at this point I could make so many Michaels and that's just not fair to Michael. Marriage is going to be tricky because I'm used to only worrying about myself, but I think this shopping trip is a solid step in the right direction. This shows that I'm willing to make sacrifices to better our relationship. I, Sadie Snow, don't know much about relationships, but I know it's necessary to treat it as any living being. You can't only feed and water it. It needs love and attention too.

Where were we?

Oh. The Adonis. Yes. How very superficial of me. I'm sure he had a great personality, but that just wasn't what I was after. Also. Let me tell you; this gentleman hadn't even bothered to put shorts on. He was brave enough to walk out of his room to fight me birthday suit to birthday suit. His tube steak was nothing to sneeze at, but it was his abs my eyes settled on. Felt the *thud* of them landing. Or maybe that was my jaw hitting the ground.

I could have done all my laundry against that wicked washboard. I could have played his keyboard to a full house. I could have done shots of tequila from the muscle groves, sucked that nectar up like a god slurping from the prettiest, most frozen crevasses of earth's remaining glaciers.

Michael. I was here for Michael. It was only fair that I think about those abs as Michael's future abs. How he'd use them to halfway sit up and let me ride him into the sunset like a horse from an old Wild West movie. Giddyup.

Adonis ran towards me. Can I just say there is

something very primal when a naked man runs at you. I dropped the ax and extended my arms for the embrace. It was going to be fantastic. Since we're pretending with the weather, let's say there was a break in the wind and rain. A shaft of pale moonlight beamed down and landed on those perfect abs. I swear I'm not exaggerating when I say they sparkled. Those abs were a mystical mountain range, and I was Smeagol sprinting up Mt. Doom to see my *precious.*

(No, I've never read *Lord of the Rings,* but Michael loves it and talks about it all the time.)

He hit me with a shoulder into my gut. The air rushed out of my lungs. We went down. I wrapped my legs around him. His mitts for hands reached up around my neck. Choking just isn't what I'm into, but his abs were still above my belly, and there wasn't a whole lot of room for thought. I pulled my pelvis up more and ground against Michael's future eight pack mountainous range.

"What the hell?" he looked confused, the way his eyes were darting back and forth and maybe he shook a little. His Sergeant Serpent stood erect. He loosened his grip. It was enough.

I shot up and bit into his neck. Not lovingly. No. I was a viper. I was hungry like the wolf. A lioness bringing down the most fantastic of antelope for her perfect, ponytailed king of the jungle. I bit into his jugular. When I tore? I screamed into the stream of blood that spurted out.

So glad I wore make-up that day. Can you imagine

if I was covered in red without eye-liner? As a white girl, I'd have just looked like a zombie. Or Carrie. No, the eye make-up had totally been a good move.

The giant crashed down on top of me. His abs (soon to be Michael's!) pressed against my low belly, greeting the Lady Elizabeth. They were so perfect. How would I get them onto Michael, though? Would I have to replace Michael's torso? You should never want your spouse to change, but I felt like whoever coined the phrase wasn't considering this particular, sensitive situation. It was an upgrade. An improvement. I patted the back of what would be Michael, loving the thick bunches of muscle against my body.

I'd be lying if I said I didn't close my eyes for a minute, just resting and reveling in my nest of perfect new Michael parts. It's hard work, killing fraternity jocks, but someone's got to do it.

Second to last chapter. I know that much. If that's not good enough for you well, you're beyond help.

I had to make a quick stop at my place. I'd completely forgotten extension cords and while I didn't have any extension cords, I did have Christmas lights. It was almost New Year's Eve and the fraternity had shockingly taken theirs down. Oddly timely. So, I needed to stop by my apartment because I still had some on my balcony and around my front door. There's only so much you can do when you live in an apartment.

I went in and looked down. I was, needless to say, quite filthy.

While I love the cold, let's get one thing straight, only psychos like cold showers. I love a hot shower as much as the next person. Unless I want to bring in my vibrator. That's when I'll turn the water cold while I let the *Ding of all Dongs* (don't look at me, I didn't come up with that lame-ass name) work and it always does. This time through though? I wanted the heat for my muscles, to get the blood off my hands. And belly. And face. And legs. My legs were pretty awful. Looked like I was wearing a pair of red stockings. I'd been knee-deep in dead jock and don't pretend you don't want to be me a little bit. Come on. Who wouldn't jump at the chance to swim around in dead douche canoes the way Scrooge McDuck swims in money?

I'm dressed and out of the shower gathering Christmas lights to use as extension cords when there's a knock on the door.

This is a really, really bad time for carolers, Mormon brothers, and Jehovah's Witnesses. While I know that I'm bringing my love back for perfect, regular, socially acceptable reasons, I did recognize that other people might not feel that way. At least not until they could see him and understand.

I tiptoed to the door to avoid those two floorboards that creaked and peaked out. It was Tyler.

He'd traded his fatigues for civilian clothes. He had on a ridiculous hat that said Y2K in glittery gold and purple. His navy, faux fur-lined coat was snug around him, but I could still see the tips of a new tattoo rising up to touch the nape of his neck. I knew they were dragon wings. He'd told me all about getting his chest tatted up. It sounded painful but when I saw his mock-up, I was sort of underwhelmed. I thought he should have gone way bigger. But, to be fair, that's how I feel about most things.

I'd forgotten. Which means it was New Year's. Which means kissing at midnight!

I loved my brother, but I didn't exactly want to smooch him at midnight when I had Michael waiting for me all hard and frozen back at the plant where I'd left him—on meat hooks.

"Sadie, I know you're here. Your rig is out front. Are you working? I thought they would have given you time off?"

My apartment was super, super covered in blood. Not like oops I spilled some marinara. No. Like, CSI would walk in and be like: 'yup, she done it.' And then leave. My boots (Michael's boots) were soaked in dead jock blood and those footprints led straight from the ambulance into my apartment. The snow must have covered it up outside, but here in my apartment? Nope. Straight path into the bathroom. Where my mask was. Where the ax was. And here I was, freshly showered, holding Christmas lights.

A dishrag! Maybe I just needed a rag. Or two. Or

three. It's not like I kept paper towels. We all have to make sacrifices to save the planet. Mine was to use less paper.

Yeah, I know then I'm just using more water to wash rags and towels, but I like trees and that was my contribution. Gosh. Maybe you should write the story next if you're so wise.

"Sadie?"

Or. Or I could just be quiet.

Slowly, without letting the Christmas lights rattle, I plopped onto the floor. Better to not move around. He'd hear me. We shared a wall for sixteen years. No way he didn't know my movements, couldn't tell when I was annoyingly close.

I heard Tyler shuffle around. His shadow under the door got bigger when he (I assume, not like I have x-ray vision) set his pack down. He fumbled around some more and I heard a little *click*.

My phone, stuck somewhere in the couch, started to ring *Ode to Joy*.

I exhaled a sort of hiss. Damn those things! They were a curse. Why people love them so much, I'll never know. Once those things take off (and they will) you'll never get a moment to yourself. People will be just calling and calling and calling because they can. I mean, what else could you use them for?

"Damn her," I heard Tyler swear outside the door. "I told her to have her phone on her. Fuck."

His shadow did a spin. He was probably wondering what he was going to do, where he was going to go while he waited for me to show up. I so, so hoped he would. Or I could show him?

Or I could show him!

Because if the plan was to get Michael to a stable place where he only needed to be jumped occasionally like the Impala he was, well, then people would see him. They would know. I'd never kept anything from my brother before, why should that change now? Especially when I'm on the precipice of something so huge! My brother should be a part of it. No. He'd *want* to be a part of it. Sure, it was a little bit early, I still couldn't get Michael to stay on for very long and I needed to sew all those new parts onto him so he didn't look well, dead, but Tyler should know.

I opened the door.

"Ty!"

"Whoa! You're home!" I wrapped my arms around him and inhaled the scent of his favorite Axe Body spray: Phoenix. I couldn't help but smile. Gross as it sounds, that's the smell of home to me. His room was right next to mine and it wouldn't be Tyler if I didn't have to fight through a cloud of scented mist in the morning to get downstairs for breakfast.

"Hey, sis." He hugged me back. "I'm so sorry about your...um...partner." His grip slackened and I could feel something in his neck go tight. "Um, there are like, a hundred bloody footprints in your apartment. What's going on? Are you okay?"

"Oh, yeah, I uh, had some period problems." I nodded along with my words for effect. I hoped it came across as reassuring.

Tyler froze a little under my embrace, and then backed up a bit. He was a little green under his eyes and at the corners of his mouth. Never fails. Mention your period and men get so grossed out.

"And you tracked it around your apartment? This is a huge amount of blood. Are you okay? I could drive you to the hospital."

Okay, so it wasn't a rock-solid solution. When did he learn about periods? Asshat must have had some lady friends and not told me about them.

"I have something to show you," I said. "Will you come with me?"

Tyler looked around my apartment, then to me.

"What the fuck is this?"

"Come with me?" I tugged Tyler through the open door toward the parking lot.

"I was hoping for a normal New Year's Eve," he complained.

"This is better, okay? Just trust me. I've been waiting for you to get here."

I led him outside. I was going to have him ride in the rig, but I still had, like, so many pounds of fresh jock meat steaming back there. Probably better if we drove separate vehicles.

"Follow me in the Mustang?" Like me, he had a type.

Tyler nodded, still looking at my apartment, then at me, his sister who was standing in jeans and an old, thin, *Lightning Response!* T-shirt in the middle of winter, holding Christmas lights.

I get it, is what I'm saying.

"Are you sure you're okay? Look, I don't want to dig into your personal life, but I really think I should get you to urgent care or something."

"I promise I'm okay."

He regarded me. His eyes did this weird non-blinking serious thing that he would do when he was waiting for me to tell the truth. I'd seen it when we were kids and I lied about stealing his bike. Under this gaze, I'd broken down and told him I'd borrowed his bike because I hated that mine had stupid pink streamers. I'd just wanted to see what his cool blue off-roading bike was like. After I told him, he'd helped me paint my bike bright blue and we burned the streamers in the fireplace. Our house smelled like melted plastic for days.

His Superman laser-gaze made me want to tell him everything, but not yet. Not yet. He finally nodded defeat. Yes! He was in.

"Fine," he said. "But I better be following you to a Hell of a Y-two-K party."

"It's going to be insane and super electrifying," I assured him.

That seemed to do it. He walked to his car, climbed in. I waited to get into the ambulance until Tyler was out of eyesight. See, when I opened the door, more than a trickle of blood washed out across the threshold. It soaked the bottom of my feet and I was super annoyed that my socks were wet and soggy again. I hate having wet feet.

I climbed in and adjusted the review mirror. Tyler was pulling his seatbelt across his chest. No way had he seen the blood pour out of the ambulance. I caught sight of my apartment and I had a feeling I wouldn't be back. Probably because Michael and I would want to live together. I should have grabbed more stuff, but it's so much better if you start a new relationship with new stuff. Old stuff has bad juju on it.

"Bye, apartment." We left and you know how I feel about narrating driving and transitions. It's dumb. No one wants to hear about people driving. We spend enough of our lives in cars.

We got to the plant. Tyler pulled up behind me. He got out and seemed very aware of the slushy snow mud that clung to his Doc Martens.

"This isn't a party, Sadie."

"Just come with me?" I walked ahead of him towards the slaughterhouse.

"What is this? Be real. You were super weird on the phone. I've come to check on you and party and, hell, you can even talk and cry and stuff about your partner, but seriously? What the actual fuck? I used *leave* for this."

I kept walking while he talked. We moved through the first set of doors, then deeper in, towards the freezer room.

"Jesus. It's so cold. And what's that *smell*?" He was shivering in his jacket. The air felt perfect to me. It greeted my skin with a chilled hug. I felt surrounded and confident. Tyler would see. Tyler was going to understand.

I opened the final door. There was Michael, my love, on a metal table. Weird. I thought I'd left him on hooks? Huh.

Also? I wished I'd been able to sew his new limbs onto him before Tyler saw. Without his new parts, my boyfriend looked really, well, dead. His skin had greyed and there was a pool of pinkish liquid underneath him. Looked like he was floating in a sea of pink lemonade. His arms were rigid. His ground up legs were a little whiter than the rest of his body. Veins and arteries stared out of the crush injuries like worms checking for sunlight. The de-fib pads dotted Michael's body. At least those were where I'd left them.

"Tyler? Meet Michael." I'd just realized I should have brought Michael back to life first so they could shake hands. This was just rude.

Tyler threw up.

It spattered the floor and I remember holding my nose because while I was super used to people barfing on or around me (nature of the job) I am a sympathetic barfer. The LAST thing you want to do as a sympathetic barfer is smell someone else's puke.

Just, I didn't expect Tyler to react so poorly, but I guess most brothers don't, like, throw a party of support when they meet their baby sister's boyfriend.

Still covering my nose, I went over to pat his back. Throwing up is so unpleasant.

"Sadie, what the fuck? What the fuck!" He started

to back up, to back away from me. To shrug my hand off his back and shoulders.

"No, no!" I tapped his shoulder twice to punch the words in. "Watch, okay?" I left him and went over to the de-fib units. They were plugged in. I pressed the red buttons.

"Clear? Stand clear. Shock advised."

I pressed the shock button.

Michael's body jerked and fell back down. Nothing. No.

"Sadie? What are you doing. Get away from that. Sadie? Please!"

"No, no something's wrong. It just needs to, I don't know, warm up for a minute." I shocked Michael again, again, and again. I walked closer each time until I was close—too close. Each shock that was supposed to give him life just made him flop around in his own chunky liquid. It made a weird wet fart squelching noise. A sour, old chicken smell curled around inside my nose.

No.

"This isn't right. He should be coming back! Why isn't he coming back?"

A door slammed. Tyler was so, so gone.

"Tyler! Ty, wait!"

I ran after down the halls and through the doors to outside after my brother. It was muddy and just starting to snow again. There'd be a storm later, I could tell from the deep bone chill. Like the wind had teeth.

"Tyler, stop!"

He was at the car, fumbling with keys.

"I don't know what you're doing, but I'm leaving. I'm getting you help."

Help? No. Michael wasn't ready to see people.

"He's not ready! We're not ready. Our relationship isn't fully developed yet!"

"Relationship? Sadie! That's a corpse. Not only are you fucking sick, but you're desecrating the dead. What about his family? What about his friends? Stay here. Please. I'll be back with people."

People? People would take him away. Would take me away.

I went to the ambulance and opened the door. My fireman's ax fell next to me, made a sort of *pluck* sound when it hit the slushy mud.

Tyler's car roared to life. He was going to get away. He was going to go get the people who would take Michael away before I'd perfected the science that kept him coming back.

Pun intended.

I couldn't let him get away. I picked my ax back up and charged. And yeah, maybe I was fifteen again, watching my big brother sign up to go to the military. Maybe I was watching him leave all over again and some unresolved issues boiled up.

"Don't leave!"

So, disclaimer? I hate it when I hear this. The whole: *two things happened at once* thing.

I think it's a total cop-out. But, I, Sadie Snow, try to keep an open mind and admit when I am wrong. And I'm wrong.

Two things happened at once: I swung my ax into Tyler's windshield to persuade him to stay, and he stepped on the gas, which, maybe because he couldn't see, careened his car into the side of the plant.

I screamed. I know I did. I felt my hands around the corners of my mouth when I yelled. I felt my breath.

"Tyler!"

A blink. A minute. A thousand years.

And then the driver's side door opened, showering the ground in broken pieces of windshield. Tyler fell from his seat to the side of his car and started to crawl away from me on his elbows. His leg leaked blood and I could hear him cussing against the ground.

The army crawl made me remember the night I stayed up when they came to get him for boot camp. He'd somehow managed to get some sleep, but fifteen-year-old me had stayed up, watched his sleeping form, and begged him with my thoughts *don't leave*.

"You're leaving me again!" When I needed him. He was leaving without even considering *me*.

I swung the ax and cut into his back, then kicked him over and swung into his chest, just next to his heart.

The blade went deep, maybe all the way through. I think this, because it got stuck and I couldn't quite pull it clear of him.

Tyler's face turned up to the sky and his eyes had time to flick over. They locked on me, confused, and then sad. They returned to the sky. Didn't close.

Oh. Oh, no.

I collapsed next to him. I wrenched the ax from his body. My hands shook over his wound. The wound I'd inflicted. My brother. Oh god. He'd never forgive me.

I held pressure trying to keep the blood in but it pooled out and stained my hands and soaked his clothes. The familiar tang, the consuming smell of iron hit me. I breathed through my mouth to keep the tears down, to keep the scream in because it was all right. He was okay.

He was.

I could bring people back to life, so this just wasn't a serious problem.

But could I? It hadn't worked with Michael this time. What if? No. I couldn't think like that. He just needed more juice.

But what if something else was wrong?

I smoothed Tyler's hair and slowly backed off the wound.

The bleeding had already slowed—no heart to keep blood dumping out of the wound. Just needed some stitches. It would be an easy fix, and after I brought him back, he'd be in a much better state than Michael. He only had an opening over his heart.

His heart.

What if that's what was wrong with Michael? And if I put Tyler's heart in Michael, well, that would be like reviving both of them, right? I only had so many de-bib units, so I had to pick. I couldn't possibly choose between the Harry-to-my-Sally and my own brother.

This would be how I saved both of them. How I could keep them both. Yes. Tyler's heart would continue beating forever inside of Michael.

Final Chapter even though I'm sure you're way bummed. This has been such a cute love story, I know.

So, remember where we are? From the beginning? I'm straddling Michael's corpse on a gurney and he's wired to every de-fib unit I could get my hands on?

Like Ricky Martin, I'm just *Livin'* my very best *La Vida Loca*.

Now, I'm not just saying this because I'm an early twenty-something female, but Christmas lights are a solid year-round decoration. The colors bounce off the walls and add an ambiance of *happy* and *joyful*.

Also. I'm super done writing, so you'll just have to be here with me. I don't care what you think. I make the rules. You want to hear the ending or not? Are we Cool?

Cool.

I hop off, place my goggles on, pull up Michael's rubber-soled boots because safety first. Time to put the monument back onto my Washington. Into, rather.

And then I hear noises coming from outside. Lights *and* sirens.

No.

I climb the chains and use the hooks as little footholds. Outside there's an array of vehicles. One says *psychiatric* and another says *military*.

One for me, one for Tyler. Like our presents. Like Christmas at the Snows' all over again.

And the worst part? Among them? The two women who must have figured it all out. Nancy and Vicky-with-an-i. I'm sort of pleased her nose looks smushed.

Well, now or never. Michael and I would have to make a run for it. Normally people say Mexico but Canada is much closer (and colder). I hop down.

I have everything plugged into a long power strip, so all I have to do is press a single, red button until it glows. The grey box of the power strip is cool against my hands. It feels like everything I've ever wanted. It feels like everything women so very rarely get: choice.

With a breath, I press down. Electricity runs through Michael, shakes him back and forth more violently than before. I don't back away.

Michael's body flails, falls off the gurney, and I can't help but hope that the stitches hold together. A moan. I kill the electricity.

"Michael?" I go to him.

"Babe?" He turns. His eyes are white and grey. No blue. "What have you done to me?" He raises his new hand up, studies it. "This isn't mine." The stitches run along his arms, holding him closed and together, pulled tight like a corset across a bodice.

I kneel down and take his hand. I place it on my face, trying to show him he can still feel. "The better to touch me with, my darling."

"I'm the wrong color!"

"That's rude. There isn't a wrong color."

"That's not what I'm suggesting! I'm saying I just want to be my color."

"Really? Did you learn nothing in our sensitivity training? Also, you're a very difficult color to match. Who's tan in winter, anyway?"

He smiles, or, tries to. The muscles there are starting to die.

"I don't think I can keep doing this, babe," he says, but that's because he doesn't know yet. About his new heart.

"But remember? You said you were missing parts? I gave you new limbs! And? My brother's heart!"

"What?"

"Surprise!"

He's not blinking. Doesn't even move. He's silent as, well, yeah, the grave. Okay, this isn't going the way I planned. Why isn't he happy?

Michael clears his throat. "Sadie? Did you kill Tyler?"

"No!"

"Oh my god, you killed your brother!"

"How can that be true when his heart is alive in you?" Hot tears run down my face because I can see how disappointed he is, and what's even worse? There's something else, something soft in the way he's looking at me. Is it pity? Pity!

Michael wipes the tears from my cheek and I don't

like the touch of some other person's hands on me. Love, it's cruel, isn't it?

"I love you," he says. "But what have you done?"

"I'm just trying to make you last longer. Make *us* last longer. We could put you on more ice. I'll order a walk-in freezer. We can just do it in there. They're made of steel. Maybe we could, I don't know, fashion some kind of electric chair?"

"I'm done coming back."

"Done with me, you mean."

"That's not it. I mean I don't want to live being held together by other people! I don't want to live waiting in the dark for you to shock me back life. I'm not really living, Sadie."

Why is he doing this? We're so happy.

"It's not the life we wanted, and I admit that. But, like, big deal. All couples make sacrifices. Everyone has to adapt, just like the frogs do in *Jurassic Park.* Look, people are coming to get us as we speak. Can't we just, I don't know, show them?" I'm shaking and my hands are all clenched up. Does he not love me the way I love him?

"I said I don't want to live like this." He moves his arm to gesture to himself, but instead, it sort of flings around and the hand flops forward uselessly. Oh, no. His handshake would be a dead fish handshake. Nothing is worse than a dead fish handshake.

He moves to kiss me, but his lips can't quite form a pucker right, and he more smears me with dry, cracked lips.

"I don't want to live like this, but that doesn't mean I don't want to be with you. I love you."

Asshole. After everything I've done.

But, what I'd done didn't exactly make him better. It made him worse. The hands. The lips.

It's just not what I'd pictured when I'd been a little girl, dreaming of my Prince.

But does that matter?

I get up from him. I run my hands through my hair, against my face trying to wake up from this strange nightmare I've created. I became a paramedic to preserve life. Have I taken it too far? He's the Richard Gere to my Julia Roberts. The Heath Ledger to my Julia Styles.

Voices outside, followed by a rattling of doors.

There's no escaping. For either of us. What's worse? There's no picket fence. There's no electric bill. We'll never buy a house or make babies or have that one stupid fight to bring up on a random night when we each have time to kill. We'll never play rock-paper-scissors for who's turn it is to get the baby and then I'd end up going anyway because I'd be the mom and being a woman sucks.

We'll never be old and have to lean on each other when we have surgeries and replacements and treatments.

We'll never slow dance to favorite songs and whisper about all those *remember whens?* All of those secret, private jokes. We wouldn't remember where they came from, only that they were ours and ours alone.

A friend. A partner. A husband.

My husband.

Our future was gone.

As they say in Romeo and Juliet (the Leo version, duh. That version is so Britney Spears), a plague on both our fucking houses.

But that gives me an idea.

"Michael?"

"Yeah?"

"If you're going to go, I'm going with you." I stare at him, daring him to protest. If anything, his eyes have the smallest bit of blue back in them.

"It's your decision." It looks like he's trying to reach for me, but his arm just sort of wiggles like cooked spaghetti. "I am really lonely out there. I miss you all the time."

That's all I need. Love. And? One hell of an electric current.

The de-fib pads cover his torso. I unstick half of them from his body, slap them on mine and then I ease down onto his cold, dead cock.

"You're sure?" he asks, groaning a little in pleasure.

"Yes. I'm sure."

I move with him and press my forehead against his. He's clutching me, running his cold tongue on my skin.

"I love you."

"I love you more."

The voices are getting closer. The sound of boots

and a flicker of flashlights from outside our room. It's time. The barbarians are at the gates. The villagers are here for their monster. Little do they know their monster just wanted love. Acceptance. A good, normal life.

I press the button and before we both explode, I can feel the lightning, the electricity from the charge in the air. The lights burn bright bright bright and our hair stands on end. The Christmas lights go as hot as their little caskets will let them before they start popping. Their breaking glass and orbs of light surround us like our own fantastic galaxy and I want to tell Cher that yes, yes I do believe in life after love.

This is what we would look like if we were frozen in a lake and above us were fireworks. Their colors would have danced on the crystals and showered us in an eternal rain of sparkle. The electrical charge pricks at the moisture on my lips and the tears on my cheeks. It dances between us, loops Michael and I in a connection of pain and pleasure, freezing us. It's the first snowflake that falls and sends a shiver up your spine. A lake I'm floating in, where white and blue hands from below grip my arms and legs and neck, and pull me down, down, down.

—

Cold. I feel cold.
Everywhere.
Finally.

ALL YOU NEED IS LOVE AND A STRONG ELECTRIC CURRENT

Acknowledgements

Thanks very much for the UCR Palm desert MFA low residency program. Like Avicii says, I didn't know I was lost. But I was. And you found me. Thank you.

Thank you, Kathryn, for daring me to write the short story version of this. Big crazy thank you to Richard Thomas for reading the short story version of this and saying that maybe I'd found a good voice and should follow it deeper.

Thanks to my writing/reading people because writing a book takes a village: Eli, thanks for the perfect notes, the attention to detail, and telling me I should name Sadie's vagina. Thank you, Megan, for saying you couldn't look away or stop reading. Kathryn, every step of the way, you were in my corner, cheering for more *Frankensex*. You also told me to maybe replace the term 'sexy' with 'Britney Spears.' You're a goddamn genius. Thanks to Stephen Graham Jones for the read, the thoughts, the zel gel idea.

Thanks very much (or maybe the better phrase is *I'm sorry*) to Sean who always squirrels his way into my books.

Thank you to all of the artists whose song lyrics/titles I lifted. And special thanks to the late, great George Carlin. Most of the dick names in here are from his head.

Thank you, Unnerving, for your hard work, dedication, and of course, for taking on such a peculiar little book.

And Lisa, fuck. I mean, more than thank you for encouraging me to write this as a novella. You always push me to go that first, second, tenth overwhelming step. I guess what I'm saying is: you challenge time itself. You're a force of fucking nature.

Thanks, finally, to my family. Thanks to Mom for always railing against the patriarchy and demanding I challenge old fashioned traditions. A special thanks to Dad, for always wanting to read whatever I'm writing, and then for giving me an honest opinion. I watched you write on your lunch breaks, after dinner, and way late at night. Your motto of 'put your head down and swim' instilled in me the idea that to get things done, sometimes, you don't stop for silly things like air. You have an iron will and indefatigable work ethics. I hope I have inherited even a little bit of that.

Finally, thank you to my husband, my Atlas, for balancing the world on your shoulders while I podcast, work, and write. Nothing I do gets done without your strength. You are so wonderful, amazing, smart that I sometimes catch myself wondering who you are and how I tricked you into marrying me. Thanks also for the ponytail, because...well, you know.

REWIND OR DIE

www.UNNERVINGMAGAZINE.com

Made in the USA
Monee, IL
30 October 2020

NO TI___
FOR
TOMBSTONES

Life and Death
in the
Vietnamese Jungle

No Time for Tombstones

LIFE AND DEATH IN THE VIETNAMESE JUNGLE

James and Marti Hefley

TYNDALE HOUSE PUBLISHERS, Inc.
Wheaton, Illinois

COVERDALE HOUSE PUBLISHERS, Ltd.
London, England

Library of Congress Catalog Card Number 74-80772.
ISBN 8423-4719-4 cloth; 8423-4720-8 paper.
Copyright © 1974 Tyndale House Publishers, Inc.,
Wheaton, Illinois. All rights reserved.
Second printing, December 1974.
Printed in the United States of America.

*To the
foreign missionaries
who remain
at their posts
in still-troubled
Viet Nam*

Contents

TET in the western year of 1968. Fireworks and feasts to celebrate the beginning of the Vietnamese "Year of the Monkey." A welcome truce proclaimed by the warring parties. A holiday from horror—hopefully.

CHAPTER

1

Captured

On *Tet* Eve, Monday, January 29, Vange Blood turned in bed and gently shook her husband awake. "Hank, that's awfully loud for firecrackers, don't you think?"

Hank lifted his head and listened. "I wouldn't worry. They get louder every year."

His reassurances to the contrary, the lanky Bible translator to the Mnong Rolom people was fully awake. There had been rumors that the Communists would try something big during *Tet*. He'd heard such stories in Kontum where he had taken their daughter Cindy to mission school. And the tribespeople in the Radê village where they lived on the southern outskirts of the highland town of Banmethuot had been warning the missionaries to leave.

He wondered if Vange had done the right thing in returning from Saigon so soon. She'd gone there to take their four-year-old Carolyn for an eye examination, taking along baby Cathy and leaving five-year-old David with him. She would have stayed longer if she had not felt sorry for them, left at home without a cook.

Boom!

"Mamma! Daddy!" Carolyn called.

"Go back to sleep, honey. It's *Tet*, remember."

Boom! Boom!

By 2:30 Tuesday morning the sounds of war were unmistakable—mortars pounding the South Vietnamese Army camp which was just up the hill. Machine guns rat-a-tat-tatting lethal messages. Stray bullets zinging overhead, too close for comfort.

"Let's get the kids into the bunker," Hank said in quick decision.

Grabbing the sleepy-eyed children, a flashlight, and some blankets, they rushed outside and scuttled into the dark hole. The small room below ground had a roof of logs and dirt that would ward off stray bullets and protect them from anything but a direct hit by a mortar.

They got the children settled and prayed. Then Hank began quoting his favorite Psalm for protection. *"The Lord is my light and my salvation; whom shall I fear? the Lord is the strength of my life; of whom shall I be afraid?"*

There was too much noise for anyone to sleep. They huddled together in the damp darkness, both trying to calm the growing fears of their children. "When daylight comes," Hank kept assuring them, "the VCs will go away. They always do."

Finally the mouth of the bunker began to whiten. They waited. They could see splashes of sun. But the bombardment continued as fierce as ever.

This was very serious.

Hank pulled his son toward him. He was so young, yet he wanted to be sure of David's relationship with the Lord. If the attackers should overrun the village, one grenade would be enough.

 The Bloods' nearest American neighbors were just two blocks above them. Christian and Missionary Alliance nurses Betty Olsen and Ruth Wilting lived in adjoining houses fronting Highway 14. Across the highway, which connected with Saigon 200 miles to the south, was the steepled Radê church and the main Christian and Missionary Alliance compound backing up to the military base. Here, trapped in their two-story Italian-style villas, were the Bob Ziemers, the Ed Thompsons, and father-daughter Leon and Carolyn Griswold.

Both Betty's and Ruth's roommates were away, so the girls had pooled their morale by staying together at Ruth's house during the night. Betty, 34 and the younger, had just dared a peep through the window. "Oh, dear God," she whispered in shock. "That wasn't a Vietnamese tank we heard explode during the night. It was the Griswolds' house!"

Seeing the destruction some hundred yards up the hill, her first impulse was to try and help any survivors. Then the self-possessed, trim redhead drew back. "They'd knock us down like pigeons, Ruth, if we try to go over there. The VCs are firing across the grounds at the ARVN base. There are probably more VCs in the church."

The girls retreated into Ruth's bedroom, where the shades were already drawn, to pray and wait for a lull in the shooting.

The minutes dragged by. After a while Betty broke the silence. "I've always told people I have no fear because I know I'm in the center of God's will. I'm not so sure I can say that now, though I know this is where God wants me."

Ruth nodded. "Yes, it's like when Dan, Archie, and Ardel were captured," she said referring to the abduction of her Mennonite fiancé and two Alliance co-workers in 1962. "After the VCs took them off, we spent a fearful night at the leprosarium before coming into town."

Betty glanced at Dan's boyish picture, framed on Ruth's dresser. "And we haven't heard from them since," she sighed.

Ruth's lip was trembling. "I know. But lately, I've had the strangest feeling that Dan and I are going to be reunited soon. I've been working on my wedding dress."

A bullet zinged by the wall, causing them both to duck involuntarily. The firing outside continued unabated for another hour or so. They kept straining to hear the whirr of helicopters. "They must have knocked the chopper base out of commission, or the boys would be here to help us," Betty finally concluded.

About ten the firing lessened, but still seemed too heavy to chance a run. Suddenly they heard a motor. Someone was coming in a vehicle.

Ruth took a quick look and pulled back in surprise. "Good grief, it's Mike Benge! That's his International Scout. There's a Vietnamese boy with him. Where are they going?"

"Some people don't have enough sense to be afraid. He must be planning on rescuing us," Betty replied with a wry grin.

The AID man was past the church now, moving cautiously toward the driveway to the compound.

"Look!" Ruth whispered excitedly. "Ed Thompson is waving from his window. He's trying to get Mike to turn back."

"There's his reason," Betty declared tensely. "A dozen VC are coming onto the road up ahead. Now Mike sees them and is backing up . . . Oh, no! More VCs are crawling out of the culvert behind Mike. They've got him. Oh, why did he have to pull such a stunt?"

There was nothing they could do but watch as Mike and

the boy were dragged from the Scout and marched down into the village, out of sight.

"He tried," Ruth said admiringly. "Mike may not be what some would like him to be. But he loves people and he's got courage."

"Yes," Betty agreed. "He's really a good guy. The best man AID ever had with the tribespeople. I wonder if we'll ever see him again."

Mike's capture lowered their spirits. The feisty, wise-cracking, crew-cut AID officer was hardly the answer to a maiden missionary's prayers, but he was liked and respected by all the missionaries. Among the American AID contingent in Viet Nam, he was known as a Montagnard "freak" because of his close identification with the jungle tribespeople, but he had been decorated twice for his achievements in education and agriculture.

 By this time the Blood children were ravenously hungry and miserable in the cramped bunker. Their parents cautiously took them back into the kitchen. Hank pushed a table against the wall, piled a big foam mattress on top, and pushed the kids' single mattresses underneath. Here they could play with toys while Vange hastily assembled some food.

 In late morning the gunfire slackened and the nurses saw Bob, Ed, and some tribal helpers pulling back wreckage from the Griswolds' house. "Carolyn and her father must still be in there," Betty said. "Let's chance it now."

Grabbing the small bags they'd already packed, the two slender single women sprinted across the highway and the debris-strewn lawn to where the men were working. "We heard Carolyn moaning," Bob Ziemer reported to them. "Leon is unconscious or dead. The rest of us are okay."

"Thank God for that," Betty murmured. "I'll go get a supply of medicine." Then she raced toward the clinic warehouse behind the church before anyone could stop her.

She returned safely. After more prizing and moving of timbers, the men were able to reach Carolyn, and they lifted her, still in her nightgown, from the wreckage. They carried her into the Ziemer house where the nurses determined that she had a broken right leg, internal injuries, and was in shock. But when they finally reached Leon Griswold, he was beyond help. They removed his body to the servants' house which stood between the Ziemers' villa and the fence enclosing the military base.

They talked about escape and discussed the possibility of getting Carolyn to a hospital. Y Ngue, the pastor of the Rade tribal church, had helped remove the Griswolds. He shook his head. "The VCs are still here. They're even in the church. I'll take my crippled son and try to get help in town. The VCs know us."

The pastor took his boy, Chen, and started toward the village, leaving two other sons, one 17 and one 10, with the missionaries. The oldest son's fiancée and her sister remained also.

Occasional firing punctuated the afternoon, then about six Hank Blood and his son David appeared. Hank was quickly informed of Leon Griswold's death and Carolyn's precarious condition, and that Pastor Ngue had gone for help but hadn't returned.

"Have you heard anything from MAC V [the American military advisers quartered near Banmethuot]?" Bob Ziemer asked.

Hank hadn't and speculated that both the American advisers and the helicopter pilots had been pinned down under the attackers' fire. He also surmised that the mission compound might be safer than his rented house in the Radê village below."

"I doubt it," Bob replied. "You're welcome to stay, but Pastor Ngue said the VCs were all around."

"Then we'd better get back. When dark comes, we'll probably get it."

Returning, Hank shepherded his family into the damp bunker. He and Vange had just made the children comfortable when their landlord's wife, with her eight children and three other relatives, wiggled in to join them. Throughout Tuesday night, they heard explosions all around. Some were close enough to shake the ground, showering the roof of the bunker.

After dark they heard planes and helicopters flying overhead. Apparently the Americans had fought off their attackers and were now in the action.

The situation remained just as critical at the Alliance compound. Betty and Ruth watched over Carolyn in one room, the Ziemers and Thompsons stayed in another, and the four Radê young people huddled in the servants' house where Leon Griswold's body had been stored.

When Wednesday morning came Carolyn was still unconscious and delirious. The nurses felt they should risk another dash to the clinic warehouse for more medicines and blood plasma.

The men protested that they should go. "No," Betty insisted. "You couldn't find anything. I've just inventoried our whole stock and can run in and out in a minute. Anyway, they're less apt to shoot women."

After Betty and Ruth returned safely, Bob and Ed painted a big SOS on an old door and placed it on top of a car. They hung out a white flag, then dug out the garbage pit behind the Ziemer house to have ready as a makeshift bunker. They were preparing to bury Leon Griswold in a shallow grave when war activity picked up.

CAPTURED   7

From Bob and Marie's window they saw two black-pajamaed Vietnamese men wearing brown floppy hats shinny through a window into the Thompsons' house, then jump back out. A minute later the house blew apart in a tremendous explosion.

"This house will be next," Bob predicted. "We'd better join the Radês in the servants' quarters."

The others agreed and the men carried the still unconscious Carolyn on a cot into the small, one-story green house.

The Bloods had spent Wednesday in their house, mostly under the table, trying to keep the children reasonably content. When evening came, Hank and Vange decided to keep the children where they would be more comfortable. They feared they might cry in the crowded bunker and draw fire that would endanger the landlord's family.

About two A.M. Thursday Hank smelled bamboo burning. He looked through the shutters and saw that several neighboring houses were afire. Their house had concrete walls and a metal roof, so they were in no danger. But when the shutters on the storerooms in back caught fire, he ran out with a bucket of water and doused the flames.

"The VCs must not be too close," he said upon returning. "Nobody shot at me."

At last the children were asleep. Hank and Vange joined hands and waited. When dawn came, Vange served them breakfast under the table. At noon, they got their first news report on the radio: "The president of Viet Nam advises all people in Viet Cong-infiltrated areas to evacuate immediately."

"Let's make a break for it," Hank told Vange. "Pack some food while I check in back."

Seconds later Hank came panting back in and dived under

the table. "VC in the shower room! Shot at me. Heard the bullets whiz past my head. Now that they know Americans are here, they'll be in to get us. Nothing to do but pray."

His six-four frame bent under the table, the big ex-engineer from Portland began to pray as his wife had never heard him before.

"Lord God, you are all powerful. You control the courses of nations. Neither death nor life nor principalities nor powers can separate us from your love. You saved us and called us to give the Mnongs your Word. You brought Vange and me together. You gave us our children and healed them when they were sick. You brought us to Viet Nam and provided for our needs. You protected us at the lake when the enemy soldiers came. You kept watch over me when I hid in the pigpen just a few days ago. Nothing can harm us unless it is your will. Be our strong tower, our shield as the enemy draws near. Watch over our babies who are not old enough to understand. . . ."

Before he finished they heard voices and a hammering at the front door. "*Muc su* [preacher]," one called.

"Yes," Hank answered. "I am here."

A moment of silence passed. Perhaps they hadn't heard.

An explosion shook the house. Then came a second blast, throwing shrapnel into the kitchen. Vange cried out in pain as she took fragments in a leg and knee. Another piece creased the forehead of little Cathy, leaving her dazed.

Hank turned to Vange, quoting Proverbs 16:7: "When a man's ways please the Lord, he makes even his enemies to be at peace with him." Crawling out from under the table, he ran outside through the blown-out door, forcing a smile, hands in the air. Vange, carrying Cathy, followed by the other two children, came along behind him.

A black-pajamaed soldier motioned for them to get in a huddle on the ground. *This is it*, both Hank and Vange thought. But it wasn't. They checked Hank's pockets for a gun and asked if more Americans were in the house. One VC bandaged Cathy's head and Vange's leg. Two others tied Hank's arms behind his back with telephone wire.

"Americans, follow me," one of the Vietnamese commanded with a sweeping arm motion.

The Alliance missionaries had fared worse. Sometime before dawn they had fled to the garbage pit, leaving Carolyn barely alive in the servants' house. When daylight came, Ruth and Betty decided to get more medicines and plasma for their patient. When they reached the clinic safely, Betty impulsively said, "I'm getting a car to take Carolyn to the hospital."

She ran to one of the mission vehicles and started the motor. Before she could shift into gear, a bullet smashed the windshield, narrowly missing her head. Communist soldiers surrounded the car. One opened the door. Another dragged her out and pulled her across the highway into the tribal section and across several back yards to the house where other captives were being held. She recognized Pastor Ngue, little Chen, and several lay leaders from the church.

A short while later Marie Ziemer staggered in, the left side of her dress soaked with blood. She slumped down beside Betty who began checking her wounds.

Marie looked dazed and weak, but was able to speak. "Bob . . . with Jesus," she murmured. "Thompsons . . . dead. Ruth, too, I think. They begged for mercy. The soldiers wouldn't listen . . ."

Soon Hank and Vange were pushed inside with their frightened children clinging to them. They groped their way through the crowd to where Betty and Marie were huddled against a wall. Vange slipped down beside them, while Hank remained standing, holding their youngest child. Betty told them what had happened.

The little two-room house was so crowded the Americans could hardly move. The tribal captives and Hank Blood were bound with telephone wire. The translator towered above the others, his white face drawn.

They heard the whirr of a helicopter overhead, then its guns firing from a low altitude. One bullet slammed through the house and wounded a tribesman.

After the chopper left, an officer came in for Betty. He escorted her to the wrecked mission on the hill. She saw the bodies of the Thompsons and Ruth Wilting in the garbage pit. Bob Ziemer's body hung over a clothesline as he had fallen. As she was trying to move it to a cot, her escort asked, "Where is his gun?"

She exploded in bitter anger. "You fool, missionaries don't have guns!"

The Communist frowned. He refused to let her look at Carolyn or check on the bodies of the young Rades who were sprawled near the servants' quarters. "Get your bag, and come," he ordered. She grabbed the small package and hurried out.

The officer returned her to the crowded house where the Blood children were complaining of thirst. The guards brought a little water. Betty found more in a rice pan and strained it through a strip of Vange's slip. The youngsters drank it gladly.

As darkness approached, two soldiers came in with a bag of rice and several cans of food. The Bloods recognized the cans as having come from their house. But they were more concerned for Hank's language notes, representing eight years of study.

The officer pulled Hank aside. "Do you want to go back to America with your wife and children?"

"*Muon cho* [I sure do]!" Hank replied.

"Then give us your agency."

Hank didn't understand the question. He looked at Vange blankly, but she just shrugged her shoulders. She didn't understand either. The interrogator then took Hank outside.

They returned a few minutes later. "Go get your husband's papers," the officer ordered Vange.

Accompanied by the officer, Vange limped back to the house. The floors were strewn with books, papers, clothes, and toys, but she managed to find their passports and Vietnamese identity cards. She handed them to the officer.

They returned to the house, where all the prisoners were given a propaganda lecture on the "just cause of the National Liberation Front." A stern warning was given to make no noise; not even a match could be lit, nothing that might attract attention.

Vange was then ordered to make another trip to her home to get some extra clothing for Hank. She returned with a pair of trousers and two shirts.

"We're going to let your wife and children and the wounded missionary lady go," the officer told Hank. "You and the red-haired lady will come along with the Radê captives."

They began moving the captives out and Hank had only a few seconds to kiss his wife and children goodbye. "Kiss Cindy for me," he called to Vange as a soldier pulled him away. "And tell the gang the Lord has done a special work in my heart. I've surrendered everything to him."

They had tied Betty to Pastor Ngue with a loop of wire. Beside him stood his little son. "Come on! Come on!" the guards were yelling.

"Wait," the middle-aged tribal preacher begged. "Let the boy go."

"No," an officer declared. "He's young and can learn to follow the revolution."

The preacher reached and pulled up his son's trouser leg. "See how he has been burned by napalm. Have mercy," he begged. "Let him go back and study. Then you can teach him."

The officer pushed the boy away. "Very well, but if he talks, he is dead."

"Move!" the officer shouted, and the captives fell in line, Pastor Ngue and Betty walking together and behind them Hank Blood, his white face bobbing above the file of dark-skinned tribal captives.

CHAPTER

2

Happy Valley

After their capture, Mike Benge and the Vietnamese boy Ky had been taken to the Communist command post in the Radê village. There Mike was stripped of his wallet, watch, and prized brass bracelet, a gift from a Radê chief.

"*Chao ông Benge* [How are you, Mr. Benge]?" an officer asked.

"I'd be better if you'd let me take my friends to safety," Mike replied. "And how do you know my name?"

"Ah, we know all about you. You are an important official of the U.S. State Department. Sometimes you live in town with your American friends. Sometimes you go into villages to learn about the movements of the Liberation Army. In you, we have—how do you say it?—caught very big fish."

"Your informants are in error, sir. I am a civilian—a noncombatant helping the tribal people grow better crops. Ask any of them. They'll tell you."

"No, you are a spy for the imperialist American invaders."

Mike looked straight into the unsmiling face of his Vietnamese questioner. "You, sir, wear the uniform of the so-called National Liberation Front. But your accent tells me you are from North Viet Nam."

The face remained impassive. "I see you do not know Vietnamese very well. We are all from the south. North Viet Nam supports us politically, but has no soldiers in the south. Now if you will give us a little military information, perhaps we can be lenient with you."

Mike again emphasized that he was nonmilitary and added that he had no knowledge of battle plans or troop movements. Finally, after considerable interrogation, the North Vietnamese turned the American and his young companion over to guards.

Later that evening they joined a contingent of tribal captives for a forced march along a jungle road. When they arrived at a small military camp, Mike looked through the trees and recognized a familiar U-shaped building: the leprosarium operated by tribal nurses. The Alliance missionaries hadn't lived here since the capture of Dr. Ardel Vietti, Dan Gerber, and Archie Mitchell back in 1962. But Mike had made two or three risky jaunts into the jungle for visits and knew the place.

Nearby a crowd of fist-shaking Viet Cong were clustered around ten prisoners, hurling accusations in Radê. Mike had seen some of the prisoners around Banmethuot. Because he understood the Radê Montagnard dialect spoken by some 100,000 tribesmen in the Banmethuot area, he knew they were facing a Communist "people's court."

Powerless to intervene, Mike stood beside the thin Vietnamese boy and listened as the prisoners were sentenced to death. Then the hapless tribesmen were pushed before a firing squad. A volley of shots echoed through the jungle and ten bodies crumpled to the ground.

The shock was too much for Ky. The terrified boy broke into a run. As he dashed into some bushes, Mike heard the crack of a Russian-made AK-47 rifle, and a yelp of pain. A soldier walked out of the thicket and reported to the commanding officer, "He's hit in the leg. What shall we do with a wounded prisoner?"

"Kill him," the North Vietnamese officer snapped with cold casualness. The soldier ran back and fired again. The boy was quiet.

Mike felt as if he'd been kicked in the stomach. "Why did you have to do that?" he demanded recklessly. He was not easily frightened. He had broken wild horses and ridden rodeo bulls back in Oregon. He had taught policemen judo after serving in the U.S. Marines. Since coming to Viet Nam he had been marked for death because of his success in helping Montagnards. But now he felt the end had come. They had killed the boy. He would be next.

He waited in suspense before being taken aside for more grilling. Again he pointed out that the officers were North Vietnamese, despite their disguised clothing. Again this was denied.

He was held at the leprosarium until Thursday evening, then marched back toward Banmethuot. Early Friday morning, the column halted near the Radê cemetery which was just across a stream from the village where he had first been captured. He heard voices up ahead.

"Hey, Mike, are you okay?"

Hank Blood—speaking in Radê.

Mike gave a quick shake of the head and pursed his lips in a silent shhh. He didn't want their captors to know he understood Radê.

Behind Hank was perky Betty Olsen, tied with wire to Pastor Ngue. Farther back was a string of tribal prisoners, fifty or so.

Two helicopters fluttered overhead. Hank yelled and moved his body furiously before guards pulled him down. The choppers flew off, giving no indication the prisoners had been seen.

Herding the Americans together, the North Vietnamese hustled their prisoners back into the jungle.

When they stopped to regroup, one untied Pastor Ngue from Betty and handed him an unloaded machine gun to carry. When they moved on in single file Ngue stayed protectively close to Betty. About two kilometers from the cemetery, she saw him positioning the machine gun to strike the guard in front. "Oh, no, Pastor," she remonstrated. "We have to love our enemies and pray for them. You mustn't fight back!"

"*Vous êtes très naïve,*" he muttered in reply, slipping into French, which was like a second mother tongue for him.

After four hours' hike they stopped near the leprosarium where Mike had witnessed the executions. The North Vietnamese seemed especially solicitous of the three Americans and gave them rice and monkey meat. The captives noticed that the tribal prisoners did not receive as much.

Pastor Ngue was still seething with anger, not over the food, but because the missionaries and church leaders had not been released. "We do not fight. We help people," he kept saying. "*Amai* [Sister] Betty is a nurse. I have seen her scraping the calluses from the feet of lepers. You will not win the allegiance of the people by taking her and us."

The commander was unmoved. "Why do you plead for the Americans? Don't you know they are enemies of the Vietnamese people?"

"Ha, you are the enemies who burn and kill and destroy."

"And you are the hands and feet of the American imperialists. The two men are CIA. The woman, we do not know who she is yet. If she is as you say, perhaps we will let her go. The National Liberation Front is just."

The officer withdrew to consult with his compatriots. The result was that the prisoners were divided into two groups, with Ngue being separated from the Americans and marched off ahead of them.

"Your friends will come searching for you," the North Vietnamese informed Betty, Hank, and Mike. "We are moving you to another area for questioning."

He looked at Betty's street shoes, scuffed and battered from the 12-mile walk to the leprosarium. Her legs were splattered with red mud and her thin print dress was tattered and torn. "We will show pity to you. Put on these combat boots. They were taken from an enemy whom we executed yesterday."

The painful wire was removed and she rubbed her wrists to restore circulation. Then she changed to the heavy, cumbersome boots and got in line behind Mike, whose hands had been freed also.

The North Vietnamese pushed them rapidly along the narrow trail, making communication difficult. During a brief rest stop Betty and Hank managed to tell Mike about the massacre.

"Vange and the baby were slightly injured," Betty said. "They'll be okay. I doubt if Marie Ziemer will make it. I think Carolyn will live if she gets proper medical care. What about your people, Mike?"

"The infiltrators shot up the town Monday night. I think everybody got out the next morning. I dropped an AID nurse off at the province hospital, then came looking for you guys."

"And got yourself captured," Hank added dryly.

"All in the line of duty. Say, do you know what happened to Pastor Ngue's boys?" Mike queried. "He was asking me back at the leprosarium before they separated us."

"The crippled one they let go as we were leaving," Hank recalled.

Betty hesitated, then said, "When I went back to the compound to get my things, I saw bodies lying all over. I'm pretty sure two of them near the servants' quarters were his boys. The guard wouldn't let me examine them."

"Did you tell the preacher?" Hank asked.

"No. I thought of it once when we were tied together. But I'm not positive, so there was no need to upset him. Besides he might get so angry that he'd kill someone."

The column moved again. They walked at a rapid pace until an hour or two after nightfall when they were allowed to wash in a stream. Then Betty was given her bag.

"Mike, Hank!" she called. "They took the clinic money! When I went back to the compound I stuffed it in here—at least $3,000."

Mike called the officer and explained what had happened. He admitted the bag had been opened and searched, but denied vehemently that any money had been taken.

"Well, at least they didn't take my Bible," Betty said, though she was still upset over the mission funds.

Bowls of white rice were brought, and after eating, the captives were chained together at the ankles and made to lie on mats near several guards. There was only enough time for Hank to quote some Bible verses and to pray before a stern voice ordered quiet. Despite the strain of the past days, they fell into exhausted sleep.

The chains were removed the next morning. After breakfast the soldiers hurriedly broke camp and got everyone moving again. There seemed to be fewer tribal captives than the night before. Mike was sure some had escaped during the night.

At midmorning they started across a precarious log bridge over a steep ravine. Hank kept his eyes straight ahead and crossed with no difficulty. The steely-nerved Benge looked to see how deep it was. Impressive, but he'd seen more treacherous crevices. He hurried to keep up with long-legged Hank.

Then he heard a pitiful wail, and a sickening thud. *Betty!* he thought, whirling around and running back down the trail. Looking into the gorge he saw that her fall had been broken by another log about ten or twelve feet down.

"Are you all right?" he called.

"I—I think so," Betty replied weakly. "I lost my glasses; they fell clear to the bottom."

"Never mind that. If you don't have any broken bones it

will be a miracle. Hold on, we'll get a rope."

The hovering guards gave Mike a rope. He tied it around his middle and scrambled down the side of the ravine to help her. Cautiously she got up, holding on to Mike for support.

"Sure you're all right?" he asked solicitously.

"Yeah, I just got the breath knocked out of me."

With help from some of the other prisoners, who pulled on the rope, they made it up the bank. A couple of tribesmen scrambled down the steep incline to look for her glasses. A gleeful shout announced success.

"Praise the Lord," Betty said. "I really appreciate your effort in searching for them," she told the delighted Radê who returned them to her.

"*Mau di!*" commanded one of the guards, "Move fast!"

"Can't you give her a minute to catch her breath?" Mike asked indignantly.

"We've wasted enough time already. Move on!"

Later that afternoon they stopped at a small military encampment. The Americans were given toothpaste, brushes, soap, and mercurochrome for scratches and were permitted to clean up. The tribal captives were ordered into the woods to cut poles. Under the supervision of the North Vietnamese, two small pole cages were hastily constructed and placed about forty feet apart. Hank and Betty were put in one and Mike in the other. Then their chains were secured and padlocked for the night.

Hank and Betty agreed that they should be as open as possible with their captors. "We have nothing to hide," the Bible translator said. "Surely they'll release us when they know why we're in Viet Nam."

The camp commander, who introduced himself as Captain Son, took Hank out the next day for interrogation.

"Tell us what your employer does," he began.

Hank tried to explain how the Wycliffe Bible Translators worked. "We are linguists, translating the Bible into tribal languages. We serve in Mexico, Peru, Ecuador, New Guinea, the Philippines, Viet Nam, and several other countries. We would work in North Viet Nam if your government would permit us. My wife and I are with the Mnong Rolom group that live near Banmethuot. For a while we lived in a village, but your 'friends' made this too dangerous. We had to move into the Radê village close to town."

"That is the only reason you are in Viet Nam?" Captain Son said in evident disbelief.

"Yes, sir. When we finish the translation and it is published, we will leave. Oh, perhaps we may do some literacy work and train some teachers. But this will only be so the Mnongs can read about God and his Son, Jesus."

"How are you supported? Who pays your salary?"

"We don't have a salary. As God leads, Christian friends and churches in the United States send money to our main office. This comes to us. It's just enough to pay our necessities. If you will ask the soldiers, who searched our house, they'll tell you we live very simply. We're not here for profit but to serve God and help the Mnong people have God's Word in their own language."

"An incredible story. But go on. How do you feel about us —the National Liberation Front, and our program of revolution?"

"We don't involve ourselves with anyone's politics. We will help you, as we will help any other Vietnamese individual. If you oppose us, we cannot fight back. God tells us to love even our enemies."

"God? Ha, Ha! You are stupid to say there is a God. Where is he? Why does he not set you free? There is no God. Revolution is power. Man forms his own destiny. We are the supreme being."

"You have been misled, Captain. God has power over all of us."

"Then why doesn't he help you?"

"He will. His Book says that man's ways are not his ways, nor man's thoughts his thoughts. He doesn't forget his people. He has allowed you to take us for some purpose. Perhaps that you may hear of him. We are his witnesses."

"You are CIA. Or crazy. Maybe both. I will talk to the woman now."

Captain Son had the mild-mannered Hank put back into the cage and Betty brought out.

"When will you let us go?" she demanded in a no-nonsense tone.

"That will be our decision," he replied coldly.

"Don't you know I'm a nurse? There are wounded and sick civilians who need my care. Now that my friends are dead, the leprosy patients depend on me. If your movement is as you claim, you will let us go so we can help the people."

"I said we will decide when you can go. You will answer my questions. Give me your agency and how you are paid."

Betty traced the history of the Christian and Missionary Alliance in Southeast Asia, pointing out that the group had once had missionaries in North Viet Nam. "I am paid much less than I would receive as a nurse in the United States," she added. "We missionaries are not here for money or political intrigue. We're here to serve God and help people.

"Do you know of Dr. Vietti, the lady doctor who was captured by your people at the jungle hospital six years ago? She was taken with two men missionaries."

The North Vietnamese officer denied any knowledge of the abduction. "I have never heard this name," he insisted.

"After she and the two others were taken, we had to move to Banmethuot. Your friends wouldn't permit us to live close to the people. But we continued to send medicines out by tribal people. I'm sure we've treated some of your supporters."

Captain Son was unmoved. "How can I understand this? It is strange that a healthy lady should be out here alone, so far from home. Where is your husband?"

Betty fought to remain calm. "I don't need a husband to serve God."

Irritated, the officer ordered Betty back into her cage, then turned his attention to Mike.

The AID man was just as insistent that they be released. "I

am not military," he declared. "For five years I've been helping the tribespeople improve their economy. You have people in this camp who know me. Ask them."

"We know about you. You are here to spy on the people and the patriotic activities of our National Liberation Front."

"You are not in the N.L.F.," Mike again pointed out. "You are from North Viet Nam. Admit it."

The officer stared off into the jungle for a few seconds. Then he turned back and stared intensely at Mike. "So. Maybe we are from the north. Maybe we have come to help our brothers unify Viet Nam. That is not why you are here."

The North Vietnamese now turned the questioning back on Mike, demanding that the AID man give military information, and repeating the charge that he was CIA. Mike stood his ground, trading charge for charge, demanding that the stolen mission money be returned. The officer dismissed him in disgust.

After two weeks at this encampment, they were moved a few miles to another camp. Here all three Americans were put in a pole cage together, giving them the first opportunity to talk freely and at length.

"I was going to ask him for my Radê brass bracelet they took off my wrist," Mike said angrily. "It was given to me by the headman at Buon Kram when I was adopted into the tribe. I wouldn't have traded it for anything."

"Ask him the next time he comes over," Betty suggested. "He'll probably deny that it was taken."

"And that our watches were stolen too," Mike added, still seething inside.

Mike then speculated that they'd been moved to evade a search party. "I'm sure some Radês got away. They would have people out looking for us."

"If they don't find us, do you think we'll be allowed to go?" Betty asked.

Mike shrugged. "Who knows the minds of these people? They haven't been too hard on us. They've been feeding us."

"Yes. One fellow has been quite neighborly to me," Hank

said optimistically.

"Does either of you have any idea where we are?" Betty asked.

"We're about forty miles south of Banmethuot," Mike replied. "This area is Chu Rulach. Some call it Happy Valley, though I don't know why. It's been a Viet Cong stronghold for a long time."

"Could we escape?"

"Not the way they keep us padlocked in these chains. We'll just have to hope they'll see that it's to their advantage to let us go."

"We've been praying, Mike," Hank said. "I hope you'll join us."

Mike looked uncomfortable. "I've been a little out of touch since I was a boy."

"Tell us about it," Betty urged.

"Not much to tell. I grew up on a ranch in eastern Oregon. Near the little town of Heppner. You're from Portland, aren't you, Hank?"

Hank nodded.

"Well, uh, I went to a Lutheran church. Had four years of parochial school. Then like a lot of boys, I guess I sort of dropped out. Didn't go to church much in high school. Then came college at Oregon State, and—"

"You went to State?" Hank interrupted. "I got my degree in engineering there. So did my brother Dave."

"Small world. I finished a little later after a stretch in the Marines. Spent most of that time in Japan. Then I thought I'd try for the foreign service. Had to settle for International Voluntary Services at $77 a month. That was the forerunner of the Peace Corps. When my term was up for IVS, I got on with AID. That was in '65, three years ago last month. January 31st to be exact, the day after they grabbed me on the highway."

"Speaking of grabbing, here comes Captain Son and some strangers."

The North Vietnamese officer was smiling. "Good evening.

I hope you are feeling well. These visitors are artists and would like to sketch your pictures."

"Why?" Betty asked.

"To show others how well you are being treated."

"May we have some to take back with us?"

"Perhaps, Miss Olsen."

"And could I have one of your flags and a pair of Ho Chi Minh sandals for souvenirs?"

The officer was still smiling. "We might arrange that. If you pledge to be good."

"Oh, we'll all be good," Betty smiled hopefully. Her companions nodded in agreement. Maybe they would be released soon.

CHAPTER

3

Fading Hope

They had been with the North Vietnamese three weeks now and every morning they hoped that day would be the last. The starvation diet of rice, manioc, and occasional vegetables had made all three ravenously hungry. Though there were no roads in the wild, forested area, Mike was sure he could lead the way back to Banmethuot.

"I'm ready to go," Hank said. "After eight years, Vange and I were just getting ready to start translating books of the Bible. We had three language informants lined up to help, and now this," he sighed. Then he added quickly, "I'm sure the Lord has a purpose in our being here."

Mike and Betty were silent, content to listen to their talkative companion. Day after boring day there hadn't been much else to do in the debilitating heat except talk and listen. Captain Son had even denied them the privilege of writing letters.

"Our biggest frustration was not being able to live in a Mnong village," Hank went on. "We started out in Lac Thien, not too far from here. You've been there, I guess, Mike."

"Yeah, I know the place. Hasn't been secure for years."

"We were there back in 1960 when the Viet Cong were still called the Viet Minh. Just a short time . . . until one night the Minh came charging in, shooting up the village, looking for the district chief. Vange and I picked up Cindy and hid in a storeroom. We could hear them knocking around and talking in the other side of the house. We stayed there until 2:30 the next afternoon, just to be certain they'd left. I was pretty mad. They had killed three people, burned seven buildings, and stolen everything they could get their hands on. We had prayed hard for our friend the chief, and the Lord answered double. The chief dropped through a trap door and made it to the lake, where he escaped in a dugout. On the other side of the lake he walked into a little store where he thought he had friends. Turned out they were enemies. Two Minh tried to shoot him, but their guns failed to go off. Had to be the Lord.

"After that, the provincial authorities said we couldn't live there any more. We had to move into the Radê village close to Banmethuot and depend on language informants coming to us."

"Didn't you go back out just before Christmas?" Betty asked.

"Yeah, but not for long," Hank smiled grimly. "This was another Mnong village. One that had never been attacked. I wanted to do some checking on Luke 15 so we could prepare a small booklet. The first evening I went with the chief to a friend's house where a dozen or so Mnongs were sitting around drinking their rice wine."

"Mmmmmm. Good stuff," Mike interrupted with a chuckle, drawing a small frown from Betty.

"I guess it keeps you awake," continued Hank, "for at ten o'clock they were still gabbing and I was about to fall asleep. The chief had just taken me home when the shooting broke loose. I knocked out the kerosene light and ran around looking for a place to hide. I ended up in the chief's pigpen, pressed between two bundles of grass. The VCs overran the village, but they never found me. They did get my cameras and my favorite picture of Vange.

"When I got home, I tried to figure out what the Lord wanted to accomplish in that experience. I decided he wanted me to feel more sympathy for people who live out in villages and are exposed to attack night after night. And to impress on me the uncertainty of life so that I'd be more concerned about the spiritual condition of people I meet."

Hank paused and shifted his hip, careful not to hurt his companions by pulling too hard on the chains.

Then he looked directly at his fellow Oregonian. "Mike, are you sure of going to heaven when you die?"

"I'm not counting on dying soon," the AID man drawled laconically.

"Tough as you are, you may outlive both of us. But nobody can be sure."

"I respect you missionaries," Mike said. "You want to help the Radés and Mnongs and other tribespeople. So do I. I may be going at it in slightly different ways from you."

"And we respect you too, Mike," Betty broke in. "You're one of the best friends the people ever had, and us, too. I've heard Bob Ziemer and Ed Thompson say many times that if they needed something—cement, plane reservations, or whatever—you're the one to be counted on."

"Wycliffe people feel the same way," Hank said. "But what I'm asking, Mike, is: Do you really know the Lord? Are you sure he's forgiven your sins? If not, you won't go to heaven."

"Well, I don't think one person can judge another. I drink

a little. When I'm with the natives, I take my turn at the wine-jar. Makes them feel I'm one of them."

"I don't think that's necessary to gain their friendship," Betty interrupted.

"Jesus drank, didn't he? I've never been much of a Bible student, so correct me if I'm wrong in saying that the Bible teaches moderation."

"Yes, but Bible times were different from today," Hank interjected. "The wine was weak and there wasn't much water."

Mike suddenly burst out laughing. "Excuse me, but I was thinking of the first time I saw you, Betty. Remember that party at the AID nurses' house. I had been out in the village and came in half snockered. I was dancing with the AID gals and having a real good time. You missionaries were sitting there looking like you'd swallowed a jar of sour pickles."

"And you stopped and came over and asked if we wanted some drinks. Yes, I remember. We really thought you were far out. Now that I've gotten to know you better, I don't think you're that bad."

"Then you'll join me for a little celebration, when we get back?" Mike teased.

"Maybe we'll learn something about that now," Betty said hopefully. "Here comes Captain Son."

"How are you faring? Are you well?" the officer asked in mock politeness.

"We'd be better if you'd unlock these chains and send us away," Mike said.

"Perhaps tomorrow, Mr. Benge. Since you are civilians, I don't think we'll keep you much longer."

The captives' eyes lit up. This was the most reassuring word they'd had yet.

"Where are you keeping Pastor Ngue?" Betty asked.

"He is in another camp."

"Will he be given his freedom? And the other tribesmen?"

"I cannot say. All depends." The officer turned away, leaving the Americans to wonder and wait.

The day ended with a trip to the stream to wash up, and the evening meal. Betty marked the date—Saturday, March 2—on the tiny calendar she was keeping. She also managed to add a little to her diary.

The next day they held worship services. Hank gave an exhortation for patience, stressing that God didn't operate by man's schedules, assuring them that in good time his purposes for their experiences would be shown. Then Betty described how God had allowed Daniel to be thrown into a den of lions, and then had delivered him. Hank began his favorite hymn, "Lead On, O King Eternal," and concluded with a long, impassioned prayer. His plea that his wife and children be kept from harm brought tears to Betty and Mike.

Early Monday they were awakened by unmistakable artillery fire. Immediately they heard Captain Son barking shrill commands at his soldiers to break camp and march. Two men ran over and opened the door of their cage and unlocked their chains. Betty had just enough time to grab her bag and Bible, and Hank the small shaving kit he'd been allowed to keep.

They were pushed at a rapid pace all day. That night they camped under a thick grove of trees, and then were forced to move on before daybreak.

They kept up this pace for the next ten days, sometimes marching at night and sleeping during the day. Several times they heard planes overhead, but the thick forest cover blocked any view. From the sun, they judged they were moving west into the mountains that tower 8,000 feet, between Banmethuot and the coastal city of Nhatrang.

In Happy Valley they had benefited from vegetables bought by the North Vietnamese from farmers a day's journey away. But on the trail captors and captives alike had to supplement meager rice rations with occasional catches of frogs, lizards, monkeys, and mouse deer. Some days the Americans got no protein at all.

Near the end of the grueling trek they stopped in a small

tribal settlement. The soldiers bought pumpkins, corn, and beans from tribesmen in loin cloths and enjoyed a feast while the Americans stood by with stomachs growling.

Then, ignoring the soldiers, the headman of the village walked over to the white strangers. "How are you?" he asked kindly.

"Hungry," Mike replied in Radê. "Weak."

Without asking permission of the North Vietnamese commander, the tribesman immediately began gathering food for the captives. They enjoyed their first satisfying meal since leaving Happy Valley.

At the end of the next day's journey, the North Vietnamese set up camp in the fog on the side of a mountain. The altitude was higher here and the air colder. Nights were especially damp.

They were still kept chained at night, but the guards were more talkative. Some were Viet Cong whom the North Vietnamese had picked up along the trail.

One VC ventured to ask Mike how many letters they had written to their families. When Mike said this hadn't been permitted, he seemed surprised.

"There's a communications gap here," Mike told Betty and Hank. "The NVAs must have told these fellows we'd been allowed to write home."

The effects of improper nourishment began plaguing Hank first. Scales formed on his lower back and began spreading downward. An ugly boil swelled on his hip that made sleep difficult. He asked Betty to lance it with the razor, but she objected. "It isn't ready."

Sharp, sudden pains near his vertebral column in the small of the back were the worst. When these occurred at night, he would cry out in anguish, bellowing like a wounded buffalo and awakening his companions and their guards. Mike and Betty were sympathetic, but after the second attack the guards became angry and threatened punishment. Hank thought it was a recurrence of kidney stones, a problem he'd had three years before.

Mike, Betty, and Hank all had bruised feet. Betty's legs were covered with small ulcerous sores. Her skin and Mike's became scaly from lack of proper food. In addition, they all were plagued by the highly contagious parasitic skin disease caused by the itch mite. They itched all over. "If I ever get out of here," Betty moaned, "I'll never again take a hot bath for granted."

All three came down with dengue fever about the same time. Having passed through mosquito-infested lowlands a week before, they weren't surprised. Their bodies ached as if their bones were crumbling into little pieces. Their temperature roller-coastered up and down between high fever and chills. After three or four days they felt better, but a day later their temperatures rose again and they broke out in body rash. "The only good thing about dengue," Betty said, "is that it's almost never fatal. If for us you can call that good."

Except for the mercurochrome and a couple of sulfa pills Betty had been given to rub in her leg ulcers, they'd had no medicine. They knew there were remedies in the camp, for they'd seen soldiers treating one another. But their pleas for aid went unheeded. The best they could do was wash in the stream.

One evening after they had cleaned up, they lay under the soft half moon waiting for their chains to be padlocked. Betty recalled the return of a Vietnamese medical worker who had been abducted with a group of Radés at the leprosarium.

"He said they had to wear the same clothes they were captured in and never took them off. They weren't allowed to bathe and became covered with body lice which gave them sores all over their bodies. He still had the scars when I saw him two months after release. They had to work when they were sick, even when they had malaria. The only water they had to drink came from buffalo wallows. He said many died, especially children, and that if it hadn't been for the Lord, he would have given up. When I saw him and heard his story, I thought, 'How horrible,' never thinking that one day I'd be in practically the same fix."

"Yeah, well, they haven't made us do any work, and malaria hasn't got us—yet," Mike grimaced.

"Unless our 'protectors' have a change of heart soon, we may get malaria," Betty predicted. "Scurvy, beriberi and who knows what else?"

"Back in Happy Valley, Captain Son was talking about letting us go. Then the war got too hot for them," Hank said. "What do you think will happen now?"

"I don't know, but they've got no reason to hold us. I've told them that over and over. Now they've stopped hinting."

"Yeah, Betty," Mike said, "you've talked tougher to them than either Hank or I. As a woman you can get away with it."

Captain Son and a guard approached. "Time to sleep," the officer said indifferently.

Betty stood up and fastened her green eyes on the NVA. "Captain, have you ever dug pus and maggots out of the sores of lepers? Have you scraped the calluses off of infected feet until your finger joints ached and your knees became raw from kneeling on the floor? Have you peeled back the burned skin of babies who were the innocent victims of war?"

The North Vietnamese stood speechless, unable to reply.

"I have. All day and often into the night. Six days at a stretch, resting only on Sunday and then sometimes having to care for emergency cases. That's why I came to Viet Nam. Not for pleasure or to spy. But to heal the sick in the name of Jesus. And you, who make speeches about justice for the poor and giving land to the landless—what have you done? Taken me and my friends prisoner. Given us no medicine. Kept us chained like animals at night. Marched us through the forest until our feet were ready to fall off. If you had any compassion for the suffering people of Viet Nam, you would make us well and set us free to do our work."

Breathing hard, her face red with the ugly rash, she paused to let him reply. But Captain Son seemed interested only in watching the guard fasten and secure the chains around Hank and Mike's ankles. "Please sit down," he then asked Betty.

"Not yet," she said firmly. "I have more to say. I don't know why you continue to keep us. It must be orders from higher up. Whatever the reason and whatever you do, we will not hate you. We will feel pity. We will help you when we can. The God you say does not exist loves you. And we love you."

"Please sit," he again commanded.

"Yes," she said meekly. "I hope you will think of what I said."

The North Vietnamese didn't reply. He merely waited until the guard had fastened Betty's chains, then walked stolidly away.

A few mornings later they awoke to find Captain Son and his North Vietnamese underlings gone. Their guards were now all Viet Cong. A short distance away they saw other newcomers under the trees. Then they heard a familiar voice.

"It's Pastor Ngue," Betty said in joyful surprise. "I'd know him anywhere. I've heard him preach so many times. Pastor Ngue, over here," she called.

Ngue started in their direction and was rudely pulled back by a Viet Cong who shouted, "Go and dig manioc with the rest."

Later in the day, Ngue was permitted to talk with his American friends. He was appalled that they hadn't been given medicine and was especially troubled at Betty's sores. "I will try to find medicine in the forest," he promised.

The next morning when he went on the work detail to dig manioc roots, the Radê preacher slashed a few strips of bark from a cinnamon tree. After boiling the bark in water, he poured the solution into a bamboo cup and left it beside a rock for Betty. The soothing medicine applied to their sores was a great relief to all three Americans.

Unfortunately, Ngue was seen the next time he dropped the cup near Betty.

"What did you give her?" the Viet Cong head of the guards demanded.

"Medicine for their sores. You wouldn't do anything."

"Why are you helping these enemies of the Vietnamese people?"

"They haven't taken our land," Ngue remonstrated. "It is the North Vietnamese who have invaded."

"The Americans have deceived you. They and their Saigon puppets want to take all the land. The missionaries are their agents."

"No, the missionaries have no politics. They work only for God." The tribal preacher's nostrils were flaring, his eyes flashing.

"Bah! There is no God but Ho Chi Minh. He's our god—our leader."

Ngue pointed a finger. "Be careful about that. The Germans made Hitler a god. Now he's dead and disgraced."

"You, Ngue, are a fool. Quit following the Americans and support the revolution."

"I will follow no one but God and what I read in his Book. You are the fool."

The officer looked around and saw the guards were listening with intense interest.

"Stop your mouth," he commanded. "When the revolution is victorious, we will exterminate you preachers first. We would kill you now, except you are needed for work. Stop meddling and keep away from the American spies."

But Ngue was a stubborn and determined tribesman. He felt a fatherly responsibility toward Betty, whose own father was serving as a missionary in Africa. When he heard her crying at night, it was almost more than he could bear.

Risking possible execution, he slipped over to the little bamboo house where she lay chained with Mike and Hank.

"*Amai* Betty, don't cry," he whispered consolingly. "God will take care of us. I will pray."

Softly he began to talk to God in his native language, calling the names of Betty and the two American men, Hank's wife and children, remembering his own family, including the two who he did not yet know were dead. He also prayed for the Banmethuot congregation, that it would experience revival, that leaders would be found to direct the people in his absence. And for Ardel Vietti, Dan Gerber, and Archie Mitchell, the 1962 captives.

When he finished, there was no sound but the snoring of the guards a dozen paces away. Then a pathetic, little-girl voice broke out of the darkness. "Pastor Ngue, please help us get away."

"Shhhhh," he cautioned his "daughter." He sat and thought a long while, then leaned back to speak through the bamboo wall. "Tomorrow night. I will alert our tribal friends. We will hide sticks of wood. When the guards are sleeping we will pound their heads." His voice trailed off in bitter anger.

"No, no, no, Pastor. You cannot hurt them. They don't know the Lord. There must be another way."

Sadly he replied, "No, *Amai* Betty, there is no other way. But if you do not wish it, we will not try."

CHAPTER

4

Escape

About ten days after entrusting the Americans to Viet Cong guards, Captain Son and his North Vietnamese cadre returned to camp for a few hours.

"Are you being treated well?" he asked them.

Mike eyed him stonily. Hank looked away sadly. Neither replied.

"No, we have always been treated badly," Betty said. "It is wrong to keep people in chains who have done nothing but help your Vietnamese brothers. When can we go?"

"Are you receiving enough to eat?"

"Harrumph!" Mike snorted sarcastically.

"I have work to do," Betty continued. "Sick people are depending on me to come back. Would you rather I stay here and they suffer?"

"Very well, then," the Captain said turning on his heel to leave. "Since you need nothing from me. . ."

"Captain, we need meat," Hank pleaded. "And Miss Olsen must have a change of clothing. Most of all we need medicine."

Face had been saved for the officer. "I will ask my brothers to increase your rations. But we have no clothes for the lady. The medicine is reserved for our fighting men."

He walked away.

The food was better for a few days. They had boiled crabs once for lunch and monkey meat two evenings. And they received larger portions of rice. They were even unchained for part of each day and permitted to walk around the camp under the watchful eyes of the guards.

Mike wandered over to the cookhouse where several tribal prisoners were peeling manioc and pounding rice. In conversation he discovered their rations were pitifully small. "We will share with you," he promised.

The Americans began saving portions from each meal, which Mike took and hid in the cookhouse for their tribal friends.

The tribesmen did not forget. Two or three days later they returned from foraging in the forest with a bundle of plants. "For you," they told Mike. Mike took the plants gratefully for they had been denied greens lately.

By this time the dengue fever had subsided, but their bodies still burned from the fiery itch. Hank's boil was bigger and redder. Betty now feared that lancing might bring on infection. And the excruciating pains that struck Hank without warning continued to double him up.

They kept up their morale by reading from Betty's Bible, now soggy from being rained on. Hank memorized from a handful of soiled Scripture cards he had managed to keep. They prayed together two and three times a day with Mike joining in awkwardly. The two missionaries now sensed a change in the wiry AID man. He was quieter and not as cocky and flippant as he had been back in Happy Valley.

Hardly a day passed without the zealous Hank sharing with Mike about a personal relationship to God. To Mike's question, "How can I be sure?" Hank told how he had made certain himself at the age of fifteen.

"My family was in church every time the doors opened. My parents were Sunday school teachers. My mother even taught Greek at a Bible college. My brother Dave and I made professions of faith and were baptized as young boys. But when I was fifteen I became very worried about life after death. Would I go to heaven or to hell? Was I God's child or not? I wasn't sure. As I thought about what to do, I remembered John 1:12: 'As many as received him to them gave he power to become the sons of God.' I knew this was speaking of receiving Christ, so that night I told God, the best I knew how, that I was receiving Christ and his salvation. I said, 'God, I know you don't lie. I am taking you at your Word.' "

After pausing to let this sink in, Hank added forcefully, "I've never had any real doubts since."

"That's the only way," Betty put in quietly. "You can't save yourself by all the good you do for people. You have to look to the Savior who died on the cross for our sins."

Mike said nothing, but stared into the thick foliage, deep in thought, as old memories of his childhood flashed through his mind. How long had it been—was it really twenty-five years ago that he'd sat in the little Lutheran church in eastern Oregon and heard about Jesus? He remembered being hit by a car when in the first grade. He could have been killed then. And his mother had told him he was sickly before that. Why had he lived when other children had died?

He had determined to be tough. Playing high school football with boys taller and heavier. Pulling more than his weight among rugged loggers. Riding anything that had four legs and hair on its back. Joining the Marines. Mastering the art of judo so he could easily handle a man twice his size. Then after the Marines and college, coming to help the tribespeople in Viet Nam's Central Highlands.

Most American military counted the days until their year

was in 'Nam, but this civilian had stayed on, even after hearing that the VC had a price on his head. Once they had almost gotten him in an ambush. He had turned the corner as they were setting up, and gotten the draw on them first. If he'd been five minutes later. . . Why hadn't he? Why had he survived when friends, both military and civilian, had been shot down in the jungle?

Now, after two months in jungle captivity, he was still alive. He had thought his number was up when they had so ruthlessly killed the Vietnamese boy back by the leprosarium. But they had let him live. Why?

And in this situation, how much longer could he and his friends survive? Hank, Betty, and the Radê preacher were surely in touch with God. But was he? What was that verse Hank had quoted? "To as many as received Jesus." Certainly he could rely on that. Maybe he had believed in Sunday school. Maybe not. What counted was that he wanted to believe and rest in God's love and care *now*.

When he confided this to Hank and Betty, they rejoiced over his commitment.

Blustery March blew into cloudy April. Betty marked each day on her calendar. On April fifth Hank recalled that he and Vange had sailed out under the Golden Gate Bridge just ten years before. "We were in such a hurry that we didn't get hitched until we reached the Philippines," he said.

"Isn't Vange from Pennsylvania? And you're from Oregon. Where did you two get together?" Betty asked.

Hank grinned. "In Wycliffe's jungle training camp in Mexico where my brother Dave and I were outnumbered by the single girls. One of the fellows, Paul Marsteller, passed word along that Vange thought a lot of me. My first reaction was that this wasn't the way the Lord worked. Then I decided that he might have to use this means for somebody as bashful as me. I was already thirty-eight.

"The people supervising our training conveniently as-signed Vange and me to the same raft crew. Four of us built and launched it for the test trip down river. Turned out it was too small, so the other two let Vange and me go alone. A hundred feet from the bank we started to sink. We paddled back and unloaded some cargo and started again. When we arrived a half hour behind the other rafts, they 'punished' us by making us set the pace on a 25-mile survival hike. Vange did fine, but I came down with an infected ankle and had to ride a mule with Dave leading it and Vange walking behind.

"You figured Vange could make it in Viet Nam, huh?"

"I sure did, Mike. But neither Dave nor I has ever been one to make quick decisions. I prayed about her every day and after we left camp in the spring we wrote regularly. On July 3rd—I remember the place—I prayed the prayer of faith and claimed her for my own. A little later she accepted my proposal and the following April she sailed with Dave and me. Dave and I had always done things together."

"Was Dave married then?" Betty asked.

"No. He had his eye on a single girl in our party. But they didn't really get together until after arriving in Viet Nam. He and Doris were married in Saigon. They're working with the Chams. As you know, the Chams are modern-day representatives of an ancient Indianized kingdom in Central Vietnam. And knowing Dave, I'm sure he's doing all he can to get us released."

"If you were married in the Philippines," Betty ventured, "where did you spend your honeymoon?"

"Probably on a jungle trail," Mike interjected.

Hank laughed. "Not quite. We shared a little summer cottage with some rats. Had a beautiful view, though, out there in the mountains among the Ifugao tribespeople. While there we did a little carpenter work for a couple of single girl translators living over a ridge. I did the hammering and sawing and Vange saw that the work was done right. I never was much good with my hands, even though I was trained as an engineer."

Five more long days inched by as they remained in the miserable limbo of not knowing their future. The North Vietnamese came back again to check, but gave no hint they would be released.

They had just finished a scanty evening meal of rice and thin slices of boiled iguana when a clap of thunder echoed across the mountainside. "We'll be hearing more of that from now on," Hank said. "The rainy season will be starting soon. It's bad enough when you have shelter. Out here—I don't know what we'll do."

Mike was lost in reminiscing. "If this is the tenth," he mused, "I got out of the Marines nine years ago today."

"Where'd you spend your time?" Hank asked.

"Japan. I really learned to like Japanese food. Back in Portland I used to eat at a Japanese restaurant called Bush Gardens. It's on Fourth Avenue, across from Old Multnomah Hotel. Ever been there, Hank?"

"I know the location, but I've never eaten there."

"Yummmm. You oughta try their deep pan-fried prawns. And they have a cucumber salad with seafood. Mmmm. Couple of nights ago I dreamed I was sitting on a soft cushion in one of their little private rooms. I was just about to taste a prawn, when—"

"You woke up," Betty said.

"How'd you know?"

"It happened to me that way. I dreamed about a place in Chicago called The Pit where I used to go. I had a charcoal hamburger all the way up to my mouth. I was sinking my teeth in. I could taste the juice—when somebody pulled on my chain."

"That must have been me," Hank laughed. "I was trying to get a bite of a fruit salad Vange makes so well."

"What restaurants did you take Vange to in Portland?" Mike asked.

Hank dropped his face. "I didn't. She was there just a few days before we left for Asia. Then on our furlough in '63 and '64, we had a little apartment in Bloomington, Indiana, where I was working on my master's. We traveled quite a bit, but our budget never let us go above McDonald's. We must have eaten a thousand of his hamburgers one summer."

"Well, I'd settle for one just now," Betty drooled.

"Have you ever taken Vange to a fancy place?" Mike asked.

Hank slowly shook his head. Regret was reflected in his sad blue eyes.

"You have a furlough coming up, don't you?"

"Next year—if we get out."

Mike grinned. "Then first thing you do when you go back to Portland is call Bush Gardens for a reservation."

"Vange will love that," the big man sighed. "If we get out."

"Why so pessimistic?" Betty queried.

"Pass me your Bible."

Hank took the soggy, mildewed lump of paper. He carefully turned to 1 Peter 4, and read verses 12 and 13:

> *Beloved, think it not strange concerning the*
> *fiery trial which is to try you, as though*
> *some strange thing happened unto you: But*
> *rejoice, inasmuch as ye are partakers of*
> *Christ's sufferings; that, when his glory*
> *shall be revealed, ye may be glad also with*
> *exceeding joy.*

"By receiving Christ, we have become identified with him, right? That means we are partakers of his sufferings. I don't know what all these verses mean, but I think Peter is saying we Christians shouldn't think suffering unusual, because Christ suffered. Until this experience, I've never suffered much. Oh, it was a blow when my dad died from a fall. And my heart ached every time one of our kids was seriously ill. I had that kidney stone attack three years ago. That's almost more than a man can bear. I just can't keep from crying out when the pains hit. But they go away. And I can put up with the bad food, the itching, and even these chains. The ache of being away from my loved ones, the torment of not knowing whether I'll ever see them again—that's suffering.

"I was quite confident back in Happy Valley that they'd let us go. But now I don't know what's ahead. I still believe the Lord could deliver us. But that may not be his will. We have to accept it if it isn't."

"You're right, Hank," Betty reluctantly agreed. "We must accept, even desire his will at whatever cost. And I do, though sometimes I'm a little slow at seeing it his way. Five years ago I wouldn't have felt this way. I wasn't even sure I wanted to keep on living, I was so disappointed in my Christian life. I came to a crisis and the Lord used a counselor to show me that I really had to want God's best. I didn't dream then that his best would include this.

"Last year I finished all my language studies," the young woman continued. "I qualified as a senior missionary, meaning I could vote in mission conferences. I was just getting to where I could help some of the Radê young people with their problems."

"I understand," Hank said kindly. "I'd felt my real work was just about to begin when we were captured. Do you know that I had only one native convert in ten years?"

"Tang?" Betty asked.

"Yes. I'd been trying to show him the way for years. Last August he told me he'd come to a fork in the road and had taken God's way. He was baptized with some of the Radês Christmas Day. Before we were captured, the Lord had impressed me to spend more time with him, helping him get established in the Scripture."

"Maybe the Lord has a great work for Tang to do," Betty volunteered.

"I've been thinking that might be the case."

Hank stopped, suddenly aware that he had interrupted Betty, then asked, "What were your plans for this year?"

"I was going to take my first furlough and go home by way of Africa and see my dad and stepmother. I have an eleven-year-old brother and six-year-old twin brother and sister. The last time I was there—that was before I surrendered my rebellious heart to the Lord—I was such a stinker the missionaries asked me to leave."

Mike had been sitting quietly without expression. Now his eyebrows lifted. "I can't imagine that."

"Oh, you didn't know the old Betty," she laughed. "Then I was planning to fly to Chicago where my sister Marilyn and some of my closest friends live. But I guess those reservations will have to be cancelled."

Mike lay down and covered his eyes with his hands.

Betty and Hank sat quietly on opposite sides of their friend and watched the black cloud swelling over the western horizon. After a few minutes, Hank got up and leaned against a tree. He was careful not to arouse the suspicions of the day guards whose eyes followed every move of the Americans.

Betty turned and looked tenderly at Mike. They were less than a year apart in age and practically the same height. Their differences had narrowed during the past two months. Her respect for his courage and loyalty had grown immeasurably, and she felt that his regard for her had risen. Hank seemed more like a father, perhaps because he was fifteen years older and the more serious of the two. Mike was becoming the brother she'd never known.

She shooed a fly from Mike's nose and saw that he was perspiring. But the weather was cool. Concerned, she put a hand to his forehead. He was burning hot.

She called Hank. "Dengue again?" he asked with concern.

"Could be. More likely, he's coming down with malaria."

When Mike awoke his speech was blurred and incoherent. His fever was down, but he was suffering violent chills. He had diarrhea and had to be assisted back and forth to the dung hole.

The next day he was delirious and complained of fading

vision. Betty begged the Viet Cong guards for quinine, aspirin, anything. They refused.

The North Vietnamese came again. Captain Son looked at Mike indifferently.

"Don't you see he has malaria? He may die without help."

"Let him die," the officer said coldly. "He is of no value to us."

The next morning the North Vietnamese left.

Betty and Hank stayed close to Mike. Hank spent much of the time praying. Betty bathed Mike's face and kept pleading with him to eat and drink. Without nourishment, she knew he would soon die from dehydration.

"Please, please, if you have any mercy," she cried to the guards. "Help him."

They did nothing.

"At least let Pastor Ngue come and pray for him."

They called Ngue over. "What difference will it make?" the head guard grunted.

The preacher prayed. Hank and Betty couldn't be sure Mike had even heard. One minute he was raving, the next snoring.

That night he talked out of his head a long time. He was directing a crew of Radês in building a fish pond. Explaining how to operate a tractor. Planning how the tribespeople could make a profit by selling handmade articles in the craft shop he'd set up beside the Radê church.

The next morning Ngue was allowed to pray again. He lingered to whisper to Betty, "I overheard two guards talking in a Mnong dialect. They didn't think I understood. I am to be killed in four days."

"They wouldn't—"

"Yes, *Amai* Betty, they will. Three friends and I are going to try and escape. We will tell the Special Forces to come and rescue you."

"You must not hurt anyone," Betty cautioned.

"We will not do that. I promise."

That evening while Mike lay in semiconsciousness, Betty and Hank heard the whistling of a familiar tune. The whistler was standing with his back to them, fifty or sixty feet away. They could only make out his shape, but they knew it was Ngue. They followed the song in their memories:

> God be with you till we meet again;
> By His counsels guide, uphold you,
> With His sheep securely fold you;
> God be with you till we meet again.
> Till we meet . . . till we meet,
> Till we meet at Jesus' feet;
> Till we meet . . . till we meet,
> God be with you till we meet again.

Their beloved friend was telling them goodbye.

Betty casually strolled into the clearing. A few yards from Ngue she turned and faced away from him so the guards wouldn't think they were communicating.

"Take me with you, Pastor. Please take me with you," she blurted. She was so young and pitiful with tears coursing down her cheeks that Ngue felt his heart would break.

"I can't, *Amai*. If I had the strength I would gladly carry you on my back to safety, but we would never make it. I would be taking you to certain death."

"I—I don't know how much longer I can take this, Pastor. Couldn't I just try? If I fell behind, you could just leave me," she sobbed wiping her tears on her sleeve.

"No, the terrain is too rough and you are too weak," he explained. By this time he was crying too. "The best thing I can do is go for help. You know I will come back for you, don't you?"

"Yes, I know. But it's so hard."

"Besides, Mike is very sick. He needs you."

"Yes. That's right. Mike needs me. Very well. We'll wait for you."

"Pray for me," Ngue whispered as a guard started toward him. He went back to his hut, and Betty returned to Mike and Hank to report what had been said.

Ngue and his fellow tribesmen waited until about two hours before dawn. Then, when the patrol passed their sleeping mats, they arose quietly. They tiptoed along behind the guards, a few paces back, until they passed through the thick woods at the edge of the camp. At this point, they took off running. By the time the patrol realized what had happened, the Radês had melted into the jungle.

Betty and Hank were roused by the shouting and yelling. It quickly became clear that Ngue and some companions had made their break. As armed Viet Cong ran into the woods in blind pursuit, the missionaries prayed fervently that the Radês would be successful.

Several hours later the searchers returned. Flushed and frowning, they told their American captives nothing. Betty was confident. "If they'd caught them, they'd be bragging. Ngue will get home and bring help. I know he will."

Betty and Hank had no doubts that Ngue and his friends had gotten away when the Viet Cong broke camp and packed to move. The missionaries got Mike to his feet and helped him walk; otherwise the Communist guerrillas would have left him to die. Fortunately for Mike, they didn't go far this time. They made camp on a level spot on the bank of a cool, flowing stream.

Here Mike seemed only to get worse. His hair turned white and began falling out. For several days he was completely blind. Hour after hour, Betty kept watch beside him, forcing him to eat and drink, wrapping his blanket tight when he was chilled, cooling his face with water carried from the stream in bamboo tubes when he perspired. The only attention his guards gave was to add salt and sometimes sugar to his rice gruel.

Betty sang hymns and Hank quoted Scripture. When the guards were out of earshot she whispered of Ngue's escape. "He won't abandon us," she assured. "If he's still alive, he'll get help. I know he will. Come on, Mike. You have to eat and get your strength back for when they come to rescue us."

CHAPTER

5

Prisoners on Display

The North Vietnamese came for a check and ordered camp to be moved again. With Hank supporting Mike, and Betty staggering behind, the prisoners somehow managed to keep up during the half-day's walk in the suffocating heat and humidity. They stopped again for a week or ten days, then moved on another half day. The position of the sun indicated they had turned south into Tuyen Duc Province.

At times Mike seemed more dead than alive as he battled with malaria. Sitting beside him, Betty and Hank fought to keep him conscious; they were afraid he might lapse into a coma and die.

When he would start to pass out, Betty would slap him, shake him awake, anything to arouse him to consciousness.

When he would protest, "I'm not hungry," as he frequently did, she would press the bowl of rice gruel to his feverish lips and say, "You must eat, Mike. You can't give up now. We're depending on you."

Two weeks passed and he was still alive. Three weeks. Four. He wasn't a complainer and Betty had to drag the symptoms out of him. One symptom was obvious. He would be sitting, chained to a tree or to Hank or Betty, when everything would suddenly turn a blinding white. He'd hear a whoosh in his ears and fall over, remaining unconscious for several hours. Then a short time later he would be stricken again by the same frightening whiteness.

Mike was most talkative when delirious. One night he took them fishing for salmon in a cold, clear tributary of the Columbia River. Another evening he raced his copper sorrel horse, Satan, around the rim of a canyon.

He called the names of his mother, stepfather, sister Lynn, and boyhood friends who were unknown to Betty and Hank. He led yells for his high school basketball team, gave speeches about the customs of the tribespeople of Viet Nam, pled with superior officers for cement and building materials to start a new project. And he had words for their captors in his delirium: "Give me back my Radê bracelet and watch. Return the money you took from the lady. Free us."

On the thirty-fifth day his temperature dropped back to normal. He could see, though bright sunlight hurt his eyes. He could walk a few steps without stumbling. He even had an appetite for the unappealing food.

He asked about Ngue. "The preacher escaped, Mike," Hank said. "Don't you remember? They went looking for him and I don't think they caught him and his friends."

"Maybe he'll bring back a rescue party."

Betty forced a weak smile. "Hank and I have been praying and hoping. But they've moved us so many times. And we're 'way south of where he left us. I wonder if anyone can find us now."

The three captives looked at each other. Mike was thin and gaunt, forty or fifty pounds lighter than when they had left Happy Valley. Hank's cheeks were hollow, his blue eyes bulging in their sockets, his shoulder blades ridging the thin, short-sleeved shirt that fell loosely around thin arms. Betty's red hair, which she'd always kept bright and shiny, lay dull and straight against a scalp infested with lice. Her once pretty face was pale and pallid, with sunken cheekbones and sagging chin.

They tottered about on limbs that looked more like piano legs. Their stomachs were enlarged and distended, bloated not from food but from gas in the intestines.

Their captors began moving again, stopping for a week or two at temporary camp sites, turning southwest and remaining in the mountains. They saw occasional bands of Viet Cong, but only passed through burned-out villages from which the inhabitants had long since fled.

It was a scavenger's existence even for their Viet Cong guards, who subsisted on the same diet as the prisoners. However, it seemed Mike could eat anything. He caught lizards on rocks, small crabs in streams, and tree frogs which constantly chirped in chorus along the trails. When it wasn't convenient to boil them, he popped the frogs into his mouth and swallowed them alive.

The monsoons caught up with them in June after—according to Mike's guess—they moved into Lamdong Province, some hundred miles due south of Banmethuot. He estimated they'd walked in a roundabout, zigzag way, more than 200 miles across some of the roughest terrain in Asia.

They camped in a green depression on the side of a steep mountain and the remaining tribal prisoners were put to work cutting poles and making thatch for houses. The Americans figured this was a sign they would remain here a while.

A swift stream ran a hundred yards or so below them. Between the camp and the stream was a cave. Mike, Betty, and Hank felt this was the best place to go for shelter from the torrential rains, but the Viet Cong guards said no, and gave them a strip of plastic for a temporary roof over their heads.

When finished, the pole houses were not effective against the rain. The three again asked to go to the cave, and again were forbidden.

The skies cleared later in the evening and a luminous moon climbed into the quiet night sky. The captives were too exhausted to enjoy the beauty.

Around noon the next day, visitors arrived.

These North Vietnamese were unusually friendly. The leader, Major Phu, told the prisoners they would no longer be chained at night. "You will have the freedom of the camp, so long as you do not try anything foolish," he said.

Betty laughed ruefully, saying, "We're too weak to go far, even if we could get away."

This officer inquired about their families. Upon learning that Hank had a wife and four children, he invited Hank to write Vange. "Tell her you've been treated well and I'll deliver it to a post office myself," he promised.

Hank gratefully took a pad of paper and a pencil from Major Phu. Taking advantage of rare midday sunshine, he stretched forward on a mossy rock to write.

He wrote as positively as he could, believing that the letter would not be delivered otherwise.

He requested that she pass word to Betty's and Mike's families that they were doing as well as could be expected. Then he asked about each of the children and expressed his hope that Cindy was now with them. "I hope that the National Liberation Front will be merciful and permit me to be reunited with you soon," he added.

"This is a beautiful spot where we are now camped," he continued. "I can't name all the different butterflies I've seen. The Monarchs and Birdwings are huge! Perhaps one day we can come here and catch some for your collection."

Then he signed, "Your loving husband" and his name, and carefully slid the folded note into the envelope Major Phu

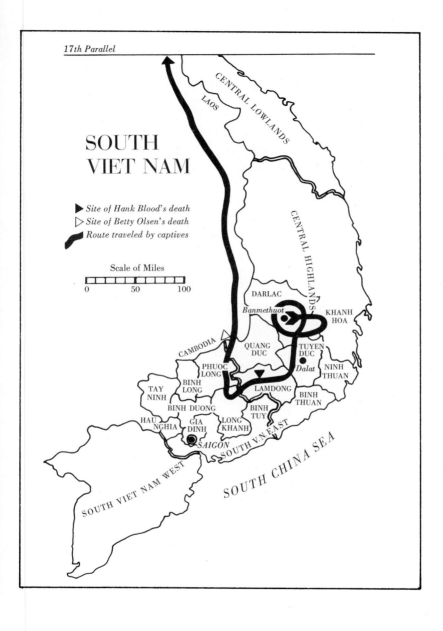

17th Parallel

SOUTH
VIET NAM

▶ Site of Hank Blood's death
▷ Site of Betty Olsen's death
Route traveled by captives

Scale of Miles

0   50   100

LAOS

CENTRAL LOWLANDS

CENTRAL HIGHLANDS

DARLAC

Banmethuot

KHANH
HOA

CAMBODIA

QUANG
DUC

TUYEN
DUC

Dalat

NINH
THUAN

PHUOC
LONG

BINH
LONG

LAMDONG

BINH
THUAN

TAY
NINH

BINH DUONG

BINH
TUY

HAU
NGHIA

GIA
DINH

LONG
KHANH

SAIGON

SOUTH V.N. EAST

SOUTH CHINA SEA

SOUTH VIET NAM WEST

▲ *The Radês, like some American Indian tribes, "bury" their dead above ground.*

▼ *Eager to be one with the tribespeople, Mike Benge often made his home in this kind of village longhouse. Here a Radê woman stands beside the horns of a water buffalo sacrificed to the spirits.*

◄ *Hank Blood in his bachelor days.*
► *A honeymoon view of Hank and Vange Blood in the Philippines.*
▼ *This rented house was home for the Bloods at the time of Hank's capture.*

In time of persecution and danger, I must remember not to fear men, but God, sanctifying in my heart Christ as Lord and being ready always to give an answer to every man a reason of the hope that is in me "with meekness and fear."

And he must needs go through Samaria.

John 4:4

See then that ye walk circumspectly, not as fools, but as wise, Redeeming the time because the days are evil.

Eph. 5:15, 16

▲ *A page from Hank's notebook expresses a thought which proved to be prophetic.*
▼ *These were among the Scripture memory cards carried by Hank during his captivity.*

▲ *Cindy Blood celebrates her first birthday with an elephant ride.*
▼ *Hank and Vange with Cindy, David, and Carolyn. Cathy later completed the family.*

Personal Disciplines of Love

1. Rom 14:7 "Don't live to myself"
   I Cor 8, 10

2. Eph 5:16 "I will make the best
   use of my time"

3. Matt 18:15 ① "I will follow
   matt 5:24 scripture when
   disharmony arises."
   ② "If bring gift & there is ought
   correct it first"

4. I Pet 2:23 — I will expect many
   opportunities to be accused
   falsely

5. Rom 13 — Cheerfully accept
   every responsibility as
   from the Lord

6. Heb 10:24 I will seek to build
   God's word in lives
   of others

_These notes came out of Betty's life-changing counseling sessions
with Bill Gothard._

◄ *Betty earned her coveted nurse's cap at Methodist Hospital in Brooklyn.*

► *Betty Olsen at age 9 and her sister Marilyn, 6, with their parents, Rev. and Mrs. Walter Olsen.*

▼ *A love of outdoor life—good preparation for Betty's service in Viet Nam.*

This beautiful memorial at Banmethuot marks the graves of some of those who died in the Tet massacre.

◄ *Back on U.S. soil, Mike recuperates from his long ordeal as a captive of the North Vietnamese. Author James Hefley took these photos during the interviews in which Mike shared the painful memories which form the basis for this book.*

► *Mike in Corpus Christi, Texas, to address rally for M.I.A. (Missing in Action) families. Here he dictates a letter to Sandy Olsen, leader of the Corpus Christi M.I.A. chapter.*

Pastor Ngue was captured with Hank, Betty, and Mike, but was able to escape and find his way back home through the jungle. Ngue is now district superintendent of the tribal churches.

Hank with Tang, his only tribal convert in Viet Nam. Tang has become a leading evangelist, winning many to Christ.

▲ *Banmethuot tribal Bible school was reopened shortly after Tet offensive. All the destroyed mission homes and buildings there have been rebuilt and a great tribal revival has taken place.*

▼ *The American troops are gone, but Alliance missionaries continue to serve Christ in cooperation with the National Evangelical Church. This literature truck in Saigon is one means of outreach.*

had given him. The officer took the letter and again pledged that Vange would get it. Hank told his companions, "I believe he is sincere."

The attempted correspondence seemed to make Hank long even more for his wife and children. He felt that Vange and the three youngest had certainly been allowed to go ahead to safety. He could not be so sure about Cindy, the oldest. Mike had said that before his ill-fated rescue attempt, he'd heard that the attack on Banmethuot was part of a country-wide North Vietnamese and Viet Cong offensive.

Hank, Betty, and Mike had frequently speculated about what might have happened at Kontum, which was some 140 miles north of Banmethuot. Eleven Wycliffe members and two Alliance couples had been there participating in a translation workshop.

"We know the 173rd Airborne pulled out just before *Tet*," Hank mentioned again. "With them gone, the enemy might have taken Kontum. Nobody in the camps has given us any information. We just don't know. I sure do hope Cindy wasn't hurt. Poor little thing, barely nine years old, up there at school, away from her family."

"She may have been better off there than if she'd been at Banmethuot," Betty mused.

"Yes, I've thought of that. And I've surrendered her to the Lord's keeping. But I can't keep her out of my mind.

"I remember her first birthday. We put her on an elephant and I took pictures. Wish I had one to show you how cute and tiny she looked on that huge beast. Vange and I thought she was really the cat's whiskers.

"Mike, you and Betty will just never understand how it is 'till you marry and have children yourselves. One of the toughest things about being a missionary is sending your children away to school."

"Remember, I'm a missionary kid myself, Hank," Betty reminded. "I don't know how many times I cried myself to sleep, wishing I could see my parents."

Hank turned his face so Mike and Betty couldn't see his tears. But they could see his bony shoulders shaking and hear the sobs.

"I'm sorry, Hank," Betty said gently. "I didn't mean—"

"I know you didn't, Betty," Hank cried. "It's just that I miss them so much. O God, if I could hold each of them just once more. Just to tell them how much I love them. It hurts. Oh, how it hurts."

Mike and Betty sat silent, trying to sympathize, but not knowing what to say.

After a while they heard Hank blow his nose in some leaves. Then he turned back to face them. The tears had dried on his face.

"The Lord's watching over them. I know he is. He watched over them in the past. He will now.

"I remember when we were on furlough and I was studying for my master's at Indiana. I came home from conference and found little Carolyn—she was just a tiny baby—looking like a chalk doll. Vange said she'd lost weight. Well, she didn't have much to lose. The doctor told us she was critical and might die. He wanted to operate.

"That evening I dug into the Word. I read about Abraham and Paul—men who dared to believe that God would work miracles. After an hour and a half of Bible study and prayer, I committed her to the Lord and slept soundly.

"We took her to Indianapolis and the doctors operated. They found her diaphragm had ruptured and her intestines were pushing up into the lung cavity and crowding the lungs and heart. They fixed her diaphragm and pushed the intestines back to where they belonged. Fifteen days later she was out of the hospital and we could hardly tell she'd been sick. Some said we were lucky to have her alive, but we knew it was the Lord who helped the doctors do what they did.

"I can point to so many times when the Lord seemed to be looking after the Blood family," Hank continued. "Back in '62 Vange and I went to Saigon for medical checkups. One of our group members had tried to make an appointment, but the nurses had said we didn't need it and should just come on in. Apparently there was a mix-up, for when we went to see the doctor, he said we had to have an appointment. That made it necessary to cancel our flight reservations.

"When we got back to Banmethuot I checked with the government security office about going on out to Lac Thien. He said we couldn't because there had been an attack the night before and the VC flag was flying over the town. If we had gone as originally scheduled, we probably would have been captured. We were saved by a misunderstanding.

"This was in March. A couple of months later we got the children ready to go see Dr. Vietti at the leprosarium. She delivered David, you know. We had planned to go earlier, but it was the 30th before we were packed up. Then someone told us to forget it, because the night before, the doctor, Dan Gerber, and Archie Mitchell had been captured. So it seemed the Lord was looking out for us again.

"But we were in the right spot this time and they got me. I don't know why the Lord has permitted this to happen, but I'm sure he has a purpose. 'All things work together for good to those that love God.' He knows what's best."

"Yes," Betty murmured. "Bad as it is, we have to believe that the Lord has reasons we don't understand."

"Yes," Hank said. "And instead of sitting here thinking about the greatness of our predicament, we should be thinking about the greatness of God. He has his eye on the world and all the things that are happening to his children. He's listening to our prayers and the prayers of others, even if he doesn't answer as we'd like him to.

"When I think of all the people who must be praying for us," he added, "I know he must have something for us to do here. Why, my mother probably has half the people in Oregon praying."

"How old is she now, Hank?" Mike asked.

"Eighty-one."

"She's certainly spry. I saw her at the dedication of your Translation Center in Kontum three years ago."

"I'd planned to be there, but my kidneys acted up and we had to extend our furlough in the States. She got to see Dave and Doris and their little son, Jeffrey. She went all the way up to Quang Tri where Carolyn and John Miller were working with the Bru. My mom is some gal, all right."

Calmer and less emotional now, Hank kept talking about his family. "Dave and I couldn't have had better parents. I remember when Dad was living, we'd pack up and go on camping trips. Cannon Beach. On the slopes of Mt. Hood. We'd take the road up the Columbia River, then loop back the long way around Mt. Hood. I guess you've been that route, Mike."

"Sure thing. Boy, I'd love to stand under Bridal Veil Falls and feel the sweet sting of spray on my face. That's one of the coolest places on earth. Then I'd like to stop at a roadside restaurant and have about a pound of bacon and a dozen fresh eggs. With some good hot coffee."

"I always thought I couldn't get by without my coffee in the morning," Betty said. "My sister Marilyn even sent me a thermos so I could have a hot cup waiting when I woke up each morning. I could drink a thermos full right now."

Hank licked his lips. "I'd settle for a half gallon of vanilla ice cream. When Dave and I were kids, Mom would treat the whole neighborhood. Drool!"

"Well, shall we order now?" Mike joked. " 'Hey, waiter, I'll have a dozen eggs, over easy, with a big side order of bacon. And six pieces of hot toast.' What'll you have for your main course, Betty?"

"With my coffee, I'd like some *duos*. That's a big African potato. Boiled, mashed, or baked. I don't care. And a bowl of peanut soup."

"And you, Mr. Blood. What's your preference on the menu?"

"Three McDonald doubleburgers. A pound of fries. And a

gallon of vanilla ice cream. Tell the cooks to hurry. I'm starved."

The three sat cross-legged, pretending to enjoy their imaginary food.

Betty giggled—the first time in days. "The guards think we're crazy."

"Oh, they've thought that all along," Hank said. "Maybe they'll send us to a mental institution where the food is better than here."

"Shhhh," Mike whispered. "Don't tell anyone, but we're in one already."

"Oh, Mike, what would we do without your sense of humor?"

"Where? What? I lost it the first day of *Tet*."

After a while they grew tired of pretending and Betty told her Bible story for the day. This one was about Queen Esther, who saved the Jewish people from mass murder.

When she concluded, Mike asked curiously, "Do the good people always win out in the Bible?"

"If you mean do they always turn out to be healthy, wealthy, and wise—no. Stephen was stoned to death. The Apostle Paul probably died in prison or had his head chopped off by the Emperor Nero."

"I remember reading," Hank put in, "that there's pretty good evidence for every one of Jesus' twelve apostles dying a violent death. Except the Apostle John, who died in Ephesus, after his exile on the island of Patmos."

After a while they lay down to nap. Mike was just dozing off when he smelled corn cooking. Someone had brought in a new supply of vegetables.

He told Hank and Betty and they waited expectantly for a little variety in the evening meal. They were served nothing but thin rice.

Stomachs aching, mouths watering, they sat licking their bowls, hungry eyes on the guards who were slurping corn and squash by the fire a few feet away.

"May we have some of the new food?" Betty finally asked.

The guards looked at the three starving Americans and laughed. Then one said, "You may search the ashes when we're done."

The three captives were desperate. They were not too proud to do that. As soon as the ashes cooled they groped on their knees for grains of corn. "Now I know how Lazarus felt," Hank said.

North Vietnamese officers came by again. The Americans were always glad to see them. When they came, food rations improved. And there remained the flicker of hope that this might be the time of release. Since the capture at Banmethuot, NVAs had always stayed in the area, maintaining regular checks on the rag-tag Viet Cong.

These new officers were polite but curt. They listened to their pleas, as had previous NVA visitors. They, as had the others, scoffed at the idea that Americans could be in Viet Nam for purely altruistic reasons. And they rebuffed Hank's usual efforts to talk to them about God and the Bible.

When the captain informed the prisoners they were going to "take a little walk," they groaned. None of them was in any condition for another hike. They were so weak from the effects of malnutrition they didn't see how they could walk a hundred yards.

"Could they be turning us loose?" Betty asked hopefully. The thought spurred the trio to try. They staggered along through the insect-infected jungle, trying to support one another as best they could. Only the leeches enjoyed the hike. They were so numerous that the marchers had to stop often to pull them loose.

It took them half a day to get to the other side of the mountain, where they stumbled into the camp of a regiment of NVA troops.

These soldiers were well fed and appeared to be in good health. The prisoners gaped at several crates of medicine stacked in a tent. Betty begged for sulfa, quinine, penicillin, anything they could spare. She was ignored.

Their escort marched them in front of the soldiers like cattle at an auction.

"What's he going to do with us?" Betty whispered to her male companions who stood protectively on either side of her.

"Maybe we'll get medals," Mike replied wryly.

The regiment commander spoke in Vietnamese, which all three understood.

"Comrades, we have brought from the prison camp three imperialist spies from America, Mr. Michael Benge, Mr. Henry Blood, and Miss Betty Olsen. We do not know why the pretty lady is without a husband. Perhaps she will tell us."

The troops guffawed.

"We have told you that Americans are accustomed to a soft life of ease and luxury. This is because they exploit poor and struggling peoples who do not yet understand the aims of our glorious socialist revolution. Americans walk very little. They ride in limousines and airplanes.

"These imperialist plotters have round stomachs and small legs because of lack of exercise. This is how you would look if you traveled as they do."

The subjects of the demonstration were grinding their teeth in frustration. If the poor dupes only knew... Finally Mike could stand it no longer. "You fools!" he screamed in Vietnamese. "Can't you see that we look this way because your comrades are starving us to death!"

The Captain's hand lashed out with a stinging blow to Mike's jaw that sent him reeling. "You are bad, Mr. Benge," he hissed through his teeth. "Very bad. You will regret those remarks!"

CHAPTER

6

Sorrow
on the Mountain

"The presence of you imperialist spies contaminates our brave fighting men," the officer shouted for all to hear. He ordered the three Americans taken back to their prison camp immediately.

"Move! Move!" their escorts shouted as they stumbled along the precipitous trail. Mike was so dizzy he could hardly stand. Betty's bare legs burned and bled from the blood-lusting leaches that clung to her. The angry North Vietnamese would not permit her to slow down long enough to pull them off. Hank wobbled in uncertain agony. The pain from the huge boil on his hip was excruciating. Ugly ulcers were breaking out on his arms. The odor from the ulcers smelled to his companions like burned beans. "Please stop, please!" he begged, to no avail.

The trip seemed endless. Besides their physical condition, the hopelessness of their situation was an added burden that weighed heavily on their hearts.

When they finally reached the little hut that was their prison cell they collapsed on the straw mats. They looked more dead than alive. Betty clawed at the leeches. Mike tried to help her, but kept falling back as his head whirled. Hank groaned, trying not to move.

Mercifully, the North Vietnamese left them alone for a while.

After an hour or two they started down hill to the stream. Betty went first, slipping and sliding, with Mike, still dizzy, hanging onto her hand. Hank inched painfully along behind them.

They stayed as long as they dared, washing their bodies, picking lice from one another's heads, rejuvenating their tortured minds with the sound of water gently gurgling over mossy rocks. "If we could only shut our eyes and be in Oregon," Hank sighed. "The streams are like this there."

"Americans! Come!"

The voice was insistent. They had never been physically assaulted in any camp, but the tone suggested this was now a possibility.

Climbing back up was torture. They made it to the cave on the side of the hill when Hank collapsed and said, "I can't go any farther."

Mike and Betty tried to help, but didn't have the strength to pull his body forward more than a few feet. They went on alone, gasping, supporting one another, half dragging their bodies until they reached the camp.

"Mr. Blood is too weak," Mike panted. "He must have assistance."

One of the North Vietnamese motioned to two tribal prisoners to go bring Hank up. When this was accomplished, an NVA officer herded the three captives together for interrogation.

"When will you admit that you are spies?" he demanded.

"When will you believe that we are here because we want to help the tribespeople?" Mike responded. "The lady is a volunteer nurse with the lepers. Mr. Blood is a Bible teacher. I am an agricultural technician."

This NVA, who had never given his name, slammed the butt of his rifle against the ground. "Ridiculous!"

He looked at Betty, huddled on the ground, trying to preserve as much modesty as her thin dress would allow. "Since you are a woman, perhaps the National Liberation Front will be lenient if you tell the truth."

Betty looked deep into the accuser's eyes. "Captain, we have always told the truth to every officer who has questioned us. No one would believe us."

"You are lying, Miss Olsen. No American would come here for humanitarianism."

"I believe you are sincere, Captain," Betty sighed weakly. "But Communism won't satisfy the deepest longings of your heart. Don't you wonder sometimes what life is all about, why you are here, where you are going when you die?"

"Man dies like all other animals. There is nothing more."

"That's what you have been taught. But man is eternal. When he dies, he goes to heaven or hell."

"Ha! That is just American imperialist propaganda. Karl Marx said religion is the opiate of the people. It makes people afraid by persuading them to believe in superstitions. Then your imperialist profiteers attach their greedy tentacles. We are going to change all that."

"Captain, we cannot persuade you. Only God can do that. We can only pray for you."

Hank had revived enough to join in the discussion. "Captain," he asked, "do you say Christianity is a tool of the West?"

"Yes. It is ammunition in the arsenal of the capitalists of Wall Street."

"Captain, history tells us that Christianity began in the

Middle East and spread first through those lands and into Europe and Asia. Jesus Christ lived centuries before Karl Marx and Ho Chi Minh."

"Jesus Christ is dead."

"He died, but did not stay dead. He rose from the grave the third day. He lives in the hearts of all those who believe in him and love him. He lives in our hearts. That is why we've come to Viet Nam. We're here as his representatives."

"Enough!" the NVA suddenly shouted. "We have more important work to do than debate such foolishness. You are either spies, or you are stupid."

"If we are stupid, we can harm no one," Mike suggested. "Why not let us go?"

The NVA didn't reply.

"Well, we tried again," Betty sighed after the NVA and his fellow officers had left.

"Don't be discouraged, Betty," Hank consoled. "If we are faithful in witnessing, God will tend to the results."

Hank shifted his body, grimacing in pain. "The devil wants to knock us out of battle. The Lord wants us to depend completely on him. Every day since we were captured, I've told him, 'Here is my life. I belong to you. Give me the right sense of perspective.'

"It hasn't been easy. I've wanted to give up. Quit. Lie down and die. Or smack a VC or NVA in the teeth. Then I think, they don't know what they're doing. Remember how the Lord prayed for his enemies on the cross: 'Father, forgive them, for they know not what they do.' "

Mike had sat silent for some time. Now he confessed, "That's easier said than done."

"We can, Mike," Betty declared. "With God's spirit living in us, we can."

"Yes," Hank said, quoting Matthew 5:44: " 'Love your enemies, bless them that curse you, do good to them that hate you, and pray for them which despitefully use you, and persecute you.' "

"Lord, help us keep on loving," Betty prayed. "Loving one another. Loving our enemies. Trusting you." Then in a weak, trembling voice, she led out in a stanza of a favorite hymn:

> *Simply trusting every day,*
> *Trusting through a stormy way;*
> *Even when my faith is small,*
> *Trusting Jesus, that is all.*

The next week the ugly boil on Hank's side burst and began draining. He seemed to have a harder time sleeping than ever. The sharp, sudden kidney pains kept recurring. The itching had never ceased. He moaned in his sleep and suffered frightful nightmares. Sometimes it seemed as if the Lord and the devil were battling for possession of his body.

Reduced to a thin shadow, Hank seemed to sense the future, noting, "Next month I'll be forty-nine. I wonder if I'll live that long."

The nights were chilly here on the mountain and sometimes the damp, cold air seemed to knife through the prisoners. One especially frigid night, Mike was trying to huddle near a tribal prisoner. The tribesman heard him shivering and chattering and offered to share his blanket. "It's full of lice, Mr. Benge," the Radê warned.

Mike was so cold he didn't care. "I'd rather have lice than freeze to death," he said, snuggling under it.

The next day the tribesman gave Mike the blanket, which he in turn shared with Hank and Betty. They begged their guards to let them boil this blanket and other lice-infested bedding and clothes, but the VCs coldly refused.

The food was the worst it had been. Usually they'd had manioc and occasional meat or dried fish, to supplement the monotonous bowl of rice. Now they were receiving only rice.

"We won't last much longer if you don't give us more food and some medical aid," Mike told the NVA, the next time they came around.

They appeared not to care. "You're of no political value to us," one officer shrugged. "If you die, we'll have three less problems."

Did they mean they were no longer considered spies? They could only guess.

The rainy season still had two months to run. They were getting a heavy downpour at least once a day and sometimes twice. Their VC guards wouldn't let them go to the cave, so they had to huddle in their leaky pole hut under the strip of plastic and wait each storm out. Invariably, either Mike or Hank got soaking wet. The covering was simply not adequate for three people.

The night of July 10th was a time, as Hank remarked, when old Noah would have felt right at home. The rain fell in drenching sheets, hour after dark hour. No matter how they positioned themselves, one was always exposed to the down-pour. Being the longest, Hank was getting soaked the most.

"I'm going to the little house on the other side of the camp," he finally said.

"The roof leaks badly. You'll get wetter than if you stayed here," Mike warned.

"It couldn't be any worse."

"He'll catch pneumonia, Mike," Betty worried. "Weak as he is, he wouldn't last long."

The two threw off their covering and braved the rain to go bring Hank back. He returned reluctantly, soaked to the skin.

The hard rains continued into the next night. "I can't stand this," Hank complained. "I'm going to the little house. Don't come after me this time."

The next morning Mike and Betty went over to check and found Hank near pneumonia. They squeezed the water from his shirt and trouser legs and dried him off as best they could. Betty tenderly covered him up with the last dry blanket they had, while Mike summoned the head guard.

"He must have medical aid," Mike said grimly. "Can't you send a man to the military camp for medicines?"

"Those supplies are for the soldiers," the guard replied stonily. "If your troops and planes weren't here, they wouldn't need them."

"Will you let him die?" Mike declared. "Let an innocent man die? Leave four children without a father? A wife without a husband?"

"If he dies, okay. We won't be bothered. Don't worry about him. Go back to your house."

Mike and Betty would have gotten on their knees if they had thought it would help Hank. They begged and pleaded to no avail.

Finally Mike said, "Let Miss Olsen and me carry him to a hospital. We'll come back. We promise."

The Viet Cong laughed in their faces.

They could only stand watch and keep Hank as comfortable as possible.

By noon he was talking out of his head. Telling his children how to pose for pictures. Questioning a tribal informant about a Mnong legend. Leading devotions for the Wycliffe gang at Saigon. Then, in a quavering voice, trying to sing the hymn he'd chosen years before as his marching song:

> Lead on, O King Eternal;
> The day of march has come;
> Henceforth in fields of conquest
> Thy tents shall be our home.
> Through days of preparation
> Thy grace has made us strong,
> And now, O King Eternal,
> We lift our battle song.

Near the middle of the day he recognized Mike and Betty. "Has the rain stopped?" he mumbled.

Betty assured him it had.

"Let's go down to the stream and wash up." He started to rise and fell back on the blanket. "Hey, what happened? I was trying to find a dry place in here, and . . ." His voice trailed off in a dry whisper.

Betty read to him from her Bible, which by now was in such condition that she could hardly hold the sections together. Mike sat nearby, head bowed in thought and prayer.

Later in the afternoon Hank came to his senses again.

"If I don't get back, hug Vange for me, Betty. Tell her I may not be much good at building a raft, but I love her. And kiss each of my children. Cindy is big enough to understand, and maybe David. Their mother will have to tell Carolyn and Cathy when they're older why this happened.

"When you see my brother Dave, tell him he's the greatest, the best. And Mike, when you go home to Oregon, look up my mom. Give her my love. Thank her for praying for me . . .Thank . . ."

He fell back into sleep. Betty felt his forehead. "A hundred and four at least," she murmured.

He came back in a few minutes. "The Mnongs must have the Bible . . . didn't get much done . . . Vange, ask Tang to help . . . Vange. . . you're strong . . . you can do it."

Then, "Tang . . . don't forget the Bible verses you learned . . . Give your people God's Word . . . I can't . . . can't . . . please help . . .

"Betty . . . Mike, you're still here . . . Oh, how my hip hurts . . . Betty, give me a shot . . . help me . . ."

"Vange, I . . . love. Cathy . . . David . . . Carolyn . . . Cindy . . ."

The first evening stars came out in the clear sky. Hank was quieter now, snoring. But his fever was still high.

Betty saw that Mike wasn't doing so well either. She feared the malaria might be coming back, and insisted he go to bed.

She stayed beside Hank as long as she could keep her head up, then dropped into exhausted sleep. The camp lay quiet in the velvet Vietnamese night.

For another day and night Betty nursed Hank as much as she was able, while keeping a weary eye on Mike, who had become delirious again.

On the morning of July 13th, or perhaps the 14th, Hank had no pulse. Restraining the bitterness she felt, she called the guards and asked them to dig a grave.

They complied.

Mike was a little better. At his request, the guards gave them a couple of empty rice bags. He and Betty pulled one over Hank's head and the other over his feet.

Then the Viet Cong picked up Hank's long body and carried it to the shallow grave under the shade of a nearby tree. They stood by unsmiling as Betty recited,

> *The Lord is my shepherd; I shall not want.*
> *He maketh me to lie down in green*
> *pastures: he leadeth me beside the still*
> *waters. He restoreth my soul: he leadeth me*
> *in the paths of righteousness for his name's*
> *sake. Yea, though I walk through the valley*
> *of the shadow of death, I will fear no evil:*
> *for thou art with me; thy rod and thy staff*
> *they comfort me. Thou preparest a table*
> *before me in the presence of mine enemies:*
> *thou anointest my head with oil; my cup*
> *runneth over. Surely goodness and mercy*
> *shall follow me all the days of my life: and*
> *I will dwell in the house of the Lord*
> *forever.*

The body was in the shallow hole and they were ready to cover it. "Wait," commanded Betty in Vietnamese.

"Earth to earth, ashes to ashes, dust to dust. We commend the soul of our brother Hank to the God and Father of our Lord Jesus Christ."

A shovel crunched into the loose earth. The first shower of dirt slapped against the body. Betty clung to Mike's arm. They turned back to the camp.

CHAPTER

7

Betty's Victory

Hank's death was like a bad dream to Mike, whose fever lasted for several days afterward. Betty, despite her sores and the miserable diet, was more able to keep her senses together. When Mike felt better, he was chagrined to realize that throughout their ordeal, she had remained the healthiest.

"I've always considered myself tough," he admitted to Betty. "To have a woman show me up hurts my masculine pride."

Betty merely smiled and said, "Thank the Lord, one of us has always been able to keep going. If we should both go down—I don't know. . . ."

They had dried fish for dinner. "The NVAs will be here to-morrow," Mike predicted. "The VCs always treat us better when they're expected."

This time it was Major Phu. He appeared to be genuinely sorry that Hank had died. "I came to tell him I mailed his letter," he said.

"How much longer are we to be held?" Betty asked.

The NVA major pleaded ignorance. He did say that since the rainy season was almost over they would be moved again.

Mike inquired—as they had all along—if he'd heard of three American missionaries, two men and a woman doctor, being in a prison camp. "They were taken six years ago," he added.

"No, I've never seen any report of this," Major Phu replied. "But we've been told that the National Liberation Front captured 500 Americans at Banmethuot."

This was news to Betty and Mike. They didn't believe it and said so. There had never been that many Americans in Banmethuot.

"What's happening in the rest of the world?" Betty asked.

"Oh, there are very bad riots in your country. The people are rising up to protest Johnson's imperialist war."

Betty and Mike didn't know how much of this to believe.

Major Phu left, and about a week later, on July 28th, their Viet Cong guards started moving them down the mountain. Though weak and emaciated, Betty and Mike tried to memorize the features of the place in hopes they might be able to return and locate Hank's grave after release.

They camped the next time in flatlands. The altitude was still high and the heat not oppressive. Mike thought he recognized the area as being part of Longkhanh Province, about halfway between Banmethuot and Saigon.

Here they had three new guards, all Radê and more friendly to the two captives who spoke their Montagnard dialect. Mike and Betty hadn't had so much food to eat since leaving Happy Valley.

They missed talkative Hank. The four-and-a-half months with him seemed like half a lifetime. His death lay heavy upon their thoughts. They dreaded having to tell Vange.

"Why did *he* have to die, and not one of us?" Mike wondered. "He had a wife and children. He was ready to do his translation."

"It does seem unfair," Betty admitted. "So many tragedies do, when you look at them from human reasoning. But God has his reasons for allowing Hank to die. Mike, do you remember the five missionaries who were killed by Auca Indians in Ecuador a few years ago? At the time it seemed so useless. Such a waste. They were all young and talented and just beginning their work. Four of them were married and there were several children involved.

"But the shock of their deaths shook a lot of American Christians. Hundreds of young people were challenged to become missionaries. Perhaps the story of what happened to Hank and to our friends back at Banmethuot will cause many more to volunteer. Jesus said, 'Except a corn of wheat fall into the ground and die, it abides alone: but if it dies, it brings forth much fruit.'

"I'm not saying that's it, but God has his reasons. There must be a higher purpose in all this. We'll just have to wait and see."

They celebrated Mike's thirty-third birthday on August 6th. Without candles or cake, they could have only an imaginary party. Betty sang to Mike and invited him to enjoy a repast from home: a Paul-Bunyan-size salmon steak with melted butter lake surrounded by mountains of mashed potatoes, roasting ears, homemade rolls, and iced tea. "Yummmmm," Mike murmured in pretended delight and patted his swollen stomach appreciatively. That night both dreamed about sitting down before luscious dinners. Then, as in past nocturnal fantasies, they woke up just as the food reached their mouths.

A few days later they heard a familiar voice. "Mr. Benge, Miss Olsen?"

It was Major Phu again.

"I've just come from seeing your friend's widow in Banmethuot. She took the news of her husband's death very sorrowfully. But she and the children are well, and she sends you greetings."

"Well, that takes care of that," Mike said after the NVA had left. "Now she knows—if he's telling the truth."

"He seemed sincere."

"But why would Vange stay in Banmethuot if 500 Americans were captured there?"

"I don't know," Betty said. "I'd think she'd go somewhere safer with the children."

With a more balanced diet that included meat and fish, Betty became more alert and, in spite of the depressing circumstances, laughed when telling of childhood incidents in the Ivory Coast of Africa.

"I wasn't a model missionary kid," she admitted. "Definitely not."

"What did you do that was so bad?" Mike teased.

"Once I let our African house boy kiss me. Our field chairman was visiting and saw us. Boy, was he upset."

Mike laughed out loud. "I can imagine."

"I had a habit of saying just what I thought. Missionary kids were supposed to be quiet and solemn and pious. Never were they to embarrass their parents. They had to be super good."

"I can't figure you any other way," Mike said.

"Oh, I was a mischievous little girl. Seriously, some of the happiest days of my life were spent in Africa. There was an old tree in the yard just right for climbing. I'd climb up to my perch and read books by the hour."

"What'd you read?"

"Anything I could get my hands on. I loved stories about nurses. Even back then I wanted to be one.

"Marilyn was three years younger. She didn't always understand, but she was sweet. Our house was one of those big old high-ceiling things with open rafters. I was supposed to protect Marilyn from the rats and lizards that ran around in our room.

"Our folks were marvelous people, but we felt they had too much to do on the mission station. Dad was a translator and spent a lot of time in his study. Mom never seemed to catch up with her work. And they were both always leaving us, it seemed, going on trips to visit the African churches. I can remember sitting and waiting, sitting and waiting for Mom to come home and play with me. I came to resent the work that took her away.

"Oh, Mike, I hope you don't get the wrong idea about missionaries. God's work has to come first with us, and it's terribly hard to divide your loyalties, especially when your family's involved. I didn't talk about this when Hank was living. I'm sure he was a good father, but I might have made him feel guilty. Now that I've turned myself over to the Lord fully, I can appreciate my folks more. We'll have to make up the time together in heaven."

Mike squinted at Betty who was sitting with her scarred legs hanging over a rock. "This turning yourself over to the Lord—you've mentioned that before. Just what do you mean?" he asked.

Betty looked at her companion, hesitating.

"If it's some deep, dark secret. . ."

"No, no. It's just that I've never been able to feel close to very many people, to really share myself. Until five years ago, I just couldn't get close to anyone."

"That's when it happened?"

"Yes, but to really help you understand how I was, I'll have to go 'way back. You see, when I was eight my folks sent Marilyn and me 800 miles away to school. There was no school at the station where they lived. It was either send us or leave their work.

"So except for furloughs, I was away from them eight months out of every year. And in high school I was away all year with kids whose parents were all over the world. In a situation like that, you learn not to make close friendships, because as soon as you get attached to someone, they leave.

"I suppose the seeds were already there, but high school

was where I really began to show my rebellion. I thought they were too strict—there were so many rules, we couldn't do anything. I was such a stinker at one school that my dad heard about it and made me write them an apology.

"Then my dear mom got cancer. I prayed for her to get well, oh, how I prayed. She was sick for about two years and died just before my seventeenth birthday. I accepted it as the Lord's will, at least I said I did. It was hard, Mike, awfully hard."

Mike could see the tears filling her eyes. He remembered how tough it had been when as a small child he'd lost his father.

"I finished high school. Then I went back to Africa for a while to be with my dad. In a couple of years he married Gene Swain, a single girl missionary. A really sweet person.

"I still wanted to be a nurse. In 1953 I came back and took my training at Methodist Hospital in Brooklyn, and then I worked there a couple of years. This was a very traumatic time for someone like me who'd always lived a protected life. I found it hard to accept people who did things I sometimes wanted to do, yet didn't approve of.

"They assigned me to the OB ward. I loved the little black-eyed Italian babies. I would baby-sit for the Jewish doctors' families. I hoped for a family of my own."

Betty was blushing. It seemed awkward for Mike to say anything, so he just waited.

"In our culture a fellow can take the initiative in seeking a life partner. A girl has to wait.

"Sure, I had dates. Not as many as I'd have liked. Some fellows I didn't like and one or two I might have liked better if they'd shown more interest.

"Also, I was thinking God wanted me to be a missionary, and that narrowed the field considerably. I wasn't very happy in my Christian experience, but the missionary thing stayed in the back of my mind.

"The marriage problem really began bugging me when I went to our Bible college at Nyack and majored in missions.

By this time I was 24, and the social pressure to get married was tremendous. It wasn't so bad the first or second years, but by the third year I could feel people beginning to wonder, 'What's wrong with Betty?' I wondered myself. Was it my looks, my personality, or what?

"I graduated in '62 and Marilyn and I spent five months with Dad and Gene in Seattle. Their little Mark was five then and adorable. And while they were in the States the twins were born. Then our family split up, as it seems missionary families are always doing, and they returned to Africa.

"This left me adrift. Marilyn was studying to be a religious education director. I was supposed to become a missionary, but I knew our Board wouldn't appoint me. I was too mixed up and confused.

"I went to Chicago with Marilyn. I didn't know why. Now I know it was the Lord. Marilyn and I drove an old turquoise Chevy and had a ball. We stopped and roasted wieners and picked up a hitchhiker. I was feeling pretty reckless.

"After a few months working at West Suburban Hospital in Chicago, I decided to visit the scene of my childhood, thinking that being in Africa might help me get my head together. But the missionaries there thought I was a bad influence on their work and made it plain that I should leave. I must have said some pretty awful things.

"So back to Chicago and nursing and the same old grind. Marriage prospects looked worse than ever. In another year I'd be 30 and a real old maid. I didn't like the way the future looked.

"I got more and more depressed about myself. Why couldn't I be a happy Christian? Why couldn't I make close friends like other people? Why did my conscience keep bothering me about things I'd asked over and over to be forgiven for? How was I ever going to be a missionary, feeling this way? Mike, I even reached the point where I contemplated suicide. I thought if this was all the Christian life had to offer, I'd be better off dead."

Betty stopped and looked straight into Mike's eyes. "You

probably thought missionaries and Christian workers didn't have problems like this?"

Mike grinned enigmatically.

"Just hold on. I'm getting to the good part of the story.

"I was then attending Jefferson Park Bible Church on the north side of Chicago. There was a fellow named Bill Gothard who came around on Wednesday nights to talk with young people. He had personal conferences with each one in the youth group. I saw how much he'd helped them, so one night after prayer meeting I waited until he was finished with the others, and then knocked on the door of his little basement office.

"I said, 'I know you're here to work with the youth group, but I wonder if you could help me with some problems.' He said, 'I'll try, but only on one condition: Do you really want God's best for your life?'

"I was really desperate. I told him I did want God's best.

"For the next half hour he asked me many questions. He had a way about him that made it easy to open up.

"Then he showed me how I was bitter toward God about the way he had made me. I realized I didn't like myself and in rejecting myself, I had rejected God's handiwork. He asked, 'How can you serve God if you aren't satisfied with the way he made you?'

"He showed me from Scripture how God had prescribed exactly how I was to look, even before I was born. He explained how God could make his strength perfect in bodily weaknesses and how he was not finished working on me yet. I realized then that God's goal was to develop inward qualities in me so that I would reflect the beauty of Christ.

"But there was an even deeper problem that Bill detected that night. And the decision he led me to make was the turning point in my life.

"For years I had struggled with the fear of being single. I was willing to serve God, but in return I was expecting him to give me a husband. I had never realized what it meant to actually abandon to God my expectation of marriage, but that night I did. It was one of the greatest struggles of my life!

"From that day I began to anticipate and even look forward to serving God as a single person. I came to value myself, as a special person whom God would use in his work."

The eyes that had been dulled by disease and debilitating trials seemed to take on new sparkle in recollection of the life-changing experience. "Without the pressure to look for a husband, I felt a new freedom. I could start setting my life in order. I made telephone calls asking for forgiveness. I dug into the Bible to find how God wanted to build my character. And I began forming close friendships, something I had never been able to do before.

"Bill Gothard said it would probably take me a year to build new thought patterns. Whenever I had a question, I would call him on the phone. I would tell him when his answers worked and when they didn't.

"When I came to Viet Nam three years ago, where do you think God put me for language study? In Danang with 10,000 GIs! I made new friends and turned down many dates. I was able to help a lot of them with personal problems because I wasn't interested in romance.

"Then in Banmethuot I was just beginning to help some of the Radê young people with their problems when I was captured. For a while I was so confident the NVAs would let us go. I just couldn't see why God didn't want me back on the job. And you know how hard I talked to some of the NVAs.

"Now I don't know what they're planning to do with us. God knows, though. We're in his hands. Hank was right in saying we should think about his greatness instead of the magnitude of our problems. I'm not going to worry about the future."

Though he wasn't the type to display much emotion, Mike was profoundly moved. The slim girl who had won his admiration for her stamina had opened her life to him.

Slowly he began to share his innermost self with her, opening long-closed doors of longings and feelings, sharing his aspirations to help the suffering Vietnamese, confiding his views of what it meant to be a Christian.

During the quiet month they spent in Buon Mega, the two came even closer. As brother and sister in Christ and partners in suffering, they found themselves able to talk about every aspect of life on the most intimate level.

Ignored by their guards, they spent long hours studying Betty's weather-beaten Bible, discussing doctrine, examining the life of Christ, considering what it meant to follow him.

"Jesus," Mike pointed out, "lived among the people and got to know their needs. So I believe I was right in living in a Radê village. Some Americans thought I was nuts. To each his own, I suppose. But I couldn't see it that way. I had to learn their customs, eat their food, share their smoky longhouses."

"You have to be close to the people," Betty agreed. "But few missionaries have been bold enough to move into their longhouses. Especially with children. We like our privacy."

"That's where the Radês are different," Mike said. "They do everything together."

"How well I know. I've gone off to a quiet spot to read my Bible and meditate, only to have a Radê come and ask sweetly, 'Amai Betty, is something the matter?' "

"It's a hard adjustment to live as they do," Mike admitted. "But I think it's all mental. It can be done."

Hour upon hour they talked. Occasionally a guard would join in, and visiting NVAs coming to check on security would try to argue their propaganda line. But most of the time it was just Mike and Betty. Two starving prisoners with God, against a silent and implacable enemy.

CHAPTER

8

"Father, forgive..."

During the last part of August Mike and Betty heard planes flying over. Sometimes they spotted familiar markings through breaks in the clouds, but there was no way they could draw the attention of the pilots. It was so frustrating not to be seen.

They'd also heard distant artillery, evidence that the Communists had not advanced as far as they'd boasted. They knew that as the war came closer, they would be moved.

Early in September, their captors almost reversed directions and led them due north across Phuoc Long Province. As they marched through cold mountain passes and crossed deep valleys, Mike seldom lost his geographical perspective. "They're taking us deeper into their own territory," he told

Betty. "If we hold out, we may soon be in Cambodia. If we hold out. We'll just have to take it one day at a time."

They stopped first near an NVA base camp on a secluded mountaintop. It was so well camouflaged and tunneled that they didn't know they were there until halted by a patrol that suddenly appeared at the side of the trail.

A little hook-nosed NVA stepped forward. He wore the markings of the Viet Cong, but Mike immediately recognized his accent as North Vietnamese. "I am Captain Phung," he said. "I know who you are. You will be here only one night. After your meal, you will go quickly to sleep in hammocks. You must be rested for a presentation to our troops in the morning."

With nothing more to say, he turned on his heel and melted into the forest.

"What does he want?" Betty asked as they sipped their bowls of thin, tasteless rice.

"Probably just to show off two ferocious American aggressors," Mike surmised.

That was it.

Shortly after sunrise, Captain Phung popped out of the misty forest and stood fidgeting while they gulped down their breakfast—more rice. Then, conscripting a couple of guards, he ordered the Americans to follow him through the trees. A few hundred feet away they twisted between two outcroppings of rock and halted under the recess of a cliff. In the foggy air it took a few seconds to realize they were surrounded by a battalion or more of soldiers.

Captain Phung wasted no time. "I promised to show you, comrades, two American aggressors who were caught in the very act of perpetrating crimes on innocent civilians. One is a woman, but do not let that deceive you. The American imperialist profiteers even send women to fight their wars while they idle in luxury and count their dollars."

Mike and Betty stood silently, waiting for a chance to speak. None came. The officer wound up his lecture, ordered the troops back to their positions, then escorted the captives and their guards back to the main trail.

During the next two weeks they were pushed relentlessly through the rugged mountains, traveling sometimes by night and sleeping in hammocks during the day. As they pushed painfully along, they picked up dry pieces of buffalo hide to chew, a futile effort to ward off hunger pains.

At points along the way, they continued to be exhibited to North Vietnamese soldiers as trophies of success. When given half a chance, Mike tried to explain who they really were and how they were being unjustly held. Betty didn't protest any more, standing mute while their accusers spouted lies.

They were both weakening. Their hair turned gray. They lost their body hair, their nails stopped growing. Their teeth were now loose with bleeding gums; every time they bit down on anything it seemed a tooth was coming out. Once for some unexplained reason a guard gave them a tube of toothpaste which they rubbed on their gums. The taste was refreshing, but the bleeding continued.

Betty began suffering severe pains and cramps in her swollen legs. Both she and Mike were finding it hard to lift their legs. To step over a log, they had to lean down and pull up one leg at a time by hand. This difficulty finally became so acute that when stopping to rest, they had to be sure to sit against a tree. Without a tree to put their arms around and pull themselves up, they had to crawl to a supporting object.

To make their terrible plight worse, the wet foliage along the trails seemed to be alive with black, blood-sucking leeches. Mike's trousers gave him some protection, but Betty's legs were an open invitation. They attached themselves to her limbs and dug into the raw, open ulcers to satisfy their draculian appetites.

Betty had to pull and throw, pull and throw constantly to keep from being covered with the blood-thirsty creatures. They'd never been this bad before. Compared with this, the trip to the base camp before Hank died had been a lark.

Bringing up the rear, Mike saw she was losing the battle. "C'mon, Betty," he encouraged. "Don't let them get the best of you."

Pull and throw. Pull and throw. She resumed the rhythmic motion. Then he saw her arms slowing again.

"Betty, you've got to keep them off. They'll eat you alive!"

She tried again, but her movements were weak and jerky.

Mike ran ahead and begged the North Vietnamese officer who leading the march, to stop. "The leeches are killing her," he shouted.

"And your bombs are killing our people," the NVA officer declared, never breaking stride. "She'll have to keep going. The camp is another hour."

Mike got back in line behind Betty. "C'mon kid, only another hour, the NVA said. You can make it. Here, I'll help you."

Ignoring the disapproving guard behind, he began pulling leeches from Betty's legs.

When at last they reached the camp site, Betty dropped her pack and slumped to the ground. "Just let me rest a few minutes," she said flatly. "I'll get my strength back."

Mike flopped down nearby. After a few minutes, he was roused by the NVA. "Get the hammocks up," the officer ordered curtly. "Darkness will come soon."

Mike took poles cut by the Viet Cong guards and strung his and Betty's hammocks. He was stretching a strip of plastic over Betty's hammock for a roof when he saw that he needed two more poles. He looked back and saw Betty sitting up.

"Cut us a couple of little poles or vines," he said, handing her the knife entrusted to him by a guard.

"I can't do it, Mike. I don't have the strength." She began crying.

"Oh, c'mon, gal. Just a couple of little ones. Then we'll go clean up. There's a little creek over there."

Gripping the knife in a thin white hand, Betty walked a few steps into the bushes. A moment later, Mike heard her wail,

"I can't. I just can't."

Mike called her back and took the knife and tried it himself. The blade felt like a hundred pounds. He could hardly do it himself. It was clear that both he and Betty were very sick.

They had their toilets, ate the pallid rice, and then held devotions together as blackness closed in around them.

"Lord, whatever you allow is all right," Mike heard Betty say. "Forgive our enemies. They don't know what they are doing. They don't know who you are."

The next morning they were moving before sunrise. Mike noticed that Betty seemed incredibly weak and ghostly white. He carried her pack as well as his own and a bag of rice. The trail that led along the side of a mountain was narrow and crooked. Each was shadowed closely by a Viet Cong.

During the afternoon Mike and his guard fell behind, causing Mike to lose sight of Betty. This had happened before and he was not alarmed. In the early weeks of the captivity he and Hank had worried about Betty's being raped and had kept close to her. But they'd soon realized this fear was groundless. In the debilitating jungle, worn out from acute malnutrition, diseases, and fatiguing marches, men lost all sexual desire.

Then he rounded a sharp bend in the trail and saw her on the ground. The guard was bending over, pounding her with his fists, and yelling, "Get up! Get up!"

Disregarding the Viet Cong behind him, he dropped the packs and ran to her rescue. The guard beating her glared at him, saying, "She's pretending to be sick."

"Mike, I can't go on," she gasped in a tired, quaky voice. "Each time I fall, he beats me. But I can't go on."

Mike boiled with anger. He called the officer in charge and demanded that they rest.

"No. We have many kilometers yet to go today," the officer replied coldly.

"You may go on, but Miss Olsen is not going one step farther. Without proper food and medical help, she's too weak to travel. And so am I. You may drag or carry us or kill us. But we're not going."

The NVA saw that Mike was adamant and unyielding. He decided to camp.

Mike and Betty rested for a while. Then Mike asked if there was a stream close by. One of the guards pointed down the steep hill.

The two Americans started down the slope. The guards let them go alone, knowing they were too weak to walk far.

They waded into the cool water and began picking off lice, leeches, and ticks. They washed their faces, arms, and legs, all packed with ulcerous sores. Then they sat down to rest on a large flat rock.

"I'll never make it back up that steep hill, Mike. I'll have to stay here."

"You can't. They'll be down after us in a few minutes."

"You go on up and leave me here, Mike."

"No, I'm not leaving you. Come on. I'll help you."

With great difficulty, Betty struggled to her feet and caught hold of Mike's hand. With Mike pulling her they got back to the camp.

The next morning they started again. Soon they entered an area laced with narrow trails. In the thick jungle Mike and his guard became separated from Betty and her escort. When they backtracked, the guard became confused. "Look for blood," Mike advised. "She's bleeding from the leeches."

A little farther on they reached a fork and there were the telltale dark stains on the rocky ground. They followed the trail of blood and caught up.

At sundown they camped in a hollow and slept. The next morning they walked across a smooth road. "Highway 14," Mike called to Betty. "I've been through here. Duc Lap is just a little north and the Cambodian border is a few miles west."

They walked about two hours more and reached another NVA military camp. Here the officers made the usual display of Mike, but left Betty alone because she was too weak to stand.

Mike saw boxes of medicine stacked here and there with markings from Czechoslovakia and Poland. He pleaded that Betty would soon die without medical help. These NVA were as unresponsive as previous ones.

"Don't you care that a woman, a volunteer nurse who came to Vietnam to help poor lepers, will die?" he asked.

"What is that to us?" was the reply. "If she dies, that will be more rice for our brave fighting men of the revolution."

Mike returned to Betty, mumbling about the inhumanity of man.

That evening their captors enjoyed fresh roasted corn, while Betty and Mike grabbed hungrily at grains that popped out of the pan.

"Haven't you been getting enough to eat?" a visiting NVA asked.

"Rice, rice, only rice," Mike complained. "Nothing else. The corn is more nutritious."

The NVA smiled. "Very well, you may have corn," he said with a benevolent air.

He had the guards cook up a pot of corn and boil some bamboo shoots. The famished prisoners ate ravenously.

Within hours both were struck with diarrhea. "It's the bamboo shoots," Betty moaned. "They're supposed to be boiled twice. They must have boiled them only once."

Mike ground his teeth. "The lazy so-and-so's. They didn't care."

During the next two days and nights they could do nothing but stumble back and forth from their hammocks to the bushes. Then Mike's diarrhea slowed down.

But Betty's was worse. She lost all appetite, and became so weak she couldn't get out of her hammock. The dysentery was coming so fast she couldn't even raise her dress in time. She had to lie in her own defecation.

Mike pleaded with the North Vietnamese guards at least to

bring some water from the stream so he could clean her, but the request was indignantly refused. Mike did get one VC to help make a hole in Betty's hammock in hopes of relieving the situation somewhat. This proved to be of little value.

During Mike's ordeal with malaria Betty had forced him to eat. Now it was his turn.

"You have to eat, Betty. Your body's dehydrating."

"I can't, Mike. I just can't."

He begged, cajoled, argued, threatened, but she kept insisting she couldn't eat.

"Allright, if you don't eat, you'll die."

"I'm sorry. I just can't. Please, Mike. Don't try to make me. Just talk to me. Pray with me."

Mike was too weak himself to argue further. He put down the bowl of rice and began praying disconsolately. "Lord, help her. I don't know anything I can do for her. These . . . *men* . . . won't help. They don't care. I care, Lord, but what can I do? I can only turn her over to you."

"Father, forgive our captors," he heard her say. "They don't understand. I thank you that I feel no bitterness toward them. Be with my daddy and Gene. Take care of Mark and the twins. Keep Marilyn in your love. Comfort them . . ." She drifted into semiconsciousness.

Mike turned his face away. He choked on the sobs erupting deep within. He heart was breaking. He knew she was dying.

A hand pulled at his tattered collar. "Leave her," the NVA commanded. "There is nothing you can do."

Numb with shock and almost unable to stand alone, Mike had no strength to resist. They pulled him some fifty feet away and forced him into a hammock.

The next day Mike was allowed only a brief time at Betty's side. He tried to get her to eat or drink, but it was useless.

"Mike. Tell them I don't hate them. I love them. God loves them. He sent his Son to die for them.

"Mike. Dear Mike. You've been such a good friend . . .

such a good, loyal friend. My brother . . ." Again she drifted off.

The third day Betty spent in her soiled hammock was her thirty-fifth birthday. There was no celebrating. Mike begged every NVA who came around, for medicine. His entreaties were futile. The buzzing of the swarming flies was the only song to be heard.

"It's all right, Mike," she whispered reassuringly. "They can't hurt me any more. . . The Lord is my Shepherd, I shall not want . . . His strength is made perfect in my weakness . . . neither death, nor life, nor angels, nor principalities, nor powers, nor things present, nor things to come, nor height, nor depth, shall be able to separate us from the love of God, which is in Christ Jesus our Lord." Her voice trailed off in a thin whisper.

By the fourth day Mike was ready to crack. "Why don't you help her?" he groaned to the guards. "How can you let her die like this? An innocent woman who loves the Vietnamese people. A nurse who has saved many lives."

The captors acted as if he didn't exist. He didn't have enough strength to lash out at them. Mercifully, Betty was so weak by this time that she was only vaguely aware of her circumstances.

Mike awoke from a nightmarish sleep the fifth day. He struggled out of the hammock and walked uneasily to Betty's hammock. Her slim form lay in quiet repose. He called her name softly. No answer.

His hand groped for her pulse. He waited. He called again. No answer.

He turned away, numbed, shaking his head in grief and despair.

He was alone.

CHAPTER

9

March of Death

At last the NVAs gave Betty some attention. An army doctor examined her, pronounced her dead, and ordered immediate burial.

Mike heard the guards digging in a grove of bamboo. Sometime later—he was too weak and shaken to keep track of the time—they pulled her body from the hammock and carried it to the grave like a sack of potatoes. There was no ceremony, no service, just thud and then the scratchy shoveling of loose dirt.

Dazed and bewildered, Mike could not speak. The most unselfish person he had ever known was dead. Never again in this life would he hear her infectious laugh, see her encouraging smile, feel her soft hand on his feverish head. He knew he'd lived this long only because of the girl he had once thought to be a stick-in-the-mud.

Now he was alone, with only recollections of Betty and Hank—and his faith in their God. "Lord, I can't make it without you," he prayed. "I have no one else."

His captors didn't keep him long at the scene of Betty's death. He was glad, for he was ready to leave this place of pain. The last five days had been the greatest agony of his life. The sight of Betty lying in the dirty hammock; the sound of her voice begging for help; then when help was refused, her asking God's forgiveness for those who would let her die: these memories would be etched in his mind forever.

He stumbled along behind a guard as the sun rose behind them. The NVA officer up ahead did not announce, "We are now entering Cambodia." There were no border markers. But having crossed Highway 14 with Betty, Mike knew they were in the fabled land of the Khmers who had once dominated much of southeast Asia.

"Neutral" Cambodia—sanctuary of the North Vietnamese. Mike knew no search party would come here. The NVAs could hold him as long as they wished, deny that he ever existed, or have their Viet Cong spokesmen say he'd died of disease in the South Vietnamese jungle. With captors who seemed not to care whether he lived or died, the future looked abysmally bleak.

Suddenly he heard the rumble and roar of trucks. Breaking out of the forest, he was showered with dust. As far as he could see in either direction, a steady line of trucks was moving along a branch of the Ho Chi Minh Trail. The trucks were loaded with troops, supplies, and ammunitions going south. Others rattled along empty, going north. Throughout Mike's five years in Viet Nam, the North Vietnamese had maintained that they had no troops in either South Vietnam or "neutral" Cambodia. Here is proof of the big lie, he thought bitterly.

They turned north, marching along the dusty highway shaded by trees, left purposely to camouflage the road from planes. Kilometer after kilometer Mike walked, ten to twelve hours a day, bare feet pounding the rocky shoulders, shin bones feeling as if they were being broken into splinters. The never-ending traffic rolled past.

When his left knee began aching painfully, they wouldn't stop. "Push on, push on," the NVA in charge demanded. He could only pray, grit his teeth, and keep limping, throwing all the weight he could on his right foot.

After several days they turned off on a side road into a more secluded area and passed armed sentries. Squinting ahead through the trees Mike made out a compound of small thatched-roof buildings.

Then he heard voices speaking English. Smooth and without accent. Was he dreaming? No, they were calling, asking his name and outfit. He answered in a slow, croaky voice, his throat tight with excitement. Except for Betty and Hank, these were the first Americans he'd seen in almost a year.

Mike was so thrilled to see friendly people, people from home, that he felt like dancing a jig despite the sore knee. There were 14 GIs of different rank, captured in various parts of South Vietnam. They all shook his hand and patted him on the back. "Welcome to Camp 102," a smiling black sergeant said.

The prisoners slept under tight guard, but during the day they were permitted to fraternize. Mike was eager to hear their stories and tell his.

His voice shook when he told how Betty had died. "They had medicines close by. They said she was of no political value, and let her die. Of no value? She was the bravest, kindest, and sweetest person I ever knew."

Though toughened by the brutality of war, the POWs listened with moist eyes as Mike told of his experiences with the two missionaries. When he described how Betty kept him from dying during the nightmarish thirty-five days of malaria, his voice trembled again. "Without her, I wouldn't be here," he whispered huskily. "If only I could have saved her life. God knows, I tried.

"When I went into the jungle with those missionaries," he added, "I wasn't on close terms with the Almighty. Betty and Hank helped me find real faith. This is all that's kept me alive."

Mike's testimony raised the morale of the camp. While they weren't permitted to hold religious services as a group, each could pray individually. Their prayers and support of each other kept them strong in faith.

Whenever the prisoners mentioned the Geneva Convention agreement on treatment of POWs, the NVAs laughed in their faces. The Geneva agreement required that POWs be treated humanely, given proper food and shelter, and be permitted to receive mail and parcels from home. Prisoners were not to be tortured or forced to write confessions. "War criminals have no rights" was the stock answer,

The diet of rice and occasional monkey meat was barely enough to keep them alive. Sergeant Gale Kearns, who'd been wounded in the right arm, suffered the most. Because he was so weak and suffering from malnutrition, his fellow prisoners feared he might die unless he got more to eat.

They asked one of the NVA officers to increase his allotment. "No, he is a war criminal and does not deserve special treatment," the officer replied coldly.

"You aren't honoring the Geneva agreement," Mike declared flatly. "You're treating us worse than animals."

The officer stared glassily at Mike, who refused to blink.

"If you are humane and just as you claim," Mike said, "you will give this man more food."

"He is a war criminal. You are all war criminals. You have no rights," the NVA insisted.

"Then let us give him some of our food."

The NVA was not touched. He refused to permit even this act of mercy.

Another officer, whom they called "Charger," taunted them with news that Dr. Martin Luther King and Senator Robert Kennedy had been assassinated. "Your country is controlled by criminals," he declared pompously. "But now that Dr. King is dead, the blacks will rise up."

Charger singled out the one black in the camp for special attention. "Both your people and mine are oppressed by the American white capitalists," the NVA told Sergeant Mc-Murray. "Why not side with the brave Vietnamese people against the American policies of war and genocide?"

"Just what is it you want me to do?" the black Detroiter asked.

Charger put a tape recorder on the table and handed Sergeant McMurray the microphone. "Tell your fellow black soldiers that America is a racist nation. Ask them to lay down their arms and stop fighting against their Vietnamese brothers. We will broadcast your message to them."

The NVA turned on the tape recorder and waited expectantly. To his embarrassment, the black soldier declared, "I believe in my country. I will always be loyal. I will not speak against America."

"You are acting very foolishly," Charger replied. "But I will give you another chance to help your people and mine."

The black American glared back defiantly. "No! Never!"

At infrequent intervals the camp loudspeaker was turned up for the prisoners to listen to Radio Hanoi. Every show was so much alike that eventually they could predict what the speaker would say next. Over and over, they heard the slogans:

"America is run by capitalist, war-mongering profiteers from Wall Street.

"These warmongers have deceived the people about the illegal, unjust, and immoral war.

"The Vietnamese people want only freedom, happiness, and independence.

"American soldiers are being used as cannon fodder for the Wall Street capitalists."

The news from America, as Radio Hanoi reported it, was so obviously distorted that they didn't know what was true and what wasn't. One broadcast presented a lecture by a doctor on the effects of malnutrition. The NVA assumption was that millions of Americans were like this.

Mike was scrubbing his skinny naked frame when this program began blaring from the loudspeakers. Having nothing better to do, he presented his own parody of the descriptions.

"The teeth become loose . . ." the speaker said.

Mike wiggled his mouth. "Yes."

"The stomach is distended and bloated . . ." Mike pushed out his inflated stomach. "Yes."

"The collarbones protrude . . ." Mike raised his bony shoulders up and down. "Yes."

Mike continued mimicking every symptom until the announcer concluded: "This is the condition of millions of starving Americans." Then he shouted loud enough for everyone in the camp to hear, "Yes, and there are fifteen more right here!"

Fall drooped into winter while the prisoners kept count of every boring, listless day. When the first anniversary of Mike's capture came, it seemed to him he'd been gone a lifetime.

The prisoners treasured every pin, piece of paper, and scrap of metal they could find. Mike made playing cards from tissue paper and whittled a chess set from bamboo. He could only rummage in his memory for verses of Scripture and Bible stories from his time with Betty and Hank. The NVAs had confiscated Betty's lumpy, worn Bible after her death. Her comb was the only possession he had been able to keep. He hoped to give it to her sister Marilyn someday.

The food got no better. Their rations of rice were cut.

Whenever one of the Americans protested, he was told by an NVA, "You will suffice"—whatever that meant. Mike heard this answer so often that he wrote a mournful song:

> *In Camp one oh two,*
> *Somewhere north of Pleiku*
> *The Dink he served bugs,*
> *The Dink he served stones.*
> *We never got meat,*
> *Not even the bones.*
> *We went to the Dink;*
> *We asked for some rice;*
> *All that he told us was*
> *You will suffice—*
> *You will suffice.*

Spring turned to summer and there was no hint of when they might be leaving. The fifteen prisoners saw no other Americans, but NVA groups dropped by periodically. For any arriving NVA willing to talk, Mike had a standard question: "Have you seen an American lady doctor and two civilian men in one of your camps?" Every answer was negative. In view of what had happened to Hank Blood and Betty Olsen, Mike could understand how the missionaries captured in 1962 could have vanished in the jungle.

In late July 1969 they heard indirectly of a major news event. The Hanoi propagandist was saying that America was capable of putting a man on the moon but couldn't end the Viet Nam War. A few days later they heard a broadcast praising the great scientific technology of the Socialist world that had landed a robot machine on the moon.

But the American achievement was of little comfort to the fifteen prisoners. They couldn't eat moon landings. They could only live from one day to the next, hoping and praying for a miracle.

One of the thinnest POWs was Billy Smith, a boyish, fresh-faced young private from Boston. He was one of Mike's favorites. Hour after hour they sat recalling memories of home and discussing what they would do when they were released.

When they were finally marched out of the camp in September 1969, Mike hung close to Billy, concerned that he might fall. This was, as they later learned, near the time of Ho Chi Minh's death—a time when prisoners in North Viet Nam began getting better treatment. But there was no letup in the rigors of the men from Camp 102.

As they stumbled northward, with Mike limping from his old knee injury, trucks roared past without slowing. Mike begged the guards to stop one of the trucks and give Billy a ride. They laughed and kept going.

Finally what Mike had feared happened. Billy collapsed on the road. He and some other prisoners started to the private's aid, but were restrained.

While the Americans watched in horror, the NVAs kicked the boy into the bushes, where one picked up a rock and smashed his head. Billy was beyond help now.

The Americans were ordered on. Hour after dusty hour they trudged up the Trail, each day fearing they could not last another. Quite often they heard dull booms in the west, evidence that American planes were keeping the North Vietnamese under heavy pressure.

Just when Mike felt he could go no farther, they stopped at a military camp. The next morning he was unable to walk. His left knee was too sore to stand on. On the right, he had lost all feeling in his side, arm, and leg.

A guard saw him trying to get up and called the camp doctor. The NVA medic gave him the first medical attention he'd received since being captured: a semisterile intravenous infusion of sugar and water. When after an hour only about an inch had drained from the pint bottle, the doctor poured what was left into a dirty bowl and ordered Mike to drink it.

Mercilessly, the soldiers forced the fifteen prisoners to resume the torturous trek. How he kept going, Mike himself didn't know. He could only cry inwardly to God for strength and keep moving his pain-wracked body.

From the distance they had traveled since leaving Camp 102. Mike knew they were in Laos now. Did they plan to force them to walk all the way to Hanoi?

He was dimly aware of crossing Highway 9, which runs east-west across South Viet Nam, just below the Demilitarized Zone, and into Laos. Just beyond the highway the guards led them down a side road. A short distance on they reached a field hospital.

"You will rest here and receive medical treatment," an NVA doctor told them.

Dizzy and feverish, Mike squinted through his glasses that were held together with a makeshift piece of rubber. He'd broken them several days before. His fellow prisoners looked like pictures of Jews in a Nazi prison camp. Disheveled and dirty, with hair turned white from insufficient diet, and tottering on swollen legs, they were one step from the grave.

He didn't need a mirror to realize he was seeing himself.

CHAPTER

10

Moment of Destiny

At the hospital an NVA doctor briskly examined Mike and diagnosed his condition as advanced beriberi and severe scurvy, both caused by extreme malnutrition. Mike could have told him that himself, for at Oregon State University he had taken courses in human nutrition.

The medic immediately ordered repeated intravenous injections of Vitamins B and C, plus more vitamins to be given subcutaneously. Because Mike was so emaciated, they tried—unsuccessfully—to feed him with injections of glucose. When it was evident this wasn't working, they let him drink the solutions.

After three weeks in the NVA field hospital, Mike was not a new man. But the fever was gone and the vitamin deficiency was less severe. At least he could walk. The health of the other prisoners had improved also, but Sergeant Kearns's injured arm hung limp by his side. It had been neglected too long.

Forced to resume the march in October, they turned east into North Viet Nam just above the 38th parallel. Days and days they walked, driven by shouting and goading guards. Each day seemed worse than the one before. Mike ached all over. Breathing was difficult. His heart pounded under a skeleton cage of ribs. With the sole of his right foot gone and gravel pinching tender flesh, every step was torture. But he wouldn't complain. His buddies were hurting, too.

How long, O Lord, how long? How much more could they stand?

Drawing on strength beyond themselves, they kept stumbling ahead, gasping mutual encouragement, trying to get through one day at a time, all remembering the fate of Private Billy Smith.

Then when it seemed the prisoners could go no farther, the guards stopped a truck and shoved them in. They were driven to a small prison south of Hanoi and given faded uniforms.

When Mike had eaten and rested, the political commissar summoned him for an interview.

Patting a thick folder, the NVA said smugly, "We have a large file on you, Mr. Benge. We know all about your CIA activities for your American Department of State. It will be to your benefit to confess."

Because of his broken glasses, Mike had to tilt his head to look at the officer. "Confess what?" he demanded.

"That you are a spy."

Mike pulled back his bony shoulders and frowned. Not expecting to be believed, he again described his work and why he had come to Viet Nam. Then he quoted the Geneva Agreement on treatment of prisoners.

The NVA merely laughed. "We will give you some time to think. Perhaps then you will be more truthful."

A guard grasped Mike's arm, led him down a corridor, and

shoved him into a dark room. It took a while for his eyes to adjust. The room was about nine by ten. The walls were painted black. The only ventilation and light came from a small round hole near the eight-foot ceiling and another hole under the door.

He felt something furry rub against his bare foot. Peering down, he counted seven rats. When he kicked at the rodents, they merely ran to the other side of the room. In a couple of hours or so a guard opened the door and shoved in a bowl of cabbage soup. He ate. Slept. The guard brought another bowl of soup plus a small loaf of brown French bread. He ate again. Shooed rats. Slapped at flies. Did exercises, physical and mental. Prayed for strength.

He heard a tap, then a scratch. Tap-tap-scratch. Someone was trying to communicate in Morse Code. Mike answered back with his name. The man at the other end gave his.

Mike was tied into the prison network. By coughing, whistling, scratching, and tapping they shared stories, swapped jokes, mocked their captors, and kept everyone informed about the latest interrogations. When a new prisoner was brought in, everyone knew within hours his name, outfit, and circumstances of capture. When a code was broken and violators punished, the prisoners changed to another.

All took turns in facing the camp commander. Mike was among the most adamant in refusing to make false confessions and write antiwar statements. He was always demanding that the North Vietnamese start observing the Geneva Agreement. For such obstinacy, he was beaten with a rubber hose and forced to sit at attention for up to sixteen hours a day. He was also required to bow at a 90 degree angle whenever the guard peeped through his door.

The days dragged by until one morning an NVA poked his head in and said, "Mr. Benge, do you know what holiday is coming?"

Mike thought and thought. He finally had to admit, "I don't know."

"Ah, Mr. Benge, you do not know American traditions and

holidays very well. On this holiday you are not permitted to eat meat." Mike chuckled bitterly. He had had no meat in months.

A couple of days later the guard brought around a soybean cake—"for a special treat," he said. Then he turned on a radio and invited Mike to listen to an Easter service broadcast from Hanoi.

A tremulous Vietnamese voice announced in English: " 'Render unto God that which is God's and render unto Ceasar that which is Caesar's.' Why do you not allow the Vietnamese people to have their freedom? Why do you continue your evil war of aggression?" The propaganda was so blatant, so obvious. How stupid do they think we are? Mike thought.

A few days after Easter Mike was called again before the political commissar. The NVA repeated the old demands: confess and write a statement of repentance. Mike refused and again called for adherence to the rules of the Geneva Agreement.

The commissar's face reddened with anger. "You are our prisoner. We will do with you as we wish." He called the guard and ordered that Mike be beaten and put back in his cell.

Spring passed into the hot months of summer. Mike sat in his black cell, praying, waiting, hoping, kicking rats, slapping flies. He relived old memories, devised new plans for helping the Vietnamese tribal people, recited to himself the Bible verses and stories he had learned from Betty and Hank.

Then in his eleventh month of solitary (November 1970), he heard Hanoi Radio admit that U.S. commandos had tried —unsuccessfully,—to rescue some prisoners. Soon after that, the NVAs loaded Mike and his companions in the country camp into trucks and moved them to a more secure prison near Hanoi.

Mike's hopes for roommates were dashed when he was put back in solitary. Six days passed. The prospect of more interminable isolation lay heavy on his mind. He considered giving in and writing a letter. He could say what the NVAs wanted him to say in a way that would indicate to American readers he was writing lies. At least his mother, stepfather, and sister would know he was alive.

He was almost ready to write, when on the seventh day they moved him without explanation to a room with two roommates. He felt that with their encouragement he could hold out.

Through communications the three learned there were 102 Americans in the old warehouse that had been converted to a prison. It was called Plantation Gardens, but Mike suggested changing the name to the Animal Farm because some prisoners got more lenient treatment than others. He dubbed one section the Bull Pen, another the Sheep Shed, and the area he and his roommates were in, the Hog House.

The NVAs knew that the prisoners were talking to one another, and set out to find and break a weak link. The POWs knew someone was finking when their captors started beating certain resistance leaders, including Mike.

Mike himself finally discovered the leak and changed the code and the room numbers. Again the NVAs were baffled.

As in the last prison, Mike passed on the accounts of how Betty and Hank had died, and shared his own personal experience with God. Many of his fellow prisoners testified of finding a closeness to God they'd never known before.

Sergeant Joe Anzaldua, a twenty-two-year-old Marine of Spanish descent, from Corpus Christi, Texas, told of being captured in South Viet Nam and taken to join twelve other Americans who were the survivors of a contingent of twenty-five prisoners. The thirteen missing, two of whom were German nurses working at a civilian hospital, had died of malnutrition and dysentery. "When I came into the camp," Sergeant Anzaldua recalled, "a black man named Isaiah McMillan was reading Scripture to a boy named Dennis Hammon. Dennis was near death, but before dying he found his Creator and came to love God's Word. Before long, I was talking to my Lord in the most personal way possible."

Mike and Joe Anzaldua found they had a lot in common. Both spoke Vietnamese. Both had subsisted on rice, manioc, and roasted lizards and bugs. Both had been close to death. "I came down with meningitis," Joe said. "I thought every day was going to be my last. I had a pretty strong faith, but I kept asking God, 'Why?' A couple of guards asked me, 'If your God is so good, why can't he get you out of here?' I tried to explain that he didn't work that way, but they were never convinced."

The Animal Farm POWs were forbidden to participate in religious services or exercises, except during holidays. For Christmas 1970, Mike was allowed to paint six biblical pictures for aids in worship. Although he had studied drawing only in high school, he set to work, sketching the Nativity and other scenes from the life of Jesus. The NVAs allowed him to hang these alongside a cross in a "Christmas room." Then on Christmas morning, a little guard they called "Cheese" came and said, "You are now permitted to go one at a time and pray to your God."

A few days after Christmas, Mike was summoned before the political commissar. "You will please to write about the pacification program among the civilians in South Viet Nam," the NVA said.

"And if I don't?" Mike asked.

"You will be given special education."

Mike was sure he meant beatings followed by propaganda and another stretch in isolation. Reluctantly, he took the pencil and paper and wrote about an imaginary goof-up without mentioning any names or nationalities.

"You left out the part about the Americans," the commissar said after reading the paper.

Mike forced a grin. "Yes. This is a new style of writing started in America by a man named Alfred Hitchcock."

The commissar appeared puzzled. Then he said, "You will please to write about American failures in pacification."

Mike started again and wrote page after page of redundant nothingness. The commissar was not amused. "When are you going to cooperate?"

"When are you going to observe the Geneva Agreement?" Mike shot back.

The NVA eyed him coldly. "You are belligerent, obstinate, and odious."

"Yes, sir," Mike responded. "I am odious because I am so seldom allowed to take a bath."

"Silence! You are acting like a commander. This is a crime punishable by death. Don't you realize we can kill you at any time?"

He paused, waiting for Mike to speak.

"Aren't you afraid?"

Mike adjusted his glasses and looked hard at the NVA. "I am very sorry, but you do not have the power of life or death over me. I should already have died twice. The only reason I did not is that Somebody up there is looking after me. He has the power of life or death over me. You do not have that power. If God chooses that I die today, I will die. You cannot kill me."

The commissar sat silent, glaring at Mike as if he were crazy. Finally he shouted, "Enough! Guard, take him back to his room."

Mike sat in his room waiting for something to happen. He was still waiting when Cheese came to take him and his two roommates out for exercise.

In the exercise yard Mike picked up a stick of bamboo, a string, and a piece of wire. He carried these back to his room and used a stolen razor blade to whittle out a cross. Then he hung the cross defiantly around his neck.

The next session with the commissar didn't end so well. After turning in the usual written nonsense, Mike asked for a clean water bucket to wash in before meals. "The defecation bucket we are required to use doesn't smell so good," he explained.

The NVA's response was to summon guards for a beating.

They pounded him unmercifully with clubs, but because Mike knew judo, he was able to protect his groin, kidneys, bowels, the back of his head, and other especially vulnerable parts of his body.

When the beating was done, they tied his hands behind his back and attached leg irons. Then the commissar and another officer began kicking him in the head and ears and mouth, demanding, "Will you confess?"

When Mike groaned, "Yes," they stopped. "I confess," he gasped, "that I failed to wash my face in the defecation bucket."

Mike continued to be "belligerent, obstinate, and odious" in the eyes of his captors. He was repeatedly beaten and sometimes kept for weeks at a time in isolation. Many of his fellow prisoners suffered similar treatment.

However, they were never denied specially selected reading material. They got a steady diet of the Communist *Daily Worker* and *The Great Speckled Bird*, an antiwar, sex tabloid published in the United States. When passing out the *Bird*, the NVAs would call attention to articles lauding homosexuality and sexual promiscuity, pointing to these as evidence of social decadence in the U.S. In contrast they were always praising Communism as the solution to all evils. "We will build a perfect state in which machines will one day do all labor," they predicted. "There will be no wars. Everybody will live together in peace. In such a society, God will be only a hindrance."

In September 1971 Mike and some other Animal Farm prisoners were transferred to another prison, Mike's third in North Viet Nam. With elections coming up in both North and South Viet Nam and in the U.S., the NVAs made politics a key topic of discussion.

When they cited the two-man election in South Viet Nam as evidence of a corrupt dictatorship, Mike asked the commissar, "How can you say this when you have only one man running for each office in your country?"

"Oh, we are united. Everybody agrees with the government—except a few reactionaries," he conceded.

Mike tried to explain how democracy operated in the United States. "Political candidates can run against the government. They can criticize the government, point out its faults. When election comes, voters have a choice from the smallest to the highest office."

The NVAs didn't seem to understand how this could possibly be.

The following January, Mike was moved with a group of prisoners to the celebrated Hanoi Hilton in downtown Hanoi. Some of the over 500 POWs in "Hilton" were quartered in groups of fifteen, thirty, and more in assembly rooms. Mike, however, was put in a whitewashed room about ten by ten with four roommates.

It was equipped with bunk beds built onto the walls, with each bed having built-in leg stocks at the foot. All the guards had to do to keep a man in bed was to place his ankles in the iron bracelets and snap them shut.

A large window high on one wall was covered by a double set of bars. Through the window Mike could see a high wall ridged by jagged slivers of embedded glass.

Communication took a little more ingenuity here, for cell walls were not joined. A hall or some other air space lay between each room and the next, making tapping noises difficult to hear. Still they found ways to talk from room to room and soon Mike was "broadcasting" the story of how his missionary companions had died on the trail.

His first nine months in the "Hilton" were the hardest. As in previous camps, the NVAs wanted statements and confessions for use in propaganda. Mike was as uncooperative as before, writing pages of foolishness that kept his roommates in stitches. And as before he kept reminding the NVA officers that they weren't complying with the Geneva Agreement for treatment of prisoners.

Here, too, he was called "belligerent, obstinate, and

odious," and rewarded with more beatings. He was forced to kneel with hands up for painfully long periods of time. He was placed in solitary confinement. Through the network he learned of men who had withstood worse abuse and torture for over seven years.

Mike and his roommates were not allowed to participate in the group religious services permitted men in other sections of the Hilton. They could only pray in their rooms and whisper assurances from hymns and Bible verses.

In conversations about religion, various NVA officers had always assured Mike there was freedom of religion in North Viet Nam. When a Hilton NVA made this statement, Mike asked for a New Testament.

"We don't have one in English," he was told.

"Then French will do."

"Sorry, we have Bibles only in Latin," the officer rejoined.

"Bring us that," Mike asked. But it never arrived.

Later a new prisoner brought in a New Testament taken from the body of a dead GI. The precious book was passed from prisoner to prisoner. Mike had it for two wonderful days.

In October 1972 the prisoners were told that peace negotiations were in process. They were put on a heavy starch diet to fatten them up. When the negotiations stalled, their rations were cut again.

The food improved just before Christmas when they heard over the loudspeakers that U.S. B-52 raids had been launched against Hanoi. Mike and his roommates stood under their window and saw the bombs falling. One missile fell close enough to kill a bird within sight.

In January the Hilton underwent an amazing transformation. Instruments of torture were removed. The courtyard was cleaned. A volleyball net was strung across the court. Basketball backboards were nailed into place.

The jubiliant prisoners began expecting to be released any day.

An officer came to Mike's room with pen and paper. "Since the hostilities are ending, we will allow you the privilege to write a letter home."

"I've waited almost five years without sending or receiving a letter from home," Mike said. "I can wait a little longer." The NVA left and returned later. Again Mike refused. But the third time he agreed to write and when the letter was finished he handed it to the officer.

The officer read it and objected to Mike telling his folks, "Contact Sister Benedict at her convent in Saigon and tell her I am all right."

"We cannot permit you to use the word *convent*."

"There is nothing in the peace agreements that says I cannot write that," Mike declared.

"We tell you you cannot."

"Show it to me in the agreement," Mike demanded.

"We say you can't," the NVA snapped in impatience.

"Then take your paper and cram it," Mike said in disgust and threw the letter in his face.

In February communications reported the arrival of two male missionary prisoners from Laos. But they were not Archie Mitchell and Dan Gerber, who had been captured in 1962 and about whom Mike had asked so many times. Samuel Mattix and Alexander Wirt had been marched forty days up the Ho Chi Minh Trail from Laos to Hanoi. GI prisoners coming from Laos reported more chilling news. They told of two women missionaries being bound by Communist soldiers and left to burn to death in their flaming hut.*

Mike was still reflecting on this atrocity when about a hundred men were called out and fitted with new clothes. To his consternation, he wasn't among them. He wondered why, for a story had swept the prison that civilians were to go first.

---

*Evelyn Anderson of Coldwater, Michigan, and Beatrice Kosin of Federal Way, Washington, members of the Christian Missions in Many Lands, a Brethren-affiliated mission.

The next day, February 12, this first contingent of to-be-released POWs left the prison in buses.

A second group followed and still Mike waited, hoping every day he would be next.

February ended and still his name hadn't been called. Why were the NVAs waiting so long?

Finally: "Mr. Benge. You are pleased to follow me."

Had the time really come?

Mike followed the NVA out the door and down the corridor to an area where other prisoners were changing into new uniforms.

His heart beat wildly. He was so excited he could hardly get his feet into the trouser legs.

The guards were standing around looking solemn. Mike suddenly felt sorry for them. All they knew was the propaganda that was dinned into their ears day after day.

An NVA officer stepped out to lead the prisoners to the bus. A few minutes later they were at Gia Lam Airport walking toward the most beautiful plane Mike had ever seen. He wanted to kiss every square inch of the big C-141 Starlifter with the Red Crosses on its tail, to hug the escort officer who shook his hand at the foot of the stairs.

He climbed into the plane and found a seat with the other prisoners. Besides Mike, there were two more American civilians, two German medical workers, two Filipino employees of the Voice of America, and twenty-seven GIs on board.

The big plane taxied across to the main runway. The seconds seemed to Mike like hours as the plane stopped, then swung into position for takeoff. Then his heart rushed into his throat as the motors roared.

It sped down the runway. Clickety, click, click over the cracks in the pavement. Faster and faster. Mike held his breath, waiting. . . Was it all a cruel dream?

The wheels lifted off the ground. A tremendous shout drowned out the roar of the engines.

"God bless America, land that I love . . ." someone

croaked, too full of emotion to sing clearly.

"Stand beside her and guide her . . ." Mike joined in with the others.

Two hours later they landed at Clark Field in the Philippines. The cheering crowd, the waving flags, the bobbing signs brought more tears of gratitude to Mike's eyes.

Since there were two Filipinos in their group, President Ferdinand E. Marcos headed up the welcoming committee. With thoughts whirling, Mike solemnly shook the Filipino's hand. As he was greeted by the American Ambassador and a line of U.S. military brass a feeling of unreality gripped him.

"It's real," he kept reminding himself. "I'm free! I'm really free! I'm on my way home!"

A short religious service was held at the Clark Field's military hospital. Then the returnees trooped to telephones to place calls to loved ones in the States.

As Mike waited for the connection to be completed he wondered if he would even remember what she sounded like. It had been so long.

"Hello," said an anxious woman. Emotion overwhelmed Mike as he immediately recognized the beloved voice.

"Hello?" she repeated, as Mike tried to control himself enough to speak.

"Mother," he blurted. "It's Mike."

"Oh, Mike! Darling. It's really you! We've waited so long. All these years. We didn't even know you were alive. There'd been no reports about you until the names were released of the prisoners who had been set free.

"How are you, Son? I can't wait to see you."

Still rejoicing over the phone calls, the former prisoners entered the dining hall. Mike felt he was in a dream as mounds of food were placed before him. Thick, juicy steaks, heaps of mashed potatoes, steaming fried eggs, and gallons of delicious ice cream. He ate until he hurt. Then ate some more.

After a quick medical check Mike was told he had a visitor. As he entered the reception room he recognized the tall woman—it was Vange Blood, waiting stoically to ask her question.

"Is it true, Mike? Is Hank really dead? I've heard so many conflicting reports over the last years, I can hardly believe this one is real."

"Yes, Vange," Mike replied tenderly. "He's dead. I helped bury him."

A long moment passed.

"Well," she responded slowly, fighting to control the tears that streamed down her cheeks. "At least I know for sure. The uncertainty has been hard to bear. Tell me about it."

Haltingly, Mike recalled Hank's trials on the trail. His witness. And his death. "His last thoughts were of you and the children," he told her. "And he hoped you would continue working on the Mnong translation."

"I knew he would," Vange replied, managing a weak smile. "That's why the children and I are here at Wycliffe's Philippine base. It's slow, hard work, but I'll finish it," she declared with quiet determination.

Mike nodded his approval, then asked, "What happened after we left Banmethuot? Carolyn Griswold—Betty was so concerned about her. Did she make it? And Marie—Marie Ziemer. She was wounded too. Did they survive?"

"The tribespeople helped get Marie, Carolyn, my children and me to the U.S. military advisers' headquarters. We were evacuated from there to the U.S. Army's 8th Field Hospital at Nha Trang.

"Carolyn never regained consciousness. She died at Nha Trang. Marie had an injured ear drum and severe shrapnel wounds along her left side and leg. She had it pretty rough for a while, but she's doing fine now. Little Cathy and I suffered only minor cuts."

"And your Cindy?" Mike asked. "Hank was so concerned because she was separated from her family during the crisis."

"We were reunited with Cindy at Nha Trang. She had had a narrow escape at Kontum, but she had been protected by the missionaries there. Dalat, Pleiku, Hue and some other places were hit hard too. But the only missionary casualties were at Banmethuot.

"The bodies of Bob Ziemer, Mr. Griswold and Carolyn were flown home for burial. Ruth Wilting and Ed and Marie Thompson were left in the garbage pit where they died. A beautiful memorial has been erected around the grave."

"And Pastor Ngue, the Radê preacher? Was his escape successful? Did he make it back?"

"Yes, he did," Vange replied. "But I was told that he looked so pitiful that his wife had difficulty recognizing him. He had quite a story to tell of escaping from a tiger, swimming deep rivers, even falling into a snake pit.

"He tried to get the U.S. Special Forces to send out a rescue team. But they wouldn't follow his plan."

"When I get back to Viet Nam, I'll sure look him up," Mike vowed. "He's quite a man."

"When you get back!" Vange exclaimed. "You mean after all you've been through you're planning on returning?"

"Certainly. Those tribespeople are going to need all the help they can get," Mike declared as he wearily rose on tottering legs. "It's nearly time for the flight to the mainland," he explained.

"Did you receive a letter from Hank after he was captured?" he asked as they walked along.

"A letter?" Vange asked, perplexed. "What letter?"

"That so-and-so!" Mike scowled in disgust. "He told us he had given you the letter personally. Typical!"

As the two were about to separate, Mike had one more question. "Hank's tribal convert, Tang? How's he doing?" Mike asked hesitantly.

Vange smiled. "Tang is a beautiful Christian, Mike. After Hank was captured he grew in the Lord by leaps and bounds and has become the spiritual leader of his people. He's won thousands of tribal people to Christ."

Mike swallowed hard, trying to control his emotions. "Then Hank's sacrifice wasn't in vain," he declared.

"No, I know it wasn't," Vange agreed. "A real revival has

broken out among the tribespeople. The buildings that were destroyed have been rebuilt. The work goes on."

Arriving in the U.S., Mike had a brief but joyous reunion with his family. "Just wait until you get home from your medical treatment," his mother told him. "All of Morrow County is planning a hero's welcome for you like it's never had before."

After being examined by the doctors at the Naval Medical Center in suburban Washington, D.C., Mike was told, "You are in surprisingly good condition, considering the severe malnutrition and other prison abuses you've endured. With extra vitamins, minerals, iodine, and a high protein diet you'll soon be almost as good as new.

"There had been some damage to your eyes, but in time we feel your full visual powers will be restored. As a matter of fact, you're in such good condition we've agreed to make a special exception and allow you to have some visitors. There are some mission leaders who would like a firsthand report of what happened to their missionaries."

"Of course," Mike replied. "There must be many people who have prayed for Hank and Betty over the years who want to know. I'll share with them as well as I can."

The Wycliffe and Alliance leaders filed in. Mike greeted them. Then in slow, hesitant speech, he described the experiences in captivity, and how the missionaries had died.

"I can't express to you how very much Betty and Hank meant to me," he declared. "I grew up in a good Christian home, but I never made a full commitment of my life to God until I turned to him in the jungle.

"I'll never forget those two wonderful friends. Both praying and talking to me about what it means to be a Christian. Betty saving my life when I was blind and delirious from malaria. Then . . ."

His listeners waited patiently as he struggled to regain his composure.

"I . . . I find it hard to talk about Betty . . . what they did to her . . . how they let her die in that hammock." Mike covered his face with thin hands.

The visitors waited in sympathetic silence.

"I wanted to help her . . . I tried. They wouldn't let me. . . And she was always asking God to forgive them. . . She never hated or was bitter . . . To the end she loved everyone."

After a few moments one of the Alliance men quietly said, "Mike, did you learn anything about our missionaries captured in 1962? Dr. Ardel Vietti, Archie Mitchell, and the Mennonite, Dan Gerber. We've investigated every possible channel to find if they are still alive, and if they are, to get them back."

Mike slowly shook his head. "Everywhere I went, I asked about them. No one knew anything, or if they did they wouldn't tell me."

Mike talked on for over an hour while the visitors took notes. Before they left they bowed for a prayer of thanksgiving and praise. As they were reaching for their coats, Mike added one more thought.

"There's a lesson to learn from all this," he declared. "The Communists tried to wipe out Christianity in the Banmethuot area. But they failed, didn't they?"

Afterword

On March 20, 1973, Mike Benge was given the U.S. Department of State *Award for Heroism* "for personally insuring the safety of eleven American civilians during the *Tet* offensive of 1968."

On May 23, 1973, Mike was presented the Department of State's *Award for Valor* "for exceptional courage and stamina while held as a prisoner of war in Viet Nam." The citation to Mike and five other American civilian POWs further stated:

> *Each of them demonstrated exceptional valor in helping care for fellow prisoners, in resisting efforts of their captors to break their spirits, and in preserving their own mental and physical strength. Their very survival under the grim conditions of their captivity—conditions which took each of them to the brink of human endurance—fully merits official recognition . . .*

As this book goes to press, Mike is engaged in a coast-to-coast speaking tour (at his own expense) to rally public support for Viet Nam POWs still "Missing in Action." These include the Alliance's Dr. Ardel Vietti and Archie Mitchell and the Mennonite's Dan Gerber.

A
Word
of Thanks
from the
Authors

From the outset, Dr. Kenneth Taylor, president of Tyndale House Publishers, took a personal interest in this book. Tyndale House provided for travel to Minnesota, Texas, Georgia, Oregon, Mexico, the Philippines, and Viet Nam for background research and personal interviews with source people. We are also especially grateful for special guidance and assistance from Dr. Victor Oliver, Tyndale's managing editor, and his wife Dixie, who are both former missionaries to Viet Nam.

Mike Benge was, of course, the key source. In tribute to Betty Olsen and Hank Blood and in the desire that their story might become better known, Mike shared painful recollections of their captivity as well as remembrances from his ordeal after their death. Mike's mother also assisted with some interesting incidents from his childhood.

Pastor Ngue, who was interviewed in Pleiku, South Viet Nam, related his experiences with the captives and described his dramatic escape from the Communists. Then a Radê tribal preacher, he is now superintendent of the tribal church district for the National Evangelical Alliance Church of Viet Nam. Several other Radê tribespeople also provided information on the *Tet* massacre at Banmethuot and the early days of Mike's, Hank's, and Betty's captivity.

Hank Blood's wife, Vange, and his mother, Mrs. Helen Blood, of Portland, Oregon, provided us with a complete file of Hank's letters as well as his personal devotional diary. Dave Blood, Hank's translator brother, also gave valuable aid.

Marilyn Olsen, Betty's sister, shared Betty's letters and personal effects. Bill Gothard, president of the Institute in Basic Youth Conflicts, recalled details of Betty's spiritual crisis and how she overcame the problems that were crippling her life before going to Viet Nam. "As Betty applied biblical principles to her problems," Mr. Gothard said, "I saw her emerge as a buoyant, radiant person."

Several Wycliffe and Alliance missionaries gave valuable insights into the personalities and spiritual experiences of Betty and Hank: Dr. Richard Pittman, Julia Supple, Richard Watson, and Milton and Muriel Barker of Wycliffe; and Betty Mitchell, Olive Kingsbury, Dawn Deets, Millie Ade, Ken and Bernice Swain, Lillian Phillips, and Gene Evans of the Alliance mission in Viet Nam. Betty Mitchell remains at Banmethuot, still hoping that her husband Archie, captured in 1962, is alive and will be released. The Swains, Lillian and Richard Phillips, Dr. and Mrs. Robert Green, and two single missionary nurses are also now at Banmethuot, living in homes rebuilt after the 1968 destruction.

Dr. Louis King, director of the Christian and Missionary Alliance's world-wide foreign missions program, and Gerald

Smith, director of public relations for the Alliance, gave enthusiastic support.

Two former POWs, Sergeant Joe Anzaldua and Major Nick Rowe, broadened our understanding of prison life in South Viet Nam. Sergeant Anzaldua also was helpful in telling about his experiences in North Viet Nam where he was incarcerated with Mike Benge.

Sandy Olsen, director of the Corpus Christi, Texas, MIA-POW chapter for the National League of Prisoners' Families, gave good assistance. Mrs. Olsen's brother, Floyd, is still unaccounted for in Viet Nam.

Faye Park typed the final manuscript with her usual commitment of concern for meaning and accuracy.

We thank all of these and others who are not named for their willing assistance. They must share credit with the authors and publisher for whatever inspiration and challenge readers may receive.

To those readers who may wish to make contributions in memory of one or both of the missionaries who died in captivity:

Gifts sent to the Henry Blood Memorial, Wycliffe Bible Translators, P.O. Box 1960, Santa Ana, California 92702, will be used to help pay for the printing of the Scriptures in Vietnamese tribal minority languages.

Funds sent to the Christian and Missionary Alliance, 260 West 44th St., New York, N.Y. 10036, may be designated in Betty Olsen's memory for general missionary work among the Vietnamese people.